LESS THAN A TREASON

DANA STABENOW, born in Alaska and raised on a 75-foot fish tender, is the author of the award-winning, bestselling Kate Shugak series. The first book in the series, *A Cold Day for Murder*, received an Edgar Award from the Mystery Writers of America. Contact Dana via her website: www.stabenow.com.

DANA STABENOW

"Kate Shugak is the answer if you are looking for something unique in the crowded field of crime fiction."
Michael Connelly

"For those who like series, mysteries, rich, idiosyncratic settings, engaging characters, strong women and hot sex on occasion, let me recommend Dana Stabenow."
Diana Gabaldon

"A darkly compelling view of life in the Alaskan Bush, well laced with lots of gallows humor. Her characters are very believable, the story lines are always suspenseful, and every now and then she lets a truly vile villain be eaten by a grizzly. Who could ask for more?" **Sharon Penman**

"One of the strongest voices in crime fiction." *Seattle Times*

"Cleverly conceived and crisply written thrillers that provide a provocative glimpse of life as it is lived, and justice as it is served, on America's last frontier." *San Diego Union-Tribune*

THE KATE SHUGAK SERIES

DANA STABENOW

LESS THAN A TREASON

First published in the UK in 2017 by Head of Zeus, Ltd.

Copyright © Dana Stabenow, 2017

The moral right of Dana Stabenow to be identified as the author
of this work has been asserted in accordance with the
Copyright, Designs and Patents Act of 1988.

9 7 5 3 1 2 4 6 8

A catalogue record for this book is available from the British Library.
Library of Congress Cataloging-in-Publication Data is available

ISBN (HB): 9781786695697
ISBN (XTPB): 9781786695710
ISBN (E): 9781786695680

Typeset by Adrian McLaughlin

Printed and bound in Great Britain by
CPI Group (UK) Ltd, Croydon CR0 4YY

Head of Zeus Ltd
First Floor East
5–8 Hardwick Street
London EC1R 4RG

WWW.HEADOFZEUS.COM

For John Sims
1950–2016

Kate21 beta reader and
Danamaniac forever

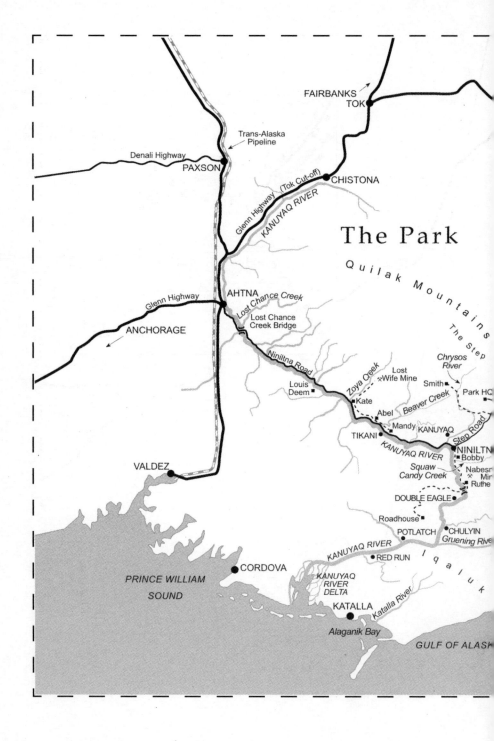

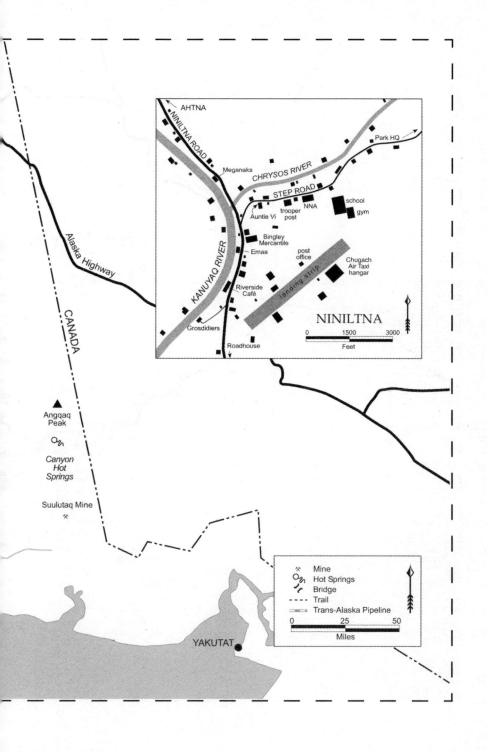

One

THE BODY HAD BEEN FOUND EARLY ON BY a raven, that inevitable first responder to carcasses in the wild. It perched on a crag and waited for signs of life before calling in the rest of the unkindness. The wolves followed the ravens. A grizzly sow with two cubs fresh out of their den followed the wolves, after which the smaller predators moved in, the coyotes and the Arctic foxes. A marmot sniffed, sneezed her disgust, and tore off one of the sleeves of the jacket to line her den. A flurry of feathers drifted out and was picked off one plume at a time by sparrows for their nests.

Encouraged by a tiny stream of snowmelt that trickled down a rusty crack in the nearby rock face, dwarf willow grew up over the remains, hiding it from anyone looking from the ridge above. A hearty stand of devil's club filled in the mouth of the cleft canyon, discouraging even the occasional moose who wandered by. A pair of enterprising black-capped chickadees, testing the northernmost reaches of their range, had built a nest on the narrow ledge that projected above the trickling stream. One year they didn't return, and their cache was found by voles, messy eaters who scattered seeds everywhere. The next spring and every spring thereafter, western columbine, chocolate lilies, wild geranium, dwarf fireweed and monkshood carpeted the strip of south-facing slope. One of the chickadees had pooped out a nagoonberry seed which had taken immediate root and runnered into a handsome patch, waiting only for a wily berry picker to discover it one August and claim it for their own.

None had, yet.

Two

JULY 16, LATE
The Park

DARKNESS.

Light. Bright, dim, bright again, dim again.

Vomit. Hers? Diesel exhaust. Fish. Rubbing alcohol. Wood smoke. Shit. Hers?

Beeps. Clanks. Thumps. Rubber on linoleum. Charlie Brown's teacher talking. Darth Vader breathing. Siren. Charlie Brown's teacher talking. Squawk squawk squawk.

"Ah, our favorite frequent flyer, back again."

"No, Jim, Jesus, don't, don't! Christ!"

"Get him the fuck out of here, Chief."

"Jim, goddammit, come on outta there. Let them do what they do."

Bumps. Pain. Weight on her chest. Crushing weight. Throat frozen. Who put the horseshoe on her face? And why the fuck?

Darkness.

JULY 17
Ahtna

Jim was having difficulty both seeing and hearing but when he heard the doc's voice again some tiny part of his brain switched back on, enough to distinguish individual words.

"She was unbelievably lucky. The bullet was small and jacketed and it didn't even tumble, so most everything is still more or less intact and in the right place. Lungs, heart, intestine, liver, spleen, spine, all good. That doesn't mean she didn't suffer trauma, including a massive amount of blood loss, but we got her in time to avert hypovolemic shock. We're keeping her tubed and under for the next twelve hours while we pour fluids into her. She should be off the ventilator tomorrow and we expect a full recovery, at least physically."

"And mentally?"

"Well, it's not like this is her first visit to the ER, but this is about as close as I've ever seen her come to knocking on the pearly gates. There will be a price."

"What kind of price?"

"Who the hell knows with her? She'll have to deal with the realization that bullets don't bounce off her chest, just for starters. For her, that'll be news."

"Jim. Jim! Back off!"

"Make that fucker keep his distance, Chief. I didn't shoot her. Jesus. Look, she may be mentally the toughest patient I've ever treated. Her recovery times have broken every medical estimate. And at least she wasn't hit on the head again. But so far as I know this is the first time she's been shot, and at pretty goddamn close range, too. She's in excellent physical condition, which will help. He got her here in time. We're handling the physical injury. The rest is up to her."

A babble of voices.

"Goddammit! Shut up, all of you! There are other patients in this hospital!"

The babble ceased, more or less.

A deep, long-drawn-out sigh. "All right then. She won't wake up until tomorrow so everybody go home now. Or at least half of you. Make some room for other patients' families and friends."

Another babble, shouted down. Muttering, followed by a shuffling of feet and the huff of automatic doors.

"Jim," a voice said. He became aware that it wasn't the first time that this voice had called his name. "Where's Mutt?"

Jim stared at the craggy face of Ahtna's chief of police.

"Jim." Hazen gripped his shoulders and forced the trooper to look at him and enunciated each individual word with care. "Where. Is. Mutt."

"Mutt?"

"The dog. Where is she? It'll be the first question Kate asks when she wakes up."

"Mutt."

"Yes, Mutt. Where is she?"

His eyes slid off Hazen's face to wander around the

room. Why was mint-green always the go-to for hospital interiors?

"Jim? Jim! Goddammit, where's Mutt?"

"He shot her, too."

Hazen swore. "Is she dead? Jim? Is Mutt dead?"

"I don't—" He blinked. "I don't know, I just—I got Kate in the vehicle and on the road. I didn't stop to think, or..."

"Okay." Hazen took another deep breath. "You need to go check on the dog."

"I'm not leaving."

"Yeah. You are. For one thing, you're frightening the docs. But mostly you're leaving because she's out of surgery and they're going to keep her under for at least a day."

"I don't want her to wake up alone."

"For sweet Christ's sake. Kate isn't alone. Bobby and Dinah and Katya are here, and all four aunties, and Laurel Meganack and Matt Grosdidier, and Bobby Singh and Tony Elizondo, and Reverend Anne is flying in tomorrow, and Johnny Morgan and Kurt Pletnikof won't get off the goddamn phone and neither will Brendan McCord. Plus some kid I never heard of keeps calling from Bering, and so does some guy named Andy from Dutch. It's like somebody sent out a fucking tweet and it's fucking trending. Kate's not alone. No one has ever been less alone. So go home, please, and check on the dog and get a shower and put on some clean clothes because, frankly, you're beginning to smell a little ripe."

Jim glanced down and noticed vaguely that his uniform jacket and pants had turned a stiff, spotty brown. The color of dried blood. Kate's blood. He swayed on his feet and the next moment found himself in a chair, an imperative hand on the back of his neck forcing his head down between his knees. "Breathe," Hazen said. "Just breathe, big, deep breaths, in and out. Good, good." The hand left his neck and he sat upright, closing his eyes.

When he opened them again the world seemed brighter around the edges and not in a good way. There were many haloed people in it he vaguely recognized—Bobby? Dinah?—and a murmur of indistinguishable conversation. He blinked, opened his mouth, and closed it again without saying anything.

"Yeah, okay," Hazen said. "I'm driving you home. I'll get Tod to follow in my vehicle."

Hazen's hand under his arm, urging him to his feet, propelling him down the hallway, forcibly quelling Jim's visceral need to stay where he was.

Where she was.

"What the..."

The first thing he saw when Hazen's truck cleared the alders that annually threatened to overwhelm the lane connecting the homestead to the road was Willard Shugak coming down the outside stairs. Behind him, it looked like every light in the house was on, none of which had been on when he had slung Kate into his vehicle and floored it for Ahtna.

"What the fuck!"

"Jim—"

Willard's arms were full. A twelve-pack of Alaskan Amber, one corner crushed where the beer inside was gone. The old-fashioned hand crank egg beater that so far as Jim knew Kate had never used, but kept because it had belonged to her mother. A pair of Jim's sneakers. Kate's .30-06 under one arm and her twelve-gauge double clutched by the barrel in the other hand. Some books.

Willard's big round face looking washed out in the early morning light. His mouth hung slack and the tilted eyes beneath their flyaway eyebrows were fixed on Jim with an expression of rapidly increasing terror.

Jim found his vision blanked out by a deep, red haze.

"Jim!"

The next thing he knew he was being held a foot off the ground, Hazen's arms so tight around him he couldn't breathe. Gradually he heard Hazen's voice. It seemed to Jim that he had been speaking for a long time but only now were his words making sense. They came in a steady, soothing stream. If all his senses had been functioning normally he would have heard the thread of panic running beneath. "Take it easy there, Jim. Come on. You know this wasn't Willard's idea. You know that. Come on. Calm down. Calm down now. Calm down."

He took a deep, shuddering breath and looked at Willard, who was crouching against the bottom stair with both arms over his head. Jim could hear him sobbing breathlessly, smell the beer from where Willard had dropped the six-pack and one of the bottles had broken on the step. For whatever reason the smell of beer recalled him forcibly to his senses. "I'm all right, Kenny," Jim said. "Let me down."

"You sure?"

"Let me down," he said, and surprised himself at how calm he sounded.

Hazen set him back down on his feet but he didn't step away.

Jim realized he was within arm's reach of Willard, and looked over his shoulder at his vehicle, stopped all the way across the yard, on the other side of the cache even. He remembered no part of how he'd gotten from the passenger seat to here.

He looked back at Hazen. "Where's Howie?"

"Long gone. He probably heard us coming and took off leaving Willard to hold the bag. A pickup passed us going their direction. I'm guessing it was his."

Jim nodded. Of course this hadn't been Willard's idea. Willard suffered from fetal alcohol syndrome. He was mentally still a child and always would be. His roommate and primary caregiver, Howie Katelnikof, had a habit of loading and firing Willard whenever he thought of something particularly nasty that needed doing. Nobody ever arrested Willard but everyone arrested Howie every chance they got.

Willard peeked over his arm, his eyes wide and terrified. "Are you going to hurt me, Jim?" He gulped and hiccuped.

Suddenly Jim felt every single year of his age and then some. "No, Willard," he said. "I'm not going to hurt you."

Willard sniffled and smeared snot across his face with his shirt sleeve. "You looked awful mad," he said, and added accusingly, "I was scared of you."

"I'm sorry, Willard," Jim said. "I didn't mean to scare you."

"Then you shouldn't look so mean."

"You're right, Willard. I shouldn't. I'm sorry."

Willard hesitated, and then lumbered to his feet, a big, hulking six-year-old child. "Howie said—"

In spite of his best efforts Jim felt his face change and Willard stuttered a little before he went on. "Howie said Kate was shot. Is that true, Jim? Did she get shot?"

"Yes, Willard. She did."

"Howie said she was dead. Is she dead, Jim?"

"No, Willard." Jim took a deep breath and let it out slowly. "Kate isn't dead."

"Oh." Willard thought about it for a moment, and then smiled a beatific smile, one with enough glow in it to rival the morning sun just now cresting the bristling edge of the Quilak Mountains. "I'm glad Kate's not dead, Jim. Are you glad she's not dead?"

"Yes, Willard," Jim said. "I'm glad Kate isn't dead."

"Willard," Hazen said.

"Yes, Kenny?"

"You know Tod?"

"Deputy Tod?" Willard said happily. "Sure, I know him. Me and Anakin beat him at Knights of the Old Republic! We beat him bad, didn't we, Anakin?" He patted his shirt, where an old-school action figure of the Jedi knight looked over the edge of Willard's pocket.

"That's great, Willard. Deputy Tod is up at the turnoff. Why don't you go on up there and wait for me, and we'll give you a ride home."

"But what about Howie?" Willard looked around the clearing and his face fell. "Oh. I guess Howie left." He looked saddened but not surprised. This wouldn't have been the first time Howie had stranded Willard at a scene. He looked back at Jim and his face got scared again. "Jim?" he said, his voice wavering. "You're looking mean again, Jim."

Jim got his expression under control again and shrugged out of Hazen's grip. "It's okay, Willard. Go on up to the turnoff, see if Tod has a candy bar for you."

Willard brightened again. "Maybe a Reese's Peanut Butter Cup?"

"Maybe."

"Oh boy!" Willard stood all the way up and shoved past them, one enormous foot crunching the remains of the broken bottle of beer. He moved pretty fast for such a big man but then incentive had always worked well with Willard.

Jim stepped forward and bent over the mess Willard had left behind. He picked up a small maroon colored book with the title in gilt letters. *Robert's Rules of Order (Newly Revised)*. His hand clenched on it, the knuckles white.

"Jim?"

"I should have shot him the moment he came into the clearing, Kenny."

The Ahtna police chief knew immediately that Jim wasn't talking about Willard. "Jim—"

"He was carrying a weapon," Jim said, his voice rising. "I don't recognize serious threat when I see it? What the fuck, Kenny?"

"Jim—"

Jim heard the warning in Hazen's voice and got himself back under control. "I mean. What. The absolute. Fuck. It's not like we don't train for that."

"No," Kenny said. They were silent for a moment. "I've never fired my sidearm in the line. I've never even drawn it. I don't know what I would have done if I'd been here."

Jim dropped his head, shaking it slowly from side to side. "I'd better clean up this mess. I don't want her to see it if— when—"

A big hand clasped his shoulder. "When, Jim. You heard the doc. When." A sigh. "You going to be okay?" It wasn't a question, exactly.

"Yeah," Jim said, although he was pretty sure his life as he knew it was totally fucked.

"Jim."

"What?"

"When you come back to the hospital later…"

"Yeah?"

"You won't stop off at Howie and Willard's, will you?"

Howie. Jim looked down at the two long guns and the broken bottles and the beer-stained books and Zoya's egg beater, which looked little more dented than it had before. "Willard didn't walk away with anything, did he?"

"No, Jim. He was so scared when you—he was so scared he dropped everything."

The old Deem place was right on the way to Ahtna, not fifteen, twenty minutes off the road. So tempting. And twenty million acres of Park in which to bury the body. People went missing in the Park all the time. Hell, in Alaska they went missing by the planeload. No one would ever know.

"No," he said. "I won't be stopping off at Howie's. Don't worry, Kenny."

"Well, then." Kenny scuffed one boot. "Well, then, I've got to get back."

For the first time Jim looked for Halvorsen's body. Hazen followed his gaze and said, "Tod bagged the body last night. Well. Pretty early this morning, I guess that would have been."

A vague memory surfaced. "Yeah, that's right, he told me at the hospital. He took my weapon and Halvorsen's rifle, too."

"And," Hazen said, thinking out loud, "we've bagged and tagged the bullet." The bullet the docs had extracted from Kate Shugak's chest. He shifted uncomfortably and cleared his throat. "It was a clean shoot, Jim. You have nothing—"

"To worry about?" Jim gave a short laugh that had no humor in it.

"You gonna be okay?"

"I'm fine. Go."

Hazen looked at him for a long moment through narrowed eyes, and then nodded once before heading back up the trail to where Tod and Willard waited.

Jim watched the Ahtna police chief out of sight, and then turned to look at the house. It seemed remarkably unchanged from when he'd seen it last. Well. Except for all the lights on and the mess on the stairs. A two-story Lindal cedar home with a prow front, the entire south-facing wall made of glass, two bedrooms, one up one down, and two baths, one up one down. Steps led up to a deck that surrounded the entire first floor. The steps Willard had been standing on when they pulled into the clearing. Jim had been on those same steps when—

He set his teeth and looked away, only to see the four-wheeler where Kate had been shot. There was a dry brown stain on the seat that continued down the side of the gas tank.

He forced himself to look away from that, too, and it was only then that he noticed. Mutt was not where she had fallen when Halvorsen had shot her, where Jim had left her when he bundled Kate into his Blazer and floored it for the hospital in Ahtna.

Mutt wasn't, he discovered over the course of that very long day, anywhere on the homestead. He spent every second of daylight, a little over nineteen hours, cross-quartering the entire hundred and sixty acres where they were passable and slogging through bog and bushwhacking through alders where they weren't. He only quit looking when he woke up on the four-wheeler, still in gear and still in motion as it neared the edge of the cliff on the east side of Zoya Creek. By then it was as dark as it got in Alaska in July.

He went back to the house, showered and fell into bed. He slept for twelve hours and would have slept longer if he hadn't had to pee. He showered, got dressed and drove the fifty miles back to Ahtna. He kept his eyes straight ahead while passing the turnoff to the old Deem place where Howie and Willard lived, and he didn't drive down the single lane that led there, and he didn't beat Howie Katelnikof to death with his fists. He didn't take any particular pride in it but he didn't do it all the same.

The first person he saw in ICU was the Right Reverend Anne Flanagan, the Park's flying pastor. She held up a hand, stopping him in mid-stride. "She's gone, Jim."

His vision grayed.

"No!" she said. "No, I'm sorry, no, that's not what I meant. Here, look—"

She got both hands under his elbow and kept him upright as she dragged him to the door of Kate's room.

The bed was empty.

He must have staggered, because he felt Anne grab his arm and pull him up. "Jim," he heard her say. "She didn't die, she left. Jim!" She shook him, trying to get his attention. "She didn't die, Jim, she left."

Gradually, his balance returned and the mint-green

cubicle where he had last seen Kate hooked up to every tube and monitor known to medical science came back into focus. A doc he remembered vaguely from before, standing at what he would recognize later was a safe distance, stood with both hands up and his lips moving. Jim concentrated. Eventually the lips synced with words. "She woke up this morning and insisted we remove the ventilator. She would have pulled it out on her own if we hadn't, so we did. The next time a nurse checked on her, she was gone. Left AMA."

"Against medical advice," Flanagan said, looking at Jim with an anxious expression.

All he could think was the last time he'd seen Kate Shugak, he'd thought she was dying.

JULY 19
The Park

"You know where she is," Jim said. It wasn't a question.

"You don't?" Bobby said. It wasn't an answer.

They glared at each other, both big men, one black, one blond, one in a wheelchair, one in the blue and gold of the Alaska state trooper, both of them mightily pissed off.

From behind the kitchen counter Dinah watched, her face still. Next to her, Katya peeped over the edge, big-eyed. She'd never heard her father speak in quite that tone of voice before. For that matter, she'd never seen her favorite man next to her father look that angry, either.

Jim felt his fist curling.

"Don't let the chair stop you, buddy," Bobby said, his own hands clenching.

Jim turned and yanked the door open.

"Leave her alone, Jim," Bobby said. "Jack did, for eighteen months. Be at least as smart as he was."

Three

TUESDAY, NOVEMBER 1
The Roadhouse

ERNIE IVANOFF HELD FORTH IN FINE VOICE. "Opera is not some goddamn mystical redemptive force. It's fat people singing really loud in French or Italian or Russian or some other language that ain't English. It might help Nicholas Cage or Richard Gere get laid but that's only in the movies."

"It's like Old Sam came back from the dead," Bobby said. He raised his beer in a silent toast to the group of old farts collected around the big round table, the one with the best view of the eighty-five-inch Samsung mounted flat to the wall. On that thing you could count the pores on Stephen Curry's nose from twenty feet away.

"In fact, I have heard opera, and I have loved it," said Bert Topkok, Sr., puffing out his chest and attempting to look down the pug nose that marked all the sons of long gone Park rat Amalia Mercado.

"Right," said Ernie with vast suspicion. "Sung by who?"

Bert drank beer and belched, both with style. "Roy Orbison. And he sang in English. And told real stories. And with feeling, instead of just trying to blast the ears offa your head."

Ernie, crushed, retired from the lists, and the half-dozen other old farts thumped the table to applaud his rout. Bert accepted it as his due with pretend modesty.

"See any snow in Niniltna yet?" Bernie said.

Bobby shook his head. "Here?"

"Nope. Looking like another non-winter winter," Bernie said.

Bobby drank beer, and directed a casual nod at the table beyond the old farts. "What's with Ace and Deuce over there?"

The two men he referred to were the same general size and bulk of bulldozers, with tats showing above the necks and below the sleeves of their identical black T-shirts. The younger man had his hair cut in a mullet, swear to god, while the older had a clean-shaven scalp. Both wore visible scars on their faces, and both sets of hands showed signs of broken knuckles, although the younger man looked a little puffy around the edges, compared to the older man who appeared to be all hard muscle.

Bernie gave a casual glance over his shoulder. "You mean those two ex-cast members of *Oz*? Yeah, they've been hanging around for a couple of days now. Rented one of the cabins out back. Say they came looking for jobs up the mine. Haven't noticed them looking very hard." He took a pull of beer. "Ace there did ask after his good buddy, that asshole Ken Halvorsen. Didn't seem all that surprised to hear he was dead." Bobby swirled the beer in his bottle. "Then he asked after Martin Shugak."

"Martin," Bobby said. Bobby rolled his eyes. "Martin. Jesus. He's like Gollum."

"How so?"

"Seldom in sight but always a foul rumor. Haven't seen a whole lot of Martin lately. Haven't missed him, either. You tell the trooper?"

Bernie snorted. "What's the point."

Bobby grimaced.

Bernie changed the subject. "You hear about Auntie Edna's last words?"

Bobby glanced over his shoulder at the quilting bee in the corner. Aunties Joy, Viola, and Balasha worked steadily at piecing bright squares together, the usual Irish coffees sitting neglected on the table. Annie Mike was there as well, knitting something blue and fluffy. She wasn't quite an auntie, not yet.

In late August, that oldest and toughest and inarguably the meanest of the four aunties, Edna Aguilar, had been returning from berry picking up the Step road in her ancient Chevy Suburban when a couple of yearling moose broke out of the brush and shot across the road a foot from her front bumper. It wasn't anything that hadn't happened a hundred times before during her life in the Park, but this time what the yearlings were running from was twelve feet behind them, a couple of grizzly two-year-olds who had been kicked out by their mom that fall. They were too hungry to den up for the winter and hot on the trail of dinner.

From what the trooper could make out afterward from the skid marks in the gravel surface of the road, Edna had tapped her brakes at the moose and then stamped on them at the grizz. The back end of the Chevy, empty but for a half a dozen one-gallon buckets of raspberries and blueberries picked only she knew where bungied into the back, slid first to the right and then more decisively to the left. At the end of the second slide the left front tire caught the shoulder and the pickup rolled. The gradient of the embankment made it roll twice more, picking up enough speed to severely impact a stand of cottonwood Keith Gette had been cultivating along the edge of a creek that ran alongside the lot line of the old Gette homestead. Meant to soak up the creek and dry the land out for later cultivation, on that fateful day that section instead presented an immovable object to Edna's irresistible force. Keith had been quite colorful on the subject. But then Edna had not been the most popular of the aunties by a long shot.

She had also not been wearing her seatbelt. When her body was finally located she had still been alive and conscious. "The troopers just released the official accident report," Bernie said now. "'Never mind me,' she says to him, 'get the berries.'"

Both men were silent, watching the quilting bee. The three remaining aunties looked somehow a little diminished. "I didn't like her much," Bobby said.

"Who did?"

Auntie Edna had been buried but the word had gone forth that the potlatch would be delayed until everyone got back from fishing and hunting. It was generally understood that this was code for "until Kate Shugak reappeared." If she ever did. Half of the Park rats were convinced she was dead, too.

Bobby's chair was pulled up to a table at the Roadhouse, the only drinking establishment within driving distance of the village of Niniltna, if you didn't want to drive fifty miles in the other direction to Ahtna, and nobody did. Bernie was a Vietnam era draft dodger and Bobby was a Vietnam War vet. They had arrived in the Park not many years apart and against every Park rat's expectation had bonded over that extremely ill-advised conflict, celebrating the Tet Offensive's anniversary every year at Bobby's house together with other likeminded survivors, holding the trauma of that time at bay with a boozy blowout that was as loud as it was therapeutic.

Almost as loud as the celebration going on at the next table over, where three women, not Park rats, sat drinking Bloody Marys. One was fifty-ish and zaftig with a tumbled mass of graying curls, the second a willowy blonde who was a dead ringer for Cate Blanchett, and the third a voluptuous brunette who took this opportunity to announce, apparently out of the blue, "Well, yes, but I majored in French." Bobby watched points grow on the ears of the half-dozen hopeful Park rats malingering with intent a discreet distance away. He pointed with his chin. "What's going on next door?"

"Three Anchorage businesswomen walk into a bar," Bernie said, and laughed. "They're here on a fishing trip."

Bobby stared. "In November?"

Deadpan, Bernie said, "They were misinformed."

Bobby threw back his head and laughed loud and long, only interrupted by a voice saying, "I am informed that you are the proprietor of this establishment." He looked around to see the Amazon with the curly hair looking down at Bernie with a pronounced twinkle in her eye.

"Depends," Bernie said. "You packing?"

"No, but Lorie is," she said, indicating the blonde.

"Well, then, I guess I better fess up. To what, exactly?"

"I'm Alison, and I'd like to know if this is your best effort at a Bloody Mary." She held up an accusatory glass.

"Alison," Bernie said, with the air of confessing all, "it is."

"Let me show you how it's done, cowboy," Alison said, and sashayed around behind the bar. Bernie joined her in an effort to defend his liquor supply but before long all the ingredients and then some were assembled and a raucous crowd had formed to sample the results of the Bloody Mary-Off. It was going to be one of those nights.

"Did you hear about Pat Mack?" Bernie said, returning to the table with a Bloody Mary not of his own making and a big grin all over his face that indicated some hope of getting lucky later on. He'd left Alison in charge behind the bar, which told its own story.

"Yeah, I heard. I'll put it out on Park Air this evening."

"Worse ways to go."

Bobby thought about Pat Mack, the oldest geezer of a steadily diminishing number of old geezers in Kushtaka village, dead of a heart attack after shooting and eating a mess of ptarmigan he'd flushed out of a patch of lowbush cranberries. "I suppose. What's the population in Kushtaka down to now?"

Bernie shook his head. "I don't know. That's three they lost in one year, Tyler, Pat—" he hesitated "—Jennifer. I heard her parents are moving to Healy. Dale got a job at Usibelli. So that's five gone."

A lot of villages in the Park were dwindling, their populations aging out and the kids moving to anywhere there might be a job, which was usually on the road system and mostly in Anchorage. "Kuskulaners doing fine, though, I expect."

"They usually do," Bernie said. He looked over Bobby's shoulder, and grinned.

"What?" Bobby looked around.

"That," Bernie said happily, "would be intrepid filmmaker Bo Diddley Tarantino zeroing in on Ranger One, aka Dan O'Brian of the US Park Service. Poor bastard."

"Which one?"

Bernie nudged Bobby. "Just listen."

It was easy to do, as Bo Diddley Tarantino's voice was

rising to a decibel level heard over even the usual happy tumult of a profitable evening at the Roadhouse. "You mean to tell me my production company is bringing tens of thousands of dollars per season into your Park and I can't shoot one goddamn moose?"

Bo was a thin, dark man with wrinkles he knew to be interesting or he wouldn't scrunch up his face that way otherwise. He was kitted out in L.L. Bean's idea of an Alaska tuxedo, khaki from head to toe, with snapped pockets all the way down his arms and all the way up his legs, no item of which appeared to have seen the Great Outdoors since it came off the hanger.

The way the chief ranger was spacing out his words told Bobby that he'd been pushed pretty far that afternoon. "As. I. Said. Before, Mr. Tarantula—"

"It's Travaglio, and I keep telling you to call me Bodhi anyway." Bo Diddley Tarantino tried what he obviously imagined to be a winning smile, which caused absolutely no perceptible change in Dan O'Brian's stone face.

"As. I. Said. Before," the chief ranger said, and Bobby observed with interest just how white his knuckles were where his hand grasped his beer bottle, "moose season was over two months ago. I'm afraid you missed it."

"Missed it! How the hell could we have missed it! One of those big bastards nearly ran me off the road on the way here!"

"Yes, well, perhaps you might like to reduce your speed on Park roads," Dan said. "We do have a lot of large mammals running around loose in these parts."

Bo Diddley Tarantino's voice turned wheedling. "Couldn't you make an exception in our case? One little moose, is all I'm asking for here." He waved at the crowd around the table. "All these people are depending on this hunt, Chief Ranger."

"It's Dan. Just Dan."

"Well, Dan then, come on. Surely you can relax the rules just this one time?"

"I'm out of beer," Ranger Dan said. He stood up and headed for the bar.

His audience took a moment for their dicks to unshrivel from the ranger's friendly smile and put their heads together. "Well, what the hell can we shoot, then?" Bobby heard Bo Diddley say. He snapped his fingers, the picture of sudden inspiration. "I know! I saw a bunch of squirrels running around out at your place, Howie."

"Squirrels?" Howie, a short, skinny guy with a weasel face, a battery of brand new, blindingly white teeth, and irremediably greasy hair, paused with his drink halfway to his mouth. No way had Howie paid for that drink himself.

"Yeah, squirrels!" Bo waxed enthusiastic. "There's plenty of those and they aren't protected, are they? And, Howie, my man, you've got to fill your freezer for the winter in the next episode, right? We need footage of you shooting something."

"Anakin don't shoot no squirrels," the big man sitting next to Howie said in a tone that brooked no contradiction, and he patted his shirt pocket for emphasis. If you looked for it, you could see the head of the Anakin Skywalker doll peeping over the edge of the pocket.

Bobby turned back. "Squirrels," he said, his broad black face radiating an incandescent joy. "For the freezer."

Bernie was shaking with repressed laughter. "I might have to close down the Roadhouse to watch that." He shook his head. "Who knew that rat-faced little bastard was so telegenic?"

"Howie Katelnikof," Bobby said, testing the name on his tongue as if it had never registered there before. "Television star."

"Well," Bernie said, "reality television star. Oh, and Willard's sharing screen time, too, and is getting more mail. Evidently female viewers like 'em big and dumb."

"Where are they filming this masterpiece?"

Bernie grinned. "On the auld Deem homeplace, yawl."

"Where bodies of Louis Deem's planting remain yet to be found. Is Tarnation really so clueless as to be totally unaware of the serial killer history of his show's location?"

"It appears so. And you know Howie will never say anything for fear all this will go away. Probably the first regularly paying job he's ever had, and all he has to do is get in front of a camera and repeat the lines they throw at him. Easier than bootlegging any day."

"And the name of this magnificent cinematic effort?"

"Wait for it," Bernie said. He paused for effect. "*Surviving Alaska.*"

Bobby stared. "And what are they supposed to be surviving?"

"Well." Bernie grinned. "Alaska? It's supposed to be about subsistence on the Last Frontier."

"They're on the road, for crissake! If they're hungry all they have to do is turn left out of their driveway!"

Bernie patted the air with his hands. "Don't shoot the messenger." He grinned again. "You know how much they're pulling down?"

"I don't want to know." Bobby thought about it. "Do I?"

"No, but I'm going to tell you anyway." Bernie paused for effect. "Twenty grand."

"Jesus. For the whole show?"

Bernie shook his head. "Per episode." Bernie took several moments to enjoy the expression on Bobby's face and added, "Thirteen episodes per season. That makes it $260,000 total, each. Every year. Supposing they're renewed. Which, the universe unfolding as it should, by which I mean making no fucking sense whatsoever, it undoubtably will be."

Bernie walked back behind the bar, pulled a couple of Alaskan Ambers out of the cooler, popped the tops and brought them back to the table. He sat down and handed one to Bobby. They toasted to the inexplicable ways of the Park 'verse and each drank half at one go.

"Well," Bobby said, recovering from his stupefaction. "At least they're spending some of it in your place of business. We could use a next new thing, what with the Suulutaq Mine failing its EIS and all." He reflected. "Didn't I hear something about Erland Bannister buying into a local film production company with Tom Hanks or somebody?"

"Not Tom Hanks, although imagine if it was and he brought Rita Wilson with him." Bernie's eyes went dreamy. Bernie's obsession with Rita Wilson dated from her role as the hooker in *That Thing You Do*, and had been revived by a recurring role on *The Good Wife*, all seven seasons of which he now owned on DVD.

Bobby snapped his fingers in front of Bernie's face. "Hey. Hey!" Bernie blinked and returned to his body. "If not Tom Hanks who?"

"Huh? Oh. Gabe McGuire."

"Oh. Hey. Wow. Interesting."

"Jesus, Bobby, you actually seem impressed."

"I saw *Kandahar*."

"That the one he won the Oscar for?"

"Yeah. Deserved it, too, which is more than you can say for most Oscar award winners."

Bernie carefully kept his mouth shut, because he knew from sad experience that on no provocation whatever, Bobby could go off on an hour-long rant on how *The Right Stuff* losing out best picture to *Terms of Endearment* was sacrilege and a travesty and the end of what little there was of American culture and how Oscars voters spent more time checking their hair and their pecs in mirrors than picking out the real best movie of any given year. Unchecked, he could go for another hour on *Gandhi*.

The door opened on a blast of frigid air and they looked around, every Park rat in the room with a working Y chromosome sensing the arrival of a woman over eighteen and under eighty. It happened that this one was worth looking at, five five, long blond hair, big blue eyes, a tip-tilted nose, a rosebud mouth, curves in all the right places visible even beneath a down jacket and jeans.

She looked around the room, hesitating beneath the onslaught of so many pairs of male eyes, and then straightened her shoulders and went to the bar. She waited without visible signs of impatience for Alicia Kvasnikof to leave off flirting with Dan O'Brian and come down the bar to ask her pleasure. It wasn't a drink, because no conversation that long was required for a Cosmopolitan, which is what the new girl looked like she'd drink. Alicia shook her head and pointed at Bernie.

The woman came to their table. "Bernie Koslowski?"

Bernie straightened right up. Alison might have competition. "That'd be me."

"Hi," she said. "I'm Sylvia McDonald. Could I talk to you for a few minutes?"

Bernie's smile was by no means dimmed when he looked for and found the wedding band on her left hand. "Why, surely, Ms. McDonald," he all but purred. He got up, tipped Howie Katelnikof out of his chair and held it for her.

"Hey!" Howie said from the floor.

Bernie ignored him, looking expectantly at Sylvia McDonald.

Sylvia McDonald sat down without missing a beat. Pretty woman privilege.

Bernie resumed his seat, smoothed back errant strands of

the receding hairline collected in a ponytail that reached his waist, and said, "What can I do for you, Ms. McDonald?"

"Call me Sylvia, please."

"And I'm Bernie, of course."

"And I'm Bobby Clark," Bobby said. "If anyone's interested."

Bernie flipped him off where Sylvia McDonald couldn't see.

She shook Bobby's hand, too, and then sat for a few moments, her brows knit together, chewing on her bottom lip, which Bobby was sorry to see, as it was a very nice lip. She looked up and offered them a smile that was half apologetic, half embarrassed. "I'm looking for my husband." Her gaze traveled around the room and her smile faded. "I can only imagine how many women have walked in here on the same errand."

Bernie's beam dimmed but only a trifle. "Well, the Roadhouse is where a lot of husbands end up around here, Sylvia."

"His name is Fergus but everyone calls him Mac. He's a geologist."

"He work up at the mine?"

"The Suulutaq?" She mispronounced it, Sooltack instead of Soo-oo-loo-tack. "Yes."

"Have you been up there?"

"Yes, just today. Mr. Perry very kindly let me ride along with him on one of his supply runs."

"I just bet he did," Bobby said.

"Pardon?"

"Never mind," Bobby said. "I take it your husband wasn't up at the mine?"

"No. They say he was on personal leave, which I knew, but he stopped texting and calling three days ago and that's just not like him. They haven't seen him since he left."

"On personal leave where?" Bernie said.

For the first time her eyes shifted away from his. "In the Park." Her laugh was unconvincing. "Sort of a busman's holiday, you could say. One of the reasons he took this job was so he could wander off with his rock pick and poke around places he'd never get a chance to see otherwise."

"What does Fergus look like, Sylvia?" Bernie said.

She reached into her purse and pulled out her phone and held it up so both of them could see the screen. It was a photograph of the two of them, a selfie. Fergus had his arms around his wife and both of them were laughing into the camera, his arm extended to get them both in the frame. He looked to be about the same age as she did, mid thirties, with thick brown hair, dark brown eyes, a strong nose, a firm jaw. He looked, Bobby thought, a little like a younger Gerard Butler, the fucker.

"Sure, I remember him," Bernie said. "He was in here a couple of times. He liked Scotch."

"He's Scots," she said. "He liked Glenmorangie, if he could get it."

Bernie shook his head. "Too high end for me to keep on

the shelf," he said. "He had to make do with Johnnie Walker Black. I remember—"

"Yes?"

Bernie smiled. "He gave me a hard time about the Black. Said I might as well serve him watered-down molasses." He handed the phone back to Sylvia. "Nice guy."

"Have you seen him recently? Like maybe anytime during the last three days?"

There was a pleading note in her voice and Bernie shifted uncomfortably. "No, I'm sorry. The last time I remember seeing your husband was…" He appealed to Bobby. "When did the EIS statement come out on the mine? October something?"

Bobby nodded.

"Yeah." Bernie turned back to Sylvia. "We had a lot of mourners down from the mine that day, and I remember your husband was one of them." He reflected. "He didn't seem as upset as the rest of them, as I recall. Most of those yahoos were drinking down their last paycheck as fast as they could gulp. Mac was just nursing his." His brow creased. "He'd brought some work with him, took it to one of the tables."

"And you haven't seen him since?"

Bernie shook his head. "I'm sorry."

She looked around the room. "Do you think anyone else here might have?"

Bernie followed her gaze and then looked at Bobby, who shrugged, grabbed his now empty bottle and thumped it on the table, once, twice, three times. "Listen up, everybody!"

The basso profundo at full volume quieted the room but for the roar of the Warriors three-pointing the hell out of the Memphis Grizzlies, poor bastards. Bernie went for the remote and muted it.

"Meet Sylvia. Her husband has gone missing in the Park. Everybody get in line to take a look at his photo, tell her if you've seen him lately."

The room lined up and one by one shook their heads. "Might have seen him at the bar a time or two," Ernie Ivanoff said. A few of the other regulars agreed.

When everyone had filed by Sylvia McDonald slumped back in her chair. "Well, thank you, Mr. Koslowski—"

"Bernie."

She smiled, a real one this time. "Thank you, Bernie." She sat for a moment, looking a little lost.

"Have you spoken to the trooper in Niniltna?" Bobby said, looking as if the words were dragged out of him.

"No," she said, a little too quickly. "No, I, no, not yet. But of course I will."

"Do you have a place to stay tonight?" Bernie said. "I have cabins for rent out back. All the modern conveniences."

"Thank you, but I'm staying at a B&B back in town."

"Sure, Auntie Vi's. You have a ride?"

"I hitched here with someone. I hoped I could do the same back to town."

"Let's see who's in the parking lot."

Bobby watched as Bernie led her outside before getting laboriously to his feet. He didn't often wear his artificial legs because they chafed, mostly because he didn't wear them often enough to build up calluses, but keeping up with a five-year-old with opposable thumbs often required more speed and agility than a wheelchair provided. Not to mention which they opened up new possibilities into sex with his wife.

He ambled up to the bar and flagged down Alicia Kvasnikof, who fluttered her eyelashes and served up another beer with a smile and an up-from-under glance that was pure invitation. She was legal if she was working at the Roadhouse but not much over that, and she was very pretty, and he was a happily married man. He sighed, more because he didn't want anyone to revoke his man card than in longing for back in the day.

The door banged open to unloose a flood of offensively fit Millennials on the sanctum sanctorum of the Park rats, Bernie right behind them and bright-eyed at the prospect of the night's bottom line turning suddenly even blacker than after Alison got behind his bar.

Bobby had to close his eyes against the glare of technicolor spandex. "Oh god. It's the orienteers again, isn't it."

"It sure is," Bernie said happily. "They're running the Heaven Trail again." He rushed to Alicia's aid. She'd need more hands to rake in all that money.

"Where's Dinah?" Dan O'Brian came to stand next to him, studiously ignoring the quality filmmakers who were trying to get his attention.

"At school with Katya."

Dan looked at the clock on the wall.

"It's an after-hours, once-a-week music class."

Dan stopped with his beer halfway to his mouth. "Who'd they get to teach it? And are they working for free? I thought the state was broke."

Bobby shrugged. "One of the Suulutaq people who was laid off wanted to stay in the Park. Says she's got a music degree from somewhere. She offered her services to the school." He turned his glass in a circle. "They're essentially giving her a classroom for free one night a week, and she's charging a fee per student."

"How's it working out?"

Bobby shrugged again. "She might actually have a music degree. The class is open to everyone still in school, so the students are K through twelve. They're learning to read music, sing choir, and play piano and guitar. And she's reaching out to local groups to come in and do workshops, like Pamyua and the Athabascan Fiddlers. Dinah says no one has said yes yet, but no one has said no, either, so..."

"Pretty cool."

"It is, actually." Bobby cracked his neck, once left, once right. "Turns out Katya can sing." He changed the subject. "You met the new trooper?"

"I have."

"Ain't got no fucking clue."

"Some people have to be happy about that." Dan was looking at Howie Katelnikof. "And come on. Cut the guy some slack. It's a pretty steep learning curve at first. Jim always said the Park ain't for sissies."

"He coulda hung on at least until they found a grownup."

"Or they could have rotated a bunch of fifty-somethings through the Niniltna Post, all more interested in upping their retirement payout than in doing any actual serving and protecting." He pointed with his chin. "Isn't that Demetri Totemoff?"

Bobby looked over at a corner table. "Yeah."

"Who're the Cabelas with him? Can't be clients this time of year. Salmon are done, moose didn't happen, and caribou season doesn't open until January."

"Don't know."

"Bet he's happy now the Suulutaq's on hiatus."

Bobby snorted. "You're not?"

Dan sighed. "Could we not do this again?"

"Hello."

He looked around to see an attractive brunette with hair cut like Tinkerbelle only in mink brown, wearing an air of sophistication that hinted at a glass of Pernod in one hand and a smoldering Gaulois in the other. Spandex was a good look for her. She smiled at Dan. "I'm Juna."

He smiled back. "I'm Dan."

The guy was typical Irish, not very tall, built like a fireplug, topped off with red hair and freckles, yet in spite of all those drawbacks he never lacked for feminine company. It was a mystery. "Yeah, and I'm Bobby, and I'm taken, not that anyone's asking," Bobby said grumpily. "I understand the attraction—" not "—but could you kind of rein it in there for a minute, honey? This is a private conversation."

She was still smiling at the chief ranger. "I'm almost out," she said, holding up her glass.

Dan's smile widened. "Give me a minute, Juna, and I'll see what I can do to remedy that."

Juna turned, casting a come-hither look over her shoulder that made the floodlights over the bar look dim by comparison.

"Have you seen her?" Bobby said.

Dan took a swallow of beer and held it in his mouth like it had been brewed by Saint Arnold himself. He knew Bobby didn't mean Juna. "I keep hearing she's dead."

"Come on, Danny."

"No," Dan said, relenting. "I haven't seen her."

"Jesus, your office is halfway there."

The Park's chief ranger shook his head. "I have no inclination to intrude where I'm not wanted."

"How the hell do you know you're not wanted? How does anyone? She could be hurt."

Dan's expression darkened. "She was." He looked at Bobby. "She's a woman, she's short, and she's an Aleut. At first glance no one would ever see her as any kind of force or threat."

"Yeah? So?"

"So she's lived her life as both."

"And?"

"And she won't allow herself to be seen as less." Dan stood up. "You remember who told me that?"

Bobby's shoulders slumped. "Yeah, yeah."

"Yeah." Dan looked over his shoulder and smiled at Juna, who was leaning against the bar, one eyebrow raised. "In the meantime..."

Bobby flapped his hand. "Go, go. People to see, babes to nail."

He took a last look around the Roadhouse. Demetri and the tree huggers, the reality TV show people and the Park rats determined to make a good living off them, the *cough* fisherwomen *cough* from Anchorage, the Spandex Gang and their admirers, including Ranger Dan, the aunties and Annie Mike, the old farts, all looked as if they were in until Bernie threw them out. Ace and Deuce had left and as Bobby watched Bernie did a sweep and a wipe of their table, picking up the one remaining glass by splaying his fingers inside the rim. Understandable. You'd want to avoid any cooties a guy sporting a mullet might be carrying around.

He drained his beer and heaved himself to his feet. Maybe Dinah and Katya would be home by the time he got there. Maybe they could lock Katya in her room and they could see how his legs worked up against the couch.

Although he did spare a passing thought for Jim Chopin. Who also hadn't been seen much around the Park the last four months.

About as long as Kate Shugak had been MIA.

Four

WEDNESDAY, NOVEMBER 2
The Park, Canyon Hot Springs

THE HUNDRED AND SIXTY ACRES OF THE homestead was mostly vertical. Tucked away in a twisty canyon, it wasn't easy to find even by someone who had been there before. The Quilak Mountains looked loftily down from six to ten to thirteen thousand feet, peaks like swords' points permanently encased in a layer of snow and ice. The canyon ran roughly perpendicular to the north–south ridge of mountains, into which the sun shone directly only a few hours per day, even during the summer.

In contrast, the narrow floor of the little canyon was almost but not quite flat, which probably had something to do with the series of eight ponds that rose first in bubbling hot springs and then tumbled merrily one into and after the other nearly all the way to the dogleg that hid the canyon's entrance. They never froze, and sometimes in winter the snow piled high enough that visitors could pack a slick, icy slide that began ten feet back and ended with a mighty splash in the middle of the first and largest pond.

There was a spring up a little ramification behind an edgy thrust of granite on the south-facing canyon wall which created a rocky rivulet of cold fresh water, meltoff originating from the snowpack above. The spring seldom froze completely solid even in the dead of winter, making it one of the few boltholes in the Quilaks with fresh water year round, most years at any rate. There was nothing sure or certain year to year in the Quilaks, or in the Park or even Alaska for that matter, especially recently. Last winter there had been hardly any snow to speak of below five thousand feet, and it was late this year, too. It wasn't climate change so much as it was a plain damn nuisance, according to disgruntled Park rats with dogs to run and snow machines to race.

In years past, if someone did find their way through the foothills and switchbacks and bushwhacked through the dense undergrowth and the endless scramble of spruce beetle kill and perchance stumbled onto the right saddle and by accident or luck happened upon the right dogleg, there they would find a tumbledown log cabin that provided adequate shelter for a day, or even an extended weekend if they had packed in enough in the way of supplies. There was even an equally tumbledown outhouse out back, and a respectable pile of firewood for the wood stove inside.

But today no trace of that old tumbledown cabin remained. Instead, a new cabin sat in the same spot, this one built on concrete piers set deep into the ground, or as deep as one person with a Bosch hammer drill could make them. It had a fourteen-by-twenty-foot floor plan with a four-foot-wide porch built of two-by-eights on the south-facing exterior wall, sheltered by an extension of the roof. The builder had used windlock asphalt shingles for both roof and siding, a golden brown for the roof and buff for the walls. There was a single slider window on each side of the cabin, white vinyl, unpainted, and a windowed door, also white vinyl, opening in from the left side of the porch. An aluminum chimney stack with a conical cap poked through the roof at the rear of the house, a wisp of smoke trailing up into the pale blue sky.

If that adventurous wanderer opened the door—it wasn't locked—and walked in, they would have found the stack led down to a small, cast-iron wood stove with a glass inset door showing logs burning down to coals inside it. Behind the stove, another door led out the back, where, if they investigated, they would find a brand new single-holer outhouse a few steps away. It too had a door with a window in it, along with a dozen rolls of toilet paper in a plastic bucket with a snap lid and a bargain container of Purell bolted to the wall. There was even an old Folger's Coffee can, only slightly rusty with age, filled with powdered lime, a plastic scoop ready to hand, and a brand new toilet seat screwed over the hole. "Just like downtown," an old-timer might say, and not in a complimentary way, but this builder was a woman who had done her time on bare plywood.

Inside the cabin, the walls and ceiling were Sheetrocked

and painted white. The floor was laminate. The trim on base, doors, and windows was untreated pine. A two-by-four ladder led to the loft, where there was room for a mattress with a built-in headboard large enough for a row of books and a Coleman LED lantern. The wanderer might have appreciated how warm air moves up and understood why the bed had only one Army blanket tucked in over utilitarian white cotton sheets.

On the ground floor there were built-in shelves on every wall made of one-by-twelves and two-by-fours, also pine, interrupted only by the wood stove, the windows and a counter. A farmer sink was set into the counter, which drained into a five-gallon bucket. A two-burner propane stove sat next to the sink. Below it sat a cast iron frying pan and a cast iron dutch oven. On the shelves above was a small assortment of mugs, glasses, plates, bowls, and cutlery. Cans and boxes and bags of food stocked the shelves on either side, along with batteries from AAA to D, a box of candles, a six-pack of kitchen matches, a boombox, a large assortment of CDs featuring everyone from Jimmy Buffett to Zero 7 (the cabin's builder had lately discovered an interest in trip-hop), a large red toolbox, and a lot of books. A cushioned Adirondack chair with a matching footstool occupied one corner, behind which another LED lantern hung from a tall stand, designed to cast light on an open book in the lap of anyone sitting in it. A copy of Stacy Schiff's biography of Cleopatra lay open and face down on the footstool.

Every nail and screw in the cabin and its fixtures had

been placed with precision, every strip of laminate and piece of Sheetrock cut to fit exactly into the space necessary. Each of the four windows, both doors, and the window over the loft fit precisely into the openings made for them in each wall and not so much as a breath of the cool breeze outside found its way in. This was a cabin that had been built with an almost painful attention to detail: slowly, deliberately, one two-penny nail at a time. There was an indefinable sense that the insulation between the Sheetrock and the windlock shingles was the best available and had been packed or blown into every available space no matter how tiny, the joists and the trusses were built to the strictest specifications, the flashing around the stack would permit no leak. You could winter over in this cabin, provided you had enough supplies and sufficient firewood.

The cabin would not have been wonderful anywhere else in the Park, but here, back in the Quilak Mountains at the nether end of a box canyon no one ever stumbled upon except by accident and then only if they had a snow machine or a four-wheeler, it was nothing short of wondrous. It simply shouldn't be there. It was so far into the Bush that Canada was the next mountain over but one.

The nearest outpost of civilization, other than the Park Service headquarters on the Step, was Niniltna, a village of, lately, almost a thousand people. It sat sixty miles away as the crow flew on the Kanuyaq River, a broad estuary draining the Park into Prince William Sound. A gravel road passed through the village, leading south to the Roadhouse and west to Ahtna, a regional market town that served eastern Alaska from the Park north to Tok. The road was traditionally serviced by the state twice a year, in spring and fall. Any additional maintenance was left for pickups and four-wheelers to wear down in summer and the four-wheelers and snow machines in winter.

Or that was the way it had been. The discovery of copper and gold at Suulutaq in the southeast corner of the Park had led to something approaching almost monthly maintenance. Which was not to say that potholes decreased in either number or size, but when GCI began building cell towers from Ahtna to Niniltna and from there out to the Suulutaq, even Juneau could see the writing on the wall. Plans were drawn to improve a road that had existed in much the same condition since the Kanuyaq River & Northern Railroad had pulled up the railroad tracks behind it as it left in 1938, abandoning the area to a human population that was vastly outnumbered by bears brown and black, wolves, wolverines, coyotes, red fox, ground squirrels, lynx, beaver, land and sea otters, muskrat, mink, marmot, snowshoe hares and every species of bird that took wing over Alaskan skies. It was a trapper's paradise, and hunting, fishing, and trapping was how most Park rats had made their living between the closing of the Kanuyaq Copper Mine and the exploration and development of the Suulutaq Mine.

The Suulutaq had recently failed its EIS, or environmental impact statement, and the Suulutaq bosses had cut payroll at the mine before they'd been allowed to pull an ounce of gold out of the ground. With oil at its lowest price ever the state was presently busy figuring out how to pay its bills and never mind improving any roads at the end of which might or might not be any revenue-inducing construction of mines. Fortunately, the Park rats told each other, they hadn't forgotten how to hunt and fish.

At present, nowhere in the Park was there anything to suggest that any Park rat had enough money in the bank to build something even as small as this cabin. Quite apart from figuring out how to get all the building materials and furnishings to this remote location, the cost of transport-ation must have at least equaled the value of those materials themselves.

Unless...

A woman appeared around a corner. She wore leggings and a ribbed tank top, sweated through although the sun had left the canyon for the day, and a pair of Keen Revels so rigorously used that their original bright red had scuffed to a muddy brown. The muscle in her shoulders and arms was well defined and she moved easily and with assurance, every step well-placed, never stumbling or tripping over the rocky path.

Her hair was black, thick and cut raggedly around her ears. Her olive skin was tanned a light gold, as if she had recently spent a great deal of time outdoors, and her eyes were almond-shaped and tilted toward her temples with just a hint of an epicanthic fold. Their color was changeable, dark brown to today's light hazel. Her lips were full and red and unsmiling, but not frowning, either. As she reached the cabin she slipped out of the light backpack she wore and drained the bottle of water she pulled from a side pocket. Without missing a stride she continued toward the largest pool, the one closest to the cabin's front door, leaving boots and clothes in a trail behind her and jumping feet first into the steaming water. After a moment she surfaced, hair sleeked back like an otter's, head tilted up to the sky, eyes closed, water sluicing down her torso.

Someone let out a long, loud, appreciative, slightly out of breath whistle, and her eyes snapped open.

Coming up the canyon at a steady trot was a long, lean-limbed man of about thirty, a broad grin on his face. He was dressed head to toe in vibrant purple with yellow and orange stripes, and his face was covered with a light sheen of sweat. His breathing was deep and steady but not labored.

"Who the hell are you?" she said.

"I might ask you the same," he said, raising his eyes to her face. He trotted up to stop by the side of the pool. He didn't immediately grab for his knees, which confirmed his general fitness as showcased by the spandex.

"You're on private property without permission," she said. "You're trespassing." Her voice was a rough husk of sound, deep, rock steady, and she seemed unconcerned that she was naked from the waist up in front of a complete stranger.

He blew out a laugh. "There's no private property this far back in the mountains."

"Yes," she said, "there is, and you're standing on it." She climbed out of the pool and walked without hurrying to the cabin, returning with a towel wrapped around herself, just in time to see a dozen more colorfully clad strangers trot into view, move past the cabin and then disappear around the corner at the canyon's top. She watched them, frowning, and then turned back to see the first man still there, looking at a map.

"I'm Kate Shugak," she said, "and my uncle homesteaded this place before World War II. I inherited it from him. I come up here for peace and privacy—" she let her voice linger over that last word long enough for it to matter "—and now I find myself overrun by a bunch of refugees from the fashion runway at REI."

He held the map out. "It's not on our map. Your home-stead."

She didn't take it. "Then the map is wrong. What are you doing up here, anyway?" Half a dozen more Dupont ads trotted by, one a woman who reminded her of Audrey Hepburn in *Sabrina*, although Sabrina would have been far more at home in Humphrey Bogart's kitchen than in running up an obscure canyon in the Quilaks.

"Hey, Juna, slow down, you're making us all look bad," the man said.

"You're not even trying to keep up, are you, Gavin?" the Sabrina wannabe said as she blew past. "Nice towel," she said to Kate, and vanished in the general direction of the YT.

Gavin's eyes followed her ass until she was out of sight, and until Kate cleared her throat in a marked manner. "We're orienteers," he said. He folded his map and put it into a pocket that must have opened directly into his left buttock because there was nowhere else between his leggings and his skin to put it. Another three or four of his cohorts trotted by, all of them giving Kate a questioning and appreciative eye.

She tucked in her towel more securely. "How many more of you might I expect through here today?"

He winced at the acid note in her voice. "There are 149 of us registered for this event. I'm Gavin Mortimer, Ms., er, um—" He held out his hand.

"Shugak," Kate said, and didn't take it.

He let his hand fall and tried for adorably confused, as if it might have worked for him before. "Ms. Shugak, of course, and it goes without saying that I'm terribly sorry about this. We plot our routes through public lands, and your homestead didn't show up anywhere on existing maps as being privately owned." He added a winning smile to the mix. "It usually isn't a problem in Alaska."

"And am I expecting all of you back through here on your return route?" she said, not smiling back.

He was clearly thrilled to be able to reply in the negative. "No, no, no, we're coming back over a ridge to the north and west of here, and then back down into Niniltna."

He checked the gigantic multi-function stainless-steel watch on his left wrist. "I'm sorry, I have to go if I want to match my time on this route. Again, my sincere apologies. I promise you, you won't even know we were here once we're gone, and I promise you we'll retire this route at our next board meeting."

"Wait a minute," she said, to his rapidly retreating back. "You've raced through here before?"

"Yeah, we rotate the routes every four years."

"You ran through here four years ago?"

He turned to run backward. "Yeah. We lost one on our last run out here. Barney Aronson." He looked as sad as someone could look going backward up a mountain pass. "He was a friend."

"You lost someone? What does that mean, exactly?"

But Gavin Mortimer had faced forward again and picked up the pace and was now out of earshot. Kate swore beneath her breath and went back inside to put some clothes on.

Dusk had come and gone by the time the last of the runners had passed through the canyon, by which time Kate was thoroughly pissed off. Old Sam had left her his homestead at Canyon Hot Springs, her personally, Kate Shugak, and even the Park's chief ranger, Dan O'Brian, had, albeit reluctantly, acknowledged her free and clear title to it. Remote, no road, no airstrip, only the very lucky or the very savvy—or the terminally romantic— had ever found their way here, and when they had it was usually winter, when the annual thirty-foot snowfall had laid down enough cushion for a reasonably survivable welcome mat.

She had come up here, no, she had crawled up here in July after surviving a damn near point-blank gunshot wound to the chest. She had come up here for peace and quiet and to heal, principally because her chances of getting shot at here were zero to none. There were other reasons but that one would do to start with, and none of them had included being overrun by a bunch of extreme sportsmen. And women. In spandex.

Orienteers. What the hell was an orienteer when it was at home? They had maps, at least, and big-ass compasses, and water bottles strapped to their backs. She just hoped one of them didn't fall down and hurt their little selves because she wasn't into rescuing anyone but herself at the moment, thank you very much.

Mortimer. What kind of a name was that for a grown man? Mortimer Snerd, that's what kind of a name it was.

She made a chowder out of her last potatoes, corn, bacon, and stock, all of it canned, and made biscuits from the last of her flour, and took it out on the porch and ate it by the light of the barest sliver of the new moon, which was bobbing and weaving with the peaks of the Quilaks. There was hardly any snow on them. It was going to be another dark winter with no snow to reflect any ambient light back.

She set aside the now-empty bowl and sat back against the bench built in beneath the window and propped her feet on the porch railing. It was a small porch so her legs reached, which in some inexplicable way comforted her.

The great horned owl that had nested on a narrow cliff ledge high above the cabin gave its five-hoot warning before launching 747-like into the air and sailing off on one of the day's last thermal updrafts. The ledge had previously been occupied by a pair of golden eagles, who had spent the fall decimating the local marmot population before abandoning it for richer pickings somewhere else. The owl was company, of a kind, which was a good thing since it had taken out most of the smaller rodents and almost all of the smaller birds in the area as well. Kate couldn't understand why it, too, hadn't moved on.

A wolf howled in the distance. She raised her head to listen. A little while later another wolf responded from farther off.

There was no lonelier sound, although she was well aware she was guilty of anthropomorphism in thinking so. Wolves often separated from their packs to hunt. A howl was a way to find that pack again. But a wolf howl was a call on a party-line phone, and any wolf pack within earshot could hear it. If it was your pack, great. If it wasn't, that howl could get you killed by a pack who thought you were encroaching on its territory.

The wolf howled again.

But damn, that was a lonely, lonely sound.

Something tickled her cheek and when she raised her hand to swipe it away it came back wet.

Like the owl she was almost out of food, too. It was time, either to return home or get out the sat phone and put in another supply call to George. She still shied away from the former and she cringed from the cost of the latter. It had been one thing to pay him to drop off pallets of food, tools, and building supplies to construct an entire cabin. It seemed somehow less cost-effective to ask him to drop off a couple of boxes of groceries.

She should go home.

She really should. It was more than time.

The wolf howled again. The owl hooted again, a little less mournfully.

And again. She dropped her feet and stood up. That wasn't an owl. She went around the cabin to look up the canyon.

Sabrina, or whoever she was, was staggering down the trail looking considerably the worse for wear. She was scratched and bleeding, her attire torn in many places, and she was limping. She was also cradling her left arm in her right hand.

"I fell," she said when Kate had her inside the cabin and tucked into the Adirondack chair.

"I can see that," Kate said, unpacking the antiseptic cream and the Band-Aids.

"I was up on the ridge, on my way back, and I tripped. Can you believe it?" She sounded incredulous, as if she had never done such a thing before in her entire life. "I tripped and fell down the side. Ouch."

"Sorry." Kate gentled her touch. "Did no one see you?"

"No. I was way out in front. I was going to beat Gavin's time. Ouch!"

"Sorry. Did you yell for help?"

"I-I think I must have knocked myself out." Sabrina squinted out the window. "Is it really nighttime? It wasn't when I fell."

"It really is." Kate washed and dried and anointed and Band-Aided everything she could see that needed it, and made a cup of lemon tea with the last of the honey. "Careful. It's hot."

The orienteer sipped it and winced. "Ouch."

"Sorry."

They sat in silence for a while. "Sabrina—"

The woman blinked at her.

"Sorry, what was your name?"

"Juna." She seemed about to doze off.

"Juna, I'm Kate. Stay with me, okay? You could have a concussion from your fall. Not a good idea to sleep just yet."

"Oh." Juna looked out the window again as if seeing it for the first time. "It's late. It—I—we need to let them know I'm okay. They'll be worried. They'll be looking." She made as if to stand up and sat back down again, wincing.

"Relax. I've got a satellite phone. I'll put a call into Niniltna, tell them to get the word to your friends. I've got some extra clothes that'll be warmer than what you've got on. And then I'll make you something hot to eat."

"Oh. Okay." Juna subsided back in the chair. "But maybe you'd better call the troopers first."

"The troopers? Why?"

"Well, I—they'll want to see it. Won't they?"

"See what?"

Juna blinked up at her. "The body."

There was a long silence. "What body?"

"When I fell." Juna flinched a little from the expression on Kate's face. "I fell on it. The bones, anyway."

"Probably an old moose or bear carcass."

"I wish." Juna let her head drop to the chair back. "There's a skull. Part of one." She looked up and saw Kate glaring at her. "What? I didn't put it there."

Kate closed her eyes. "Fuck my life," she said, and went to get the sat phone.

Five

THURSDAY, NOVEMBER 3
Canyon Hot Springs, Niniltna

K ATE CLOSED UP THE CABIN. IT DIDN'T take long since she didn't lock the door and all she really had to do was bag the bedding against any voles that wriggled their way inside and shutter the windows against storms. She filled up the toilet paper holder and the lime can in the outhouse and they were pretty much good to go.

The morning had been spent first finding and then recovering the body, or rather, the bones. Unfortunately, Juna had been quite correct, it was a human skull, although only a partial one. She had appropriated Juna's phone—her own phone had died shortly after her arrival in the canyon—and taken pictures before, during and after collection, not that she thought any of them were going to help. She had even hiked to the top of the ridge from which Juna and presumably the deceased had fallen and took photos from there as well.

The bones consisted of a partial skull, what might have been an ulna, possibly a femur, what could have been a bit of pelvis, although it could just as easily have been the vertebrae of a humpback whale after the bears got done chewing on it, and a pile of small bones that could have come from either the hands or feet, or could just as easily have been the bones of a parka squirrel. Everything bore bite marks and there wasn't a scrap of cartilage left to tie any of the bones together. The putative arm and leg bones had been cracked for their marrow and sucked dry. The pelvic bone looked like someone had used it to sharpen a knife, or in this case possibly a set of canines. Kate was no expert but she didn't have to be to realize that identifying the deceased was going to require a DNA analysis, and she wasn't any too sure there was enough left of the deceased to do even that much.

She packed the bones away in a stuff bag and returned to the springs a little after noon, to be greeted with relief by Juna. "I thought you'd gotten lost."

"I'm not an orienteer," Kate said.

The implied insult flew right over the other woman's head. "Are we going back now?"

Kate squinted at the narrow band of sky that was all the canyon allowed. It was clear so far as she could see, and the air was still. "No reason I can see why not."

She hitched the trailer to the four-wheeler and put the bag of bones, half a dozen bottles of water, a box of energy bars and a ten-gallon can holding the last of her gas inside, along with an emergency kit, a sleeping bag and a one-man tent.

She took a last walk around the cabin, making sure everything was snugged up and the door on the latch but not locked. She stood on the deck for a full minute, listening.

"What are we waiting for?" Juna said impatiently. "Be better to get me back to town before everyone shows up here looking."

That was true enough. Kate stepped off the porch and climbed on the four-wheeler in front of Juna. "Fasten your seatbelt," she said. "It's going to be a bumpy ride."

She wasn't lying, Juna was pleased to tell her with some asperity at the end of the long trip down out of the Quilaks. Winters when it actually snowed, you waited until the pack settled some and then skimmed over the top of it on your ATV or your snowmobile. Years like these, when fall lingered on into spring, it was a matter of bushwhacking your way through the undergrowth, which if it had lost its leaves was still thick and in many places impenetrable. It took the rest of the daylight to get halfway to Niniltna. They camped overnight, sharing the close quarters of Kate's tent, all the closer because Juna snored.

They rose with the sun—mercifully, the high was holding—and packed up. By noon they had disgorged themselves from the claustrophobic brush to emerge on the road to the Step a couple of miles down from Park Headquarters. Kate debated for a moment whether they should check in with Ranger Dan first, but there was that body. In the end she headed for Niniltna, where she dropped Juna off at the Grosdidiers' clinic before making for the trooper post.

She walked in the door and a complete stranger looked up at her from behind the front desk. "May I help you?"

"Where's Maggie?"

"Maggie retired."

From the weary way this was said, Kate got the feeling it wasn't the first time the question had been asked. "Who are you?"

"I'm Estelle Kefauver, the new dispatcher," the other woman said. She was in her late thirties, early forties, with a solidity that came from muscle, not fat, dark hair cut in a bob, and dark eyes, steady and assessing. Kate got a general impression of Eyak, with maybe a little Tlingit and some Scandahoovian thrown in. Not a Park rat per se, but close. "You from Cordova?"

Kefauver looked surprised. "Yes. Have we met?"

"No. I'm Kate Shugak."

The straight, thick eyebrows went up a little. "I heard you were dead."

Kate almost laughed. "I am a sort of walking miracle, I guess."

Kefauver shifted in her chair, looking a little uneasy. Evidently not a Plath fan but who was, really. "You'd be looking for Jim Chopin, then."

"No. I am looking for the trooper, though."

"He got called out."

"Where?"

Kefauver gave her a cool look, and then relented, evidently because the story was too good not to share. "Chick Noyukpuk liberated one of the Suulutaq's front end loaders and busted into the liquor store, made off with what Cindy says was most of the Budweiser, and is currently leading the trooper on a low-speed chase up the road to Ahtna."

"Aw, hell," Kate said. "Chick's drinking again?"

"Looks like."

"Okay," Kate said. "I'll just leave this with you then." She dumped the stuff bag down in front of the dispatcher.

"What the hell! Hey! Hey, Shugak!"

She stuck her head back inside. "Yes?"

"What the fuck is this?" Kefauver was holding the skull remnant in accusing if appalled fashion.

"Well, I'm no expert but that looks like what's left of a human skull after the bears were finished with it."

"Where did you find it?

"I didn't find it. An orienteer did."

"What's an orienteer?"

"Good question. This one's named Juna and right now she's at the clinic, having Luke Grosdidier look at her arm, which she hurt when she fell off a ridge when she was, um, orienteering around the Quilaks. She landed on the bits and pieces of John Doe there. Luckily she wasn't hurt so badly that she couldn't manage to stagger back to my cabin at Canyon Hot Springs."

"You should have left it where it was so we could view them in situ."

"In this case in situ is the ass end of nowhere and John there has been dead for a while. The matter didn't seem urgent. Besides, it's November, even if it doesn't feel like it. I wouldn't go back up there myself this time of year, not unless I meant to stay until spring." Kate held up Juna's phone. "I took a bunch of photographs of the scene before, during and after I collected the bones. Give me an address, I'll email them to you."

Kefauver rattled one off. Kate opened a mail app, attached the photos and hit send. A minute later they appeared on Kefauver's desktop. She scrolled through them. "Was there anything besides bones? Any clothes fragments, personal belongings?"

"I'm guessing the clothing is in bits and pieces in various nests and dens over a hundred-mile radius. I saw no personal belongings, no wallet, no watch, no jewelry."

Kefauver blew out a breath. "Well, hell."

"Yeah, if it was easy everybody'd be doing it." Kate turned.

"Wait, where are you going?"

"To give Juna a ride to Auntie Vi's B&B, and then find a bed there myself and fall into it."

"How can we contact you?"

"Ask around."

Outside, she stood on the steps for a moment. A beautiful night, clear and cold, the Milky Way a smear of confectioner's sugar, the moon an ethereal, almost translucent crescent. A door opened, a truck started and drove off, a dog barked and was answered by another and then a third. She waited, not quite holding her breath, but she didn't hear anything else.

More noise altogether than she'd heard in four months. The sounds of human habitation grated on newly formed nerves. Not much, but a little, enough that she was forced to acknowledge it. She climbed on the four-wheeler and drove down the hill and turned left through the village, turning into the driveway of the last house on the right. It sat on the river, a dock protruding over the water, a thirty-foot drifter tied up to the dock. The house was two stories, four bedrooms and bathrooms up and the common rooms down. One of those rooms had been converted to a health care clinic when the Grosdidier brothers had taken an EMT course offered by the Niniltna Native Association and never recovered. It diverted energy that had been heretofore expended at the Roadhouse, and the feeling among Park rats was that at least the Grosdidiers were now treating injuries instead of causing them.

She walked in and halted just inside the door. Matt, Mark and Pete had returned while she was gone, and brought Laurel Meganack, Matt's girlfriend and the owner of Niniltna's only restaurant with them. "Hey," Kate said.

They all stared at her, bug-eyed except for Luke. "See," he said, "I told you." He was sitting on a stool next to a treatment table, fitting a fuzzy white sock over the ace bandage he'd wound around Juna's ankle, which didn't look all that swollen to Kate and had gotten Juna from her fall to the hot springs just fine. "There. Keep off that as much as you can—we've got a pair of crutches that should be a good fit—and you'll be fine in a couple of weeks." He gave her his best smile, which always looked good on a Grosdidier, and Juna wouldn't have been female if she didn't color just a little bit. "I'd recommend at least a little recovery time in the Park. Where are you staying?"

"I see you're still hitting on the patients, Luke," Kate said.

Luke turned that smile her way, unrepentant. "I takes my chances where I finds them, Shugak."

"Uh-huh. Come on, Juna, I'll give you a ride to Auntie Vi's."

Luke snatched the crutches from a closet and helped slash stalked Juna out the door and assisted her tenderly to a seat on the ATV. "Auntie Vi's, huh? I'll stop by tomorrow to check on you."

"I'll be flying out on the first plane tomorrow," Juna said, and made play with her lashes. "Are you ever in Anchorage?"

Kate turned the key, and stopped when Luke put his hand out. "Don't mind them," he said, jerking his head toward the house. "The thing is, Kate, we were all starting to think you were dead."

"Uh-huh," she said. "Thanks, Luke."

She dropped Juna at Auntie Vi's, who wasn't there, for which Kate sent up a silent but fervent thank you to whomever might be listening. Another woman was, curled up in a wing chair in the living room, staring into the fire in the fireplace with a lost look on her face. She was a living, breathing Barbie doll, blond hair, blue eyes and a body by Mattel. "The last time I saw Mrs. Shugak she was quilting at the Roadhouse with her sisters," she told them. "That was last night."

"Thanks," Kate said, and went to the board, where keys to all the rooms but one hung. She selected one and handed it to Juna. "I'll get the word out on Park Air that you're all right and where you are. You said you figured on flying out of here tomorrow?"

Juna nodded. "As soon as I can get on a flight. Have to get back to work."

"The airstrip is up the hill from here, just turn right out the door and keep walking. George should have at least one flight into town."

"Thanks." Juna made a face. "Sucks that I don't even know who won the race."

Sucks that we don't even know whose body you fell on, too, Kate thought.

"What's Park Air?" the Barbie doll said.

"Local pirate radio station."

"Can they hear it in Anchorage?" Juna said.

"They can hear it on the International Space Station."

As luck would have it, Park Air was up and running and Bobby was broadcasting over it in full voice when Kate walked in the door.

The A-frame had undergone some changes over the summer and fall. The door in back that had once led into the yard now opened into an extension. The king-sized bed that used to take up a full corner had vanished, so it was a good bet that Katya had reached the age of needing her own space. Or, more probably, her parents had reached the point of needing privacy from their inquisitive five-year-old. So the extension was most likely two new bedrooms. But the kitchen had new counters made of dramatically black composite with a wide, deep farmer sink that Kate envied on sight, and the cupboards finally had doors on them, and nice ones, too, some kind of distressed wood that invited the touch. Dinah, a slender blonde some twenty years Bobby's junior—chronologically, anyway—was drying dishes and putting them away. She turned when she heard the door open. When she saw Kate her face lit up in a beaming smile.

The console remained the same, a circular construction surrounding a central pillar up which snaked many cables that vanished into the roof and were connected to the 212-foot tower out back. Bobby was the NOAA reporter for the Park, or that was his day job. At the moment he sat hunched over a microphone, the very best in Bose headsets clamped over his ears. "Okay, everyone, time to take a brief commercial break. Larkin Poe, Brad Paisley and the cast of *Hamilton* coming up, so stay tuned. Oh yeah, and I got a copy of the *Hamilton* libretto and I put it up on the website, ParkAir.rad, and linked it to our Facebook page, so pull it up if you want to sing along with Lin-Manuel. Probably the closest you'll ever come to seeing it.

"The *Game of Thrones* discussion group meets at the Roadhouse this Saturday beginning at eight p.m., although Bernie sez that he's rationing the mead after what happened last month. You dudes take your Cersei seriously, that's for sure. And, Peter, by now everyone knows you read all the books and that you think the books are way better than the TV series, so put a plug in that shit, man. Saturday, eight p.m., Roadhouse, be there. At least winter is coming somewhere." Bobby sat up straight and squared his shoulders. Mighty fine shoulders, Kate couldn't help but notice. Again. "And for those of you morons still thinking Ramsay's death was appropriate, all I can say is you got your heads so far up your—"

A bamboo trivet sailed through the air and ricocheted off the hanging mike.

Bobby cleared his throat. "Sorry, folks, slight technical difficulty there. All I was saying before I was so rudely interrupted is, Ramsay was scum. Sansa shoulda took a little longer over him, payback for all that bad shit he pulled. Like maybe letting only one dog into his cell at a time, and when that dog was full, let the next one in for his share. Stretch that justice out, what I'm talking about." Bobby paused. "And maybe spreadeagle the fucker on the floor. 'Cause as we all know animals go for the soft parts first.

"Okay, enough of that, on to the Rat Out." He consulted a handful of slips of paper. "First up, Herbie Topkok needs someone to fill in at the shop while he and Alicia do their snowbird thing in Sun City. No big jobs, just flats, tire rotation, oil changes, like that, plus you make appointments for the big stuff or refer them to a garage in Ahtna, Herbie'll tell you which one. Plus you can use the shop to work on any of your own vehicles. As in inside, where it's warm. The light bill comes out of your earnings, the rest is yours to pocket. Job runs December to April. Drop by the shop anytime between now and December first to show Herbie you can tell one end of a socket wrench from the other and you're hired."

Bobby had the kind of deep, resonant voice born for on-air work. In another life he would have been a CNN host, his very timbre lending verisimilitude to whatever he was saying. It gave every woman listening the shivers, while every man listening wanted to be his new best friend. He shifted and his chair creaked. Kate took a second look and realized it was a real chair, not a wheelchair. She raised her eyebrows at Dinah, who mouthed "Later." She was still beaming all over her face, and Kate felt an answering smile spread across her own. There were some people she had missed during her sojourn in the mountains. Not many, but some.

"Next up, from Gabby Shugak to Eugene the Suulutaq pipefitter who followed me home for a month and left behind eight hundred dollars in roaming charges on my phone, I'll expect check or cash in the next twenty-four hours or I'll post every one of those pictures we took to my Facebook page and tag your mom. And she'll do it, too, Eugene, so I'd scare that money up pronto. Besides, dick move, man, really. Although, Gabby, if you're in those pictures, you can put them right up on Park Air's Facebook page. Really, anyone can post there who—ouch!"

This as a purple plastic ladle connected with the side of his head.

"Moving on," Bobby said, obviously suppressing a laugh, "for the fifth year in a row Harvey Meganack is putting his drifter up for sale. Price hasn't changed from last year so no hurry, it'll probably go up for sale again this time next year, too, same price."

The handful of slips diminished as Bobby read through them one at a time, some with editorial commentary, some not. It was mostly ads for used skiffs and kickers and trucks and fishing gear, PSAs for the annual Christmas craft sale at the school and a bake sale at the Riverfront Café benefiting the school choir's trip to the state championship, a cri de coeur for a lost cat—"Probably an eagle snack by now"—and the occasional bit of advice to the lovelorn— "Harry, for crissake, wouldja please just put Cathy out of her misery and ask her out for a drink at the Roadhouse? Or take her out to the dump to watch the bears, it doesn't have to be fancy. Jesus. Okay, that's it for Rat Out today. Next up, the soundtrack to the Broadway musical *Hamilton*. Music on the air, lyrics on our website and Facebook page, don't come crying to me if you so white you can't hiphop, children." He flipped a switch, and pulled off his headset. "What?" he said to Dinah, who was still beaming.

She pointed over his shoulder and Bobby swiveled around.

Kate enjoyed the second and a half that he was speechless.

"Where the FUCK have you been! And what the FUCK have you been up to!"

She might have had to blink away a tear at the welcome sound of that outraged bellow. "Well, first I tore down a cabin. And then I built a new one. That pretty much filled in the days."

He was up out of his chair and on his—feet?—and had her caught up in a hug that had her fearful of a return visit to Luke Grosdidier. He dumped her back down, grabbed her shoulders and gave her a shake that would have taken the head off any lesser being, and grabbed her up again. "Jesus Christ, Shugak," he said into her hair. "We were starting to think you were dead."

"I got that," she said, swallowing hard.

He pulled back for a comprehensive examination, head to toe and back. "Damn, Shugak. You look like a fucking Valkyrie. Only brunette. And, you know, short."

"Thanks," she said, wheezing a little. "Where's your chair?"

"New prostheses," he said, pulling up his pants' legs to show off his bionic ankles. "I never could work up a callus on the old ones. I read about these new ones online and went to Anchorage and they fitted me up. Check this out." He snatched Kate into his arms for a third time and cut an impromptu waltz to "Alexander Hamilton." He wasn't quite on the beat but then it wasn't a song written for waltzing.

He let her go, grinning. "How about that?"

"Impressive," Kate said.

"He heard about the father–daughter dance they have every year at the school," Dinah said.

"Isn't that only for high schoolers?"

"He says he needs the practice." Since Katya was only in first grade, Bobby was definitely getting a head start. Dinah stepped forward to take her turn at rib-cracking, and then stood back to give Kate her own once-over. "He's right, you do look about as healthy as I've ever seen you. Vitamins?"

Kate shrugged. "Tote that barge, lift that bale."

"Your hair looks like hell, though."

Kate ran a self-conscious hand over her head. "I just hacked at it whenever it got in my way."

"Looks like it." Dinah had Kate on a stool with a dishtowel around her shoulders and the scissors out almost before she finished speaking. While she worked she and Bobby filled her in on the latest Park gossip. All Kate could say in response to the info dump was, "Howie and Willard are television stars? Really?"

"Really," Bobby said, deadpan. He hooked a thumb over his shoulder. "I can fire up the promo for the first episode online if you want to see."

She held up a hand. "God, no. I'm begging you, don't do that to me."

"Yeah, well, wait till you hear about The Great Squirrel Harvest."

"I'm not asking."

"Did I tell you about Ace and Deuce? Couple of Outside bruisers looking for Martin?"

"My cousin Martin?" she said, surprised but not shocked. "What's he done now?"

"These two look fresh out of Spring Creek, so my guess is nothing good."

Kate sighed. "Great."

"Don't worry, they haven't found him yet," Bobby said, "or they wouldn't still be here."

It was noticeable during the entirety of this visit how Kate was very careful never to look in the direction of the woodbox, where the thighbone of a brontosaurus could have been reliably found every other time she had walked into this house. Bobby and Dinah exchanged glances and followed her lead. There were some wounds that never healed.

"So you're back, right?"

"It seems so, yes."

She didn't sound overjoyed but he forbore to comment. "What made that happen?"

She told them about the orienteers, and the body. "Huh," Bobby said thoughtfully. "I seem to recall they lost one the last time they were out this way. Five years or so ago?"

"Four. Evidently they run a route through Canyon Hot Springs every four years. Or that's what one of them told me, and, yeah, I figure this skeleton is probably what's left of him. Nobody else up that neck of the woods who has gone missing." Their eyes met. "That we know of." She changed the subject. "What have I missed?"

He said, gently for Bobby, "You know about Auntie Edna."

"Yes," she said. "Now and then George would include a note with supplies. Was there a potlatch?"

He shook his head. "They're holding off on that."

She didn't ask why. "What else?

"Well," he said, considering. "Suulutaq failed its EIS and there's a Crab Mafia in the Bering now."

"There's a Crab Mafia?"

When Dinah was done and the dish-towel whisked away Kate raked her hands through the cap of hair that now felt less like steel wool and more like thick silk. "What else?"

She saw Bobby look at Dinah. "What?"

"Have you seen Jim yet?"

"No."

"You know he—"

"Yeah," Kate said.

"And?"

She was spared the necessity of answering by a knock on the door.

"It's open!" Bobby bellowed without taking his eyes from Kate's face.

The door opened and a hesitant voice said, "Is this Park Air?"

It was the Barbie doll from Auntie Vi's. She saw Kate and said, "Oh."

"Hi," Kate said, trying to remember her name.

"Sylvia McDonald," the Barbie doll said. "The guy I hitched a ride with told me this was where I could find the radio station. I know it's late, but—"

Bobby waved an expansive hand. "Come on in, Sylvia, it's a night for late visits."

McDonald stared at him, her brow creased. "I—do I know you?"

Bobby smirked. "Points for being so color blind you don't recognize the only black guy in the Park."

Her blush was immediate and vivid. "I'm sorry. At the Roadhouse, right? You and—"

"Bernie," Bobby said, his delight at having to remind her of Bernie's name manifest. Kate could tell he would be informing the entire Park of it on the next Rat Out.

"You both helped me ask everyone if they had seen my husband."

"Yes. And you're here because—?"

"This is the radio station, right?" She looked at Kate. "She's the one who told me you had a radio station here in the Park."

"This is Park Air, yes."

Sylvia McDonald swallowed. "Could you maybe put out an announcement? A description of him, and ask anyone who has seen him to call in? I've been asking around town all day but I know a lot of people live outside it, and everybody says everyone in the Park listens to Park Air."

"I could do that," Bobby said. "Or you could hire someone to look for him."

McDonald's expression brightened a little. "Do you do that?"

"No," he said, and nodded at Kate. "But she does."

Kate pulled into Auntie Vi's driveway and killed the engine of the four-wheeler. She and McDonald got off and went inside.

Auntie Vi was waiting. "You," she said to McDonald, "go to your room."

"Auntie Vi—"

"You shut up."

Kate shut up, and McDonald scuttled down the hallway. When they heard the door to her room close behind her, Kate said, "Auntie—"

Auntie Vi shook her finger in Kate's face. "Finally you come back! Four months you are gone! Four! Things are happening while you are gone!"

Auntie Vi marched—there was no other word—into the kitchen and began banging pots and pans around with a vengeance, accompanied by a harangue on the new trooper—"A child! An infant! Half here, half in Ahtna! half in Tok!"—the loss of the school superintendent—"A lead teacher! What is that!"—and the capping of the

Permanent Fund annual dividend—"Veto! I veto him next election time!"

A door opened, followed by halting footsteps, and Juna appeared, looking sleep-rumpled. "What the hell?"

"If you value your life," Kate said in her best Delenn imitation, "be somewhere else."

Give her credit, Juna stood the torrent of Auntie Vi invective for at least fifteen full seconds before reeling back down the hallway.

Kate remained at a stool at the counter with head bent, saying "Yes" and "No" and "Certainly" when such comments might be safely inserted into the maelstrom. Eventually the smell of baking chocolate-chip cookies perfumed the air, and when the first sheet was yanked from the oven and slammed down on the counter in front of her she ate three without pause, partly in response to the minatory look in Auntie Vi's eye but also because she'd missed dinner and lunch had been an energy bar. Also, they were very good, with double chips and four ounces of grated milk chocolate added to the recipe. Toll House was hiding its head in shame.

Eating didn't stop her from listening, though. Auntie Vi's language seemed to have deteriorated. The aunties, like many of their generation, had been educated in BIA schools out of state and by BIA teachers in state, and when they wanted to they could deploy subject and predicate with the best of them. Now articles and adjectives and proper word order had devolved into fragments which if they couldn't be parsed still did not fail of effect. Kate wondered how much of this was due to Auntie Edna's death. She wondered, too, if Auntie Joy and Auntie Balasha were similarly affected.

The second sheet of cookies went into the oven with a little less verve than the first had. "Now what?" Auntie Vi said, shaking off her Wonder Woman oven mitts and fisting her hands on her hips. She fixed Kate with a beady eye and waited.

A bit of cookie went down the wrong pipe and Kate choked and her eyes watered. "What do you mean, auntie?"

"What next with you?" A contemptuous sniff. "You hide out—"

"Somebody shot me, auntie. I was recovering."

"—all summer into winter—"

"It was only four months."

"—and now you prance back into the Park—"

"I never left the Park, auntie," Kate said, her voice rising in spite of herself. "And I never prance."

They glared at each other. Someone cleared their throat and they both whipped around to see Sylvia McDonald shrinking beneath the combined fury of their gaze. Words withered on her tongue. Auntie Vi backhanded the plate of cookies in her direction. "You eat."

"Well, really, I just wanted to talk to—"

"You eat!"

McDonald swiped up a handful of cookies, said to Kate, "I really need to talk to you", and scurried off in practically the same breath. The kitchen timer dinged and Auntie Vi pulled the second sheet out of the oven. She paused, holding it with her back to Kate, staring at the row of hooks on the wall above the stove that held measuring spoons, cups and pot holders in a bright, colorful disarray. "Edna dead."

"I know, auntie. I'm sorry."

Auntie Vi blinked her eyes rapidly. "You go talk to that woman. Help her find husband."

"Auntie—"

"You go!"

Kate went.

A soft knock and McDonald opened her door. She had the overhead light on because Auntie Vi saw no need to put reading lamps next to the beds. The glaring light of the energy-saver bulb leached all the color out of Sylvia's face. She waved Kate into the bedroom and closed the door behind her. "Was it true, what that man said? That I could hire you to find my husband?"

Kate hesitated. Whatever Bobby or Auntie Vi said, she wasn't sure she was ready to jump back into work. She wasn't entirely sure she would ever be ready. Contrary to what some people thought, it turned out that bullets didn't bounce off her chest after all.

"Please," Sylvia said, shoulders slumping. She looked as if she hadn't slept in days. "I have to find him."

Against her will Kate said, "I'll agree to listen to what you have to say. No guarantees, though." Not wanting to see the look of hope in Sylvia's eyes Kate looked around for a chair and found an ancient wooden kitchen chair being used for a luggage rack. She moved the open overnight case to the floor. An express mail envelope, opened but not empty, slipped from the case and fell to the floor. "Oh, sorry," she said, and bent to pick it up.

"No problem," McDonald said, there before her to snatch up the envelope and tuck it into the gray canvas messenger bag on the bed, zipping it closed with a firm gesture. She sat down, shoving the bag behind her. "My husband is a geologist. He worked at the Suulutaq Mine. He calls home or texts every day and I haven't heard from him since last Saturday morning."

Kate counted back. "The twenty-eighth."

"Yes. He called and said—"

Kate listened to the story and asked the usual questions, and at the end got to her feet. "Look, Ms. McDonald—"

"Sylvia, please."

"Sylvia, people disappear in Alaska all the time. Most of them are runaways who left voluntarily and who come home again on their own." She waited for Sylvia to meet her eyes. "Unless you have some reason to believe that his disappearance is something else..."

Sylvia said nothing but continued with the cow eyes.

Kate tried again. "I can ask around, but I can promise you the word from the Roadhouse is already spreading, and when Bobby put the word out on Park Air it made it all the way to Tok, Ahtna, and Cordova. You've already got a couple of thousand people looking for him."

"Yes, but you're a professional."

Well, she had been. As recently as four months ago. And see how well that had turned out. "Are you sure the two of you didn't have an argument? A little spat?" She smiled. "I've never been married myself but I know it happens."

Sylvia's eyes fell, and she picked at a piece of lint on her pants leg. "No. Nothing like that. He just stopped texting and calling." She raised her head and gave Kate a pleading look. "Please. He's all I have."

The worst thing about a missing persons case was interacting with the family of the person missing. They wanted answers. All too often there were none. Kate had told Sylvia the truth; most missing persons in Alaska were like missing persons everywhere, teenage runaways who returned home on their own sooner rather than later. But for those who weren't, for those who had gone missing on a hike or a hunt or whose boat had never returned to port or whose plane had vanished minutes after takeoff, their families were left hanging, hoping their loved one was alive but, if they had lived any amount of time in Alaska, knowing they probably weren't. Kate thought about the scattered bones Juna had found, bones that would probably have lain there undisturbed for a lot longer if she hadn't stumbled across them. Bones too old to be Fergus's. She wondered who they belonged to, and if the family of their owner was still living in hope of seeing him or her alive again.

She hid a sigh. "I'll give it two days, no more."

"Oh, thank you, I—"

"And I'll need a retainer, full pay for both days as an advance against expenses."

Back in the hallway, she paused with her hand on the doorknob. Was that a ding she heard from inside the room? The sound of an incoming text, perhaps? She put her ear close to the door, listening.

"What you do about that man?"

Kate turned to see Auntie Vi glowering at her. She re-swallowed her heart and said mildly, "What man, auntie?"

"Your man!" Auntie Vi poked Kate in the chest hard enough to hurt.

"Oh. That man." Kate avoided another poke. "What am I supposed to do about him, auntie?"

"He quit!"

"I heard."

"Make him take it back!"

Kate contemplated the existence of an imaginary world in which she could make Jim Chopin do anything at all, ever, and kept her mouth shut.

With another poke for emphasis, Auntie Vi stormed back down the hallway. Shortly there was the clash of a pot on the stove. Probably she was going to cook up some jam from berries picked and frozen this fall. This one with the correct amount of spices.

Kate trudged off to bed. In the past thirty-six hours she'd had more interaction with humankind than she had had in the past four months combined, and it had been a long and wearisome journey down from the mountains.

And in the morning she had to get up and do some detecting. Joy.

Six

THURSDAY, NOVEMBER 3
Kate's homestead

EARLIER THAT SAME DAY JIM CHOPIN WAS running the broad blade of a rented Caterpillar grader down his brand new airstrip one last time.

He'd googled the topic of airstrip construction before he began. Guys with usernames like cubslut and avionista and bigstick had plenty of advice on picking a site with a two percent grade so you could land short going uphill and take off shorter going down. He didn't have a slope to work with, two percent grade or otherwise, just a flat piece of land that was mostly granite with a scraping of topsoil and a lot of scrub spruce falling on top of each other, corpses left in the wake of the tricentennial spruce bark beetle infestation. He did find a how-to on the state of Texas' website that had helped some, but in the end Wikipedia had more and better information.

Initially the job had required heavy equipment and people who knew how to drive it. He'd found a dirt-moving business in Ahtna that gave him a bid on clearing the land that put him into mild pecuniary shock until he remembered that his father's will had left him wealthy beyond dreams of avarice and signed on the dotted line. It took two bulldozers and one front end loader with a grapple attachment five days to clear the area he'd pegged out with stick and string.

The result was a strip of bare, packed earth a hundred feet wide and three thousand feet long (nothing succeeds like excess and he was still shopping around for an aircraft so he had no idea what kind of length he'd need), running roughly east–west to take advantage of the day breeze that blew toward the Quilak Mountains and the night breeze that blew away from them. Zero niner and two seven, easy peasy.

He ran a drainage ditch down both sides and one probably unnecessary culvert to drain down the cliff that fell into the creek, but better safe than sorry and it was going to snow again someday. He made sure any culvert would empty out on the bank well above the creek itself so it wouldn't foul the spawning grounds for the king and silver runs that called Zoya Creek home. Always thinking with his stomach.

He'd acquired what appeared to be the entire senior class of Niniltna High to limb the trees in exchange for a hefty donation toward the senior class trip. ("We're going to London," the basketball team's captain had told him. "You can drink at age eighteen in England, did you know that?" Now he did, and was ever so grateful not to live there.) The limbed trees had been neatly stacked in a small mountain and the limbs and the rotted trees in a much larger mountain waiting on winter to be burned. Given that winter had taken a pass the last two years, it might be waiting a long time.

That had been the end of July. The first of August had seen the delivery of a dozen pallets containing a pre-fab hangar broken into its essential parts. He hired help, again from Ahtna, and spent a blasphemous two weeks assembling it. Ikea this hangar was not, but when it was done he was satisfied. It was more or less the shape of a shoebox with sliding doors that opened up the long side facing the strip. The roof had a mild peak to facilitate snow removal. Aluminum–zinc alloy coated sheet steel on a steel frame bolted to concrete pillars sunk into the bedrock. With a forty-year rust warranty it ought to stand up to the worst storms Prince William Sound could scare up. He'd put in the recommended amount of strapping and bracing for earthquakes, too. He'd been born in California and he hadn't left the Ring of Fire behind when he moved to Alaska.

After that he had the hangar wired for electricity and installed a generator in a much smaller and extremely well insulated pre-fab next door. He thought about solar and did some research, which did not convince him that the tech was there yet, so in went a thousand-gallon tank on cradles next to the generator shed. Bastard weighed thirteen hundred pounds and cost twelve hundred dollars to fill, for which he ought to be able to work on his airplane in the nude for a year at least. If he was into that kind of thing.

Another tank was installed on the other side of the hangar for avgas, same size, much more sophisticated and way more expensive both to buy and to fill. After it was in, he got a card-carrying, dues-paying honest to god electrician to come in and wire everything to code. "Dude," the guy said, admiring the strip, the hangar, the tanks, even the stack of soon-to-be firewood. "Okay if I ride my 172 out here for some touch and goes?"

"Call first," Jim said, and paid in cash and didn't give the guy his number. He checked the Recreational Use Statutes for Alaska and did call his insurance agent.

That was the end of August. This November morning he woke, dressed and drove into town early in the hope he would see as few people as possible. As he pulled up at the post office, he saw George Perry in an Aero Tech Bell 212 lifting off with a plastic-sealed pallet depending from a sling. Looked like building materials and a few cases of dry and canned goods. George either didn't see Jim wave or didn't want to, pointing the nose of the Aero Tech northeast and skeddaddling out of Niniltna air space.

Jim didn't think the Aero Tech was rated for high-altitude work so George was probably headed for Park Headquarters on the Step. Although Ranger Dan or one of his minions generally bought most of the Step's groceries at the Ahtna Costco and drove it in. The Step being one of those rare locations in the Park that had a road to it.

A whine of turbofans drew his attention to the G II parked next to George's hangar, which ran up and back on its engines, pulled out and onto the runway and took off with no more ado. He watched it disappear rapidly into the west. He'd seen that aircraft overhead a lot lately.

He went into the post office, the small, square, mercifully empty room, an obvious add-on to the log cabin it was attached to. Both boxes contained only a single slip marked "Overflow." He went to the dutch door, the top half of which stood open, and dinged the bell. Noises off came from the cabin and shortly thereafter the postmistress hove into view. Hove was exactly the right word, as Cheryl Jeppsen was a generously sized woman who dressed in loose-fitting layers that fluttered like floral sails. "Jim," she said, eyeing him with more interest than he felt was strictly necessary. He was dressed in jeans worn white at the seams, a beat-up brown leather bomber jacket over a blue T-shirt and scuffed, stained Carhartt boots, the kind with the steel toes. It wasn't exactly a tuxedo, even an Alaskan one.

"Cheryl." He held out the slips.

Her lips pressed together. "No need. I haven't been able to walk a straight line back here for all the mail you've let pile up."

She disappeared for a few moments, reappearing with two overflowing tubs and had to return for a dolly piled high with packages. "You bring these tubs back now, you hear?"

"I hear." He carried them out to the pickup and returned for the dolly, pitching the packages into the passenger-side foot well of the cab and wheeling the dolly back inside with dispatch. But she caught him anyway, Cheryl. As the principal media outlet for the Park she had her responsibilities. "You look, I don't know, different."

He didn't quite know what she meant. "Probably the lack of uniform," he said, parking the dolly next to the dutch door.

"No," she said with a frown. "That's not it." She snapped her fingers. "Yeah, okay, when I look for it I see you've got a whole WWE look going on here. You been working out?"

"Not working at a real job, that's for sure," Bobby said, who had come up unnoticed behind Jim.

Fuck. "Bobby," he said, because he had to say something – the guy was standing right in front of him.

"Asshole," Bobby said, in exactly the same tone. "Cheryl! Looking good, girl!"

Jim could hear the simper. "Why, thank you, Mr. Clark, sir. And how are Dinah and Katya?"

Bobby shoved past Jim. He was wearing his legs, not driving his chair, although he managed to step on one of Jim's feet anyway. Jim took that as his congé and left the building. He climbed back into his pickup—that was new, a Toyota Tacoma standard cab in Blazing Blue Pearl, with the V6 after he'd read a scathing blog post on the 4-cylinder—and lit out of town like his pants were on fire.

He got back to the homestead with the feeling of having dodged a bullet.

Unfortunate choice of metaphor, that.

One of the packages was a wireless weather station— love love love Amazon Prime—to which he added batteries and mounted on a limbed, debarked tree trunk he'd tarred and countersunk into the ground on the north side of the hangar. The homestead already had Internet but he'd upgraded and boostered it between house and strip. The station came with an app that he immediately downloaded to his phone and there it was, light winds out of the west, fluctuating a little south by, barometer holding steady at two niner, no perceptible precip, temperature thirty-nine degrees, just plain bizarre for even the first of November in the Park. It had begun laying down frost overnight recently but there had been as yet no hard freeze. The alders lining the strip didn't know what to think and kept putting up buds only to have them knocked back by the lack of light and heat.

He spent the rest of the day rendering a very small part of the limbed logs into firewood with a chainsaw and splitter. At four-eleven the sun went down and he put the chainsaw and the splitter in the hangar, closed the big sliding doors, and added most of the cut wood to the stack against the back wall that was already six cords. The rest went into the trailer attached to the four-wheeler—also new, a very nice and very expensive Polaris Sportsman that always started and seemed to regard a forty-five-degree incline as a laugh—and he drove back to the house, having ripped through yet another Pendleton shirt, which pissed him off no end as those shirts were supposed to be virtually indestructible. They were sure as hell priced like it. Maybe Cheryl was right, maybe he had bulked up some since July. Certainly he'd been working physically harder than he'd ever worked before in his life.

He dumped the wood next to the wood pile beneath the deck, stacked it, and drove the ATV into the garage and closed it up before trudging back to the house. He stood in the shower until the hot water ran out and came down the stairs pounding the sides of his head to clear his ears. Dinner was half a pound of moose stew meat stir-fried with garlic and a package of mixed vegetables and anointed with sesame oil and soy sauce, served over the entire contents of the three-cup rice cooker.

Afterward he built a fire in the fireplace and took a beer out on the deck to watch the moon rise over the Quilaks. It was a bare sliver of silver, a waxing crescent, overshadowed and nearly outshone by Orion striding up behind it. The temperature had dropped to just above freezing according to the weather station app, and he could feel his still-damp hair freezing to his head, but he stayed where he was, his breath beginning to steam in the cool air.

Kate had run here, to the Park, to her father's homestead, after that colossal snafu in Anchorage had left her for dead with a throat slit from ear to ear. Not quite dead, though, she'd left ANMC the same way she'd left Ahtna General, against medical advice, and disappeared—as seemed her invariable habit—to lick her wound, and regain her strength away from the prying eyes of the honestly concerned and the pruriently curious alike. Eighteen months last time, before she'd returned to the world.

He'd only been holed up for four.

He heard a wolf howl far away, and he looked up again at the Quilaks, at Big Bump and Mother and Child outlined against the stars along with the rest of the Praetorian Guard, a solid line of mountains running north from Prince William Sound to the edge of the Park, where it curved west to follow the Park's border until it diminished into rolling hills interspersed with broad stretches of taiga and tundra. Cupped in the Quilaks' cold embrace was most of the twenty million acres of the Park, drained by the Kanuyaq River, meandering back and forth across the Park until it reached the Sound some hundred and thirty miles west of the Quilaks.

The wolf howled again, or another wolf howled in answer to the first one. He raised his beer for another swallow and found the bottle empty. His hand was clenched around it so tightly his knuckles gleamed white even in the darkness. He took a deep breath and went back inside.

The house was scrupulously, even painfully, clean. He went through it every Sunday morning, changing the sheets and towels, scrubbing out both bathrooms, dusting and vacuuming all the rooms, wiping down the entire kitchen with undiluted Clorox so thoroughly that he had to open up all the windows and doors afterward so his eyes wouldn't tear up.

Because when Kate came back, the fact that every flat and horizontal surface was as antiseptic as an OR table might blind her to the fact that he had nearly gotten her killed.

Not to mention the aroma of the aforesaid Clorox.

He closed his eyes and shook his head. He tossed the bottle and sat down on the couch with his laptop to resume his search for the perfect plane.

A pilot's license made a candidate for trooper that much more attractive to the State of Alaska and had been his main motivation in acquiring one, but after twenty-two years on the job, much of it in the air between crime scenes, flying was in his blood now. Besides, the very thought of driving the three hundred and fifty miles to Anchorage made his butt hurt. Now that he no longer had access to the Alaska Department of Public Safety Cessna 180 stationed at Niniltna, the only alternative was a plane of his own. His father, a wizard ("wizard" might have been his actual job title) at investment, had left Jim with more than enough money to indulge his son and heir not only with an airstrip with all the mod cons but the aircraft of his choice as well. The problem was, which aircraft.

For a while now he'd been seduced by the Cirrus SR-22, the airplane with the built-in parachute, mostly because he'd read the news articles about the instances where the parachute had saved lives, although he didn't expect to find himself flying over the middle of the Pacific or anywhere the hell near DC anytime soon. The drawback of the Cirrus was its low wing, impractical for landing on narrow Bush airstrips, but really, he asked himself, how many Bush strips was he going to be flying into in the future?

He bookmarked the Cirrus website and googled that quintessential Bush aircraft, the Piper Super Cub. (Only half a million hits? Really? For an iconic aircraft like the Cub? Google, you are drunk, go home.) The Super Cub was the take-off-almost-anywhere go-to aircraft for flying in Alaska. Put it on tundra tires and you could land almost anywhere, too. Put it on floats and every lake and seaplane base was in play. A pilot he knew took his Super Cub out to Southwest Alaska once a year to go beachcombing and had the biggest stash of Japanese floats (legal) and walrus tusks (not) Jim had ever seen. Another had landed on a glacier to rescue someone who had fallen down a crevasse. Another had landed in the middle of a running river to rescue a canoer come to grief in rapids. He'd seen with his own eyes Demetri Totemoff take off from the Kanuyaq River with two sheets of four-by-eight plywood strapped to both floats. He'd had to use the river damn near all the way to Double Eagle to build enough speed to get into the air, admittedly. For going low and slow there was nothing like the Super Cub. The downsides were, well, slow, and if he wanted to hunt with a Super Cub he'd be going after caribou because he'd never fit a whole moose into the back of one.

He bookmarked a few websites that felt more like Super Cub fan clubs than straightforward sales platforms and moved on to the deHaviland Beaver, which was way more plane than he needed, but put it on floats and keep a pair of wheel-skis in reserve and there was just nowhere he couldn't go and nothing he couldn't carry, and at any time of the year, too.

And then there was the Cessna 180, the plane he'd been flying for the last twenty years, with time off for bad behavior in a Bell Jet Ranger, as he was rated for both fixed wing and rotor, and which latter craft had given rise to his nickname (one of them, anyway), Chopper Jim. The Cessna 180 was a fast, reliable bird with a lot of room, but a little too much aircraft for too many of the smaller airstrips. But, again, how often would he be flying into smaller strips? The job that had required that was in his rear-view mirror, and he wouldn't have access to the helo anymore. Although... he shook his head. That way lay madness

He closed the laptop and set it aside, standing to stretch out his back and put another log on the fire. He got another beer and went to drink it standing in front of the bank of windows that made up the prow front of the house. The crescent moon was well over the Quilaks now, tracing their peaks with a faint iridescence that made the edges of their drawn blades seem insubstantial, even ghostly. Quite a trick when most of the time those swords' points looked like they ought to be covered with the blood of those who dared to cross them.

The vale of the Kanuyaq River lay in deep shadow as it rolled westward from the mountains. No snow or ice to reflect the moonlight, and the dark hills and hollows seemed hidden and full of mystery and danger. The deciduous trees, the birches and the aspens and the cottonwoods and the all-pervasive alders were bare of leaf, throwing the evergreens with their thick-needled limbs into prominence, looming, alert, on watch.

It was hard not to anthropomorphize the Alaskan landscape, he thought, when it was trying to kill you pretty much every time you stepped out the door. A sudden winter storm and any minor emergency like childbirth or murder was transformed into a survival story that made the voyage of the *Endurance* look like amateur hour. A warm spring melted too much snowfall too fast and a flood took out your homestead and you and every member of your family along with it. Hell, for that matter, a moose could stove in your skull with one kick and a bear could rip you four new bodily orifices with one swipe of his or her paw. It was hard not to imagine a certain native animus in the very topography. Much better to fly over it than drive it, especially in winter.

But in what? It occurred to him that in the months since he'd been searching for exactly the right aircraft, that one all-purpose super-duper utility at altitude vehicle, that he had yet to look up the price of any of them. He wondered if having unlimited funds was adding to his indecision. If you were broke you bought what you could afford. When you had money enough in the bank to buy anything up to and including a G II like the one that had taken off from Niniltna that morning, your choices expanded algebraically and it was much harder to choose. A First World problem if he'd ever heard one.

The outline of the mountains seemed to firm up for a moment, become more substantial, more assertive, more present. At a distance, he could admire their beauty and their magnificence. Up close, they were just another killer added into the Park mix.

He wondered how often Kate had stared at this same view, that time when she had come back to the Park wounded physically, mentally, emotionally. The homestead was a refuge, isolated, as Robert Service would have had it, amid a silence you most could hear. The aunties had left her alone for a while, letting her heal physically, before depositing a half-wolf, half-husky hybrid pup, abused, near starving, on her doorstep. Something to divert her thoughts away from herself. Something to help her heal.

He remembered the Aero Jet taking off from Niniltna that August morning, too.

Maybe he should get a helicopter. A small one, enough for the pilot, a passenger, and a couple of hundred pounds of freight. One that could handle a little altitude. Say an altitude similar to that of Canyon Hot Springs. With the ability to land on a space the size of a postage stamp because that was about the sum total of horizontal to be found there. A craft small enough to not shear off the rotors on the canyon walls.

He was pretty sure they hadn't built it yet.

A flash of light showed through the trees. Someone was coming down the lane from the main road. He watched as a fire-engine-red Chevy Suburban lumped and bumped its way into the clearing and pulled up in front of the house with a lunge and a jerk. A diminutive woman in jeans and a First Nations sweatshirt jumped down from the cab.

"Oh hell," he said, and went to open the door, just in time for Auntie Vi to bounce through. Not a woman so much as a force of nature, Auntie Vi never walked where she could bounce.

"She's back," Auntie Vi, never one to waste time on preliminaries, said. She tossed a gallon Ziploc filled with fry bread on the table with such vigor it slid off onto the floor.

He froze in the act of closing the door. His tongue seemed to have cleaved to the roof of his mouth.

Auntie Vi, not one to suffer fools gladly, poked him hard enough with one sharp finger to rock him back a step. "You hear me, stupid man? She's back!"

Seven

FRIDAY, NOVEMBER 4
Niniltna

IN THE MORNING KATE WENT OUT TO FIND her four-wheeler gone.

So was Sylvia McDonald.

The first they knew of this was when the new trooper thumped at Auntie Vi's door at oh-dark-thirty. He stood in the kitchen where Kate was eating her bacon and eggs and homemade sourdough bread toast dripping with butter—the great thing about Auntie Vi, she'd still feed you no matter how mad she was at you—and said, "Are you Kate Shugak?"

The new trooper was tall but looked as if his uniform weighed more than he did, the open collar displaying an Ichabod Crane neck and an Adam's apple that stuck out farther than his chin. His buzz cut was so short it was hard to determine his hair color. His eyes were big and brown and thickly lashed, making him look a little like Bambi before

Bambi grew into his legs. He didn't look old enough to vote, let alone to have graduated from the trooper academy and done his three supervised tours. "I am," she said. "And you are?"

He swallowed, his Adam's apple bobbing like a Jet Diver with a fish on. Kate watched, one loaded fork suspended halfway between the plate and her mouth. It was kind of mesmerizing. "I'm Cooper Cochran, Alaska state trooper, temporarily assigned to the Niniltna post." His voice almost broke and he flushed a bright, vivid red. "I'm new."

His blue uniform jacket and pants with the gold stripe running up the sides had yet to wash out its synthetic shine. "How can I help you?"

"Do you own an ATV?" He consulted his tablet. "A Polaris?"

"Yeah, sure," Kate said around a mouthful of toast, and hooked her free thumb over her shoulder. "It's parked right out—"

Something in his expression warned her. She swallowed and put her fork down. "It's not parked right out front, is it?"

"No, ma'am, I'm afraid not." Swallow, bob. "It's been found overturned on the side of the Step road about a mile from here. Did you leave your keys in it?"

Kate shook her head, eyes never leaving his face. There was more but he wasn't ready to spit it all out quite yet. "No, Auntie Vi makes us leave them on the board there." She pointed at a square of plywood nailed up next to the door, festooned with three rows of cup hooks. "People can come get the keys to move the vehicle that's got them blocked in." She stood up. "And I see that my keys are gone."

The baby trooper looked at Auntie Vi, standing behind the counter with her arms tightly folded and the standard glower on her face. "Did you have a Sylvia McDonald staying here last night, ma'am?"

The glower faded a little.

"Crap," Kate said. "This way, officer." She went swiftly down the hall and knocked on Sylvia's door. There was no answer. She tried the handle. It was unlocked. The small case was still sitting open on the chair, but the messenger bag was gone and so was Sylvia McDonald.

A mile up the Step road, the body lay tumbled into the ditch at the side of the road. Cochran had taped off the scene but he wasn't experienced enough to always carry a tarp in the vehicle, so she lay exposed to the sky, surrounded by crime scene tape Cochran had laid around her on the ground. Unbeknownst to Kate, the same raven that four years before had first found the body up at Canyon Hot Springs had discovered Sylvia's body in the interim, and he and the rest of the unkindness had as usual gone for the soft parts first. Cochran fell back a step and turned away to vomit, thoroughly and noisily, into a clump of grass.

"Go on," Kate said, "git, shoo!" She advanced on the body, waving her arms, and the ravens ascended reluctantly in the air, expressing their displeasure with raucous caws and a few well-placed shits.

Cochran wiped his mouth on the sleeve of his uniform jacket and looked like he might vomit again. "You really shouldn't be inside the tape, ma'am."

Kate crouched down to look at the body. Sylvia lay on her back as if she had fallen there. The ravens hadn't really gotten started on much beyond the eyes and lips before Kate and the trooper had gotten there. She bent over to look at the back of Sylvia's head. There seemed to be some darkness there other than the natural cast of shadow, and she reached out a hand to raise Sylvia's head. There was a large, deep depression visible, even through her hair, stained with blood and brain matter. Behind her, she could hear Cochran retching again. She put Sylvia's head back down.

The four-wheeler was upside down in the ditch next to the road twenty feet away. Sylvia's messenger bag was halfway between her body and the road. Kate went to the bag and picked it up. It was unzipped.

"Uh, ma'am, you shouldn't be touching that. Please put it down."

Kate rummaged inside the bag for a moment and came out with a wallet. She dropped the bag and handed him the wallet. He looked from it to her. "Verify her identity," Kate said.

"You already did that."

"Did I?" Kate went back to search the pockets of Sylvia's coat and pants. "Pockets are empty," she said, straightening up. "Have you got a body bag?"

He looked at her.

"A tarp?"

He had a truly technicolor blush.

When he didn't move she said, "Have either at the post?"

"Well, I—"

"Good, then you'd better go get one."

He turned and paused. "Am I supposed to—"

"Do you have a pad and pencil? And a tape?"

Nope. The cloud of humiliation he left behind rivaled the billow of dust. Kate got out her cell phone and took photos of the scene with the EasyMeasure app, making sure to get exact distances between the ATV, the body, the messenger bag, and the nearest trees. The keys to the four-wheeler were still in it.

She'd just snapped the last photo of some interesting tire marks on the road when Cochran returned. He wasn't alone. "Hey, Nick," she said. "Didn't know you were in town."

"Rolled in this morning. They've got us covering Ahtna and Tok as well as Niniltna."

"Constantly in motion."

"You said it." Half as tall and twice as wide as the younger trooper, with the shine on his uniform definitely worn dull, Nick was carrying an aluminum case that Kate knew from experience served as his murder bag. "I'll have to ask you to step back from the scene."

"Of course." She could bullshit the kid but knew better than to try that on the veteran. She retired down the road and found a stump to sit on. It was a nice enough morning, mostly clear and cold as hell. The high pressure system hanging over this part of Alaska had maintained a stubborn toehold on the region for more than a week. A low had to be growing up in back of it. Better it blew in sooner than keep building into a storm that when it finally pushed back the high would flatten everything from Katalla to Fairbanks.

She watched the two troopers go about their business. It was a depressingly familiar scene. Nick did have a measuring tape and put Cochran on one end and measured what Kate had measured and recorded with her phone app. He went through the vic's clothing and bag. He did everything methodically, by the book, with a calm, almost cold efficiency. Nick didn't do empathetic.

Sylvia had lied to Kate the night before and Kate had known it when she did so. And here she lay, face turned up to the sky, divested of the animating spirit that made her peculiarly herself. Her body was an offense, an obscenity even.

Please. He's all I have.

Kate could feel the anger rising up behind her breastbone, pushing to get out. It was her own peculiarly animating spirit.

Her phone rang. "Hi, Kate Shugak? It's Gavin Mortimer. I was wondering if you'd had any news regarding the identification of the body you found on your property."

"No, Gavin, I haven't," Kate said, still looking at the second dead body she'd seen in two days. "I told you I'd call when I did."

"Yeah, I know. It's just—he was a friend of mine."

"I understand." She hung up.

The two troopers slid Sylvia McDonald into a bag and zipped it up. A raven expressed his displeasure from a nearby spruce bough and launched himself up and away with a disgusted flutter of blue-black wings.

Kate waited until they had the gate closed. "You flying her back to Anchorage, Nick?"

He nodded. "I'll need to take your statement."

"How about I hitch a ride and you take it in flight?"

He shrugged. Not big with the verbal, either.

"Can I take my ATV back to Auntie Vi's?"

"Will it run?"

The three of them rolled the ATV upright. It started on the first try. "Takes a licking," Kate said.

"I'm taking off as soon as we load the body," Nick said.

"Meet you at the strip," Kate said.

She parked the ATV at Auntie Vi's, who was extremely annoyed when Kate said she was going to Anchorage and said so, pungently. Once she was out of range, Kate called Bobby to let him know where she was going and hoofed it up the hill to the airstrip in good time. The body was laid out in the back of the 180 and bungeed down. They were in the air at ten a.m. and change. Kate watched out her window as Niniltna and the Kanuyaq River fell away and behind as the Cessna leveled out and headed west by southwest.

"They give you Jim's plane?" she said.

"Yeah." Nick almost smiled.

Figured.

At almost exactly the same moment came a hammering at the door of the A-frame. "This ought to be good," Bobby said, already up, mug in hand. He strolled over to the door and opened it. "Why, Jim. What an unexpected... displeasure."

Jim pushed his way inside without being asked. "Where is she?"

"Well sure, come on in," Bobby said, closing the door behind him. "Happy to see you anytime." His grin was broad and sharp.

"Don't fuck with me, Clark," Jim said, his shoulders tense. "Where is she?"

At that moment came the distinctive growl of an airplane on takeoff.

Bobby smiled. "At this exact moment? About five hundred feet overhead and climbing."

"What?" Jim stared at the ceiling. "What the hell? Where is she going?"

"Anchorage."

"Anchorage! Why? She hasn't even been home yet!"

"She's on a case," Bobby said blandly, and he crooked an evil eyebrow. "Unlike yourself."

Ecstatic for the opportunity to relieve his feelings on the nearest available target, Jim stepped forward to go toe to toe. "Bobby, why don't you just—"

"Stop. It."

The words, handed down like lightning from Olympus, halted both men all upstanding. Dinah came out from the bedroom, tugging on the second of a pair of slippers that looked as if they'd been born in a purple shag rug left over from the Sixties. She was in robe and pajamas but she had taken the time to brush her hair, because Jim. "I'm going to make more coffee and then Bobby is going to make his justly famous Nutbush Omelet and Park Air Pancakes and the three of us are going to sit down and eat and visit like civilized. Human. Beings. And the longtime friends that we are." She glared impartially at the two of them.

Jim took a deep breath and let it out slowly. He looked Bobby in the eye and with an effort used his inside voice. "I quit. Get over it."

Bobby took a deep breath, intercepted a look from Dinah, and visibly detumesced. She pointed at the kitchen, and Bobby hung his head and stumped into the kitchen, muttering.

"I'm sorry, what was that?" Dinah said.

"Nothing," Bobby said, casting a malevolent look over

his shoulder at Jim as he pulled eggs and pork chops from the fridge.

"That's what I thought," Dinah said, and she pulled a chair out from the table. "Sit down, Jim."

Jim sat.

Eight

FRIDAY, NOVEMBER 4
Anchorage

THEY LANDED AT MERRILL AND WERE MET by an ambulance. Sylvia McDonald was loaded into the back. Nick, not a man to use one word where none would do, gave Kate a nod and they left their separate ways.

He'd taken her statement in his usual terse fashion, tapping notes into his tablet, evincing very little interest in her answers, even when she told him why Sylvia was in the Park and that she had hired Kate to find her husband. For her part, she kept her answers as brief as his questions and made only two unsolicited comments. "You didn't find a phone."

"No."

"She had one. I heard it ding after I left her room last night."

"What time?"

"About eleven."

He wrote it down. "Know her number?"

Sylvia had given Kate her phone number after writing a retainer check and Kate read it to him from her own phone. "And she had an express mail envelope in her messenger bag addressed to her husband in her room. It had been opened."

"See who it was from?"

"No."

He didn't ask her how she knew the envelope was gone because he was smarter than that. "Anything else?"

There was plenty, but there was also no point in saying so, or not yet. "No."

Nick tucked the tablet away and let his hands rest on his knees, eyes checking for traffic, feet easy on the rudder pedals. DPS's Cessna was in good hands.

The investigation into Sylvia McDonald's death might not be. Between Tok, Ahtna and the Park, Nick had to be spread pretty thin. He probably had another dozen current cases and who knew how many more hanging fire, everything from taking two more caribou than the bag limit allowed to sexual assault of too many minors to armed robbery to permanent dividend fraud. On the face of it, Sylvia McDonald had gone for either a late night or early morning joy ride on Kate's ATV, rolled it and died. Just another suicide by Alaska. Nick would drop the body at the medical examiner's, who would do an autopsy as required by Alaska statute in any accidental death. The ME, whose caseload was every bit as backed up as Nick's. Absent any adverse evidence he found, he would absolutely back up the trooper. Complications took too much time. So much better for everyone concerned if Sylvia McDonald's death was declared accidental.

Better for everyone except perhaps Sylvia McDonald, Kate thought. And Fergus McDonald, still among the missing. She fished out her phone and called a cab to take her to the townhouse.

The townhouse sat on Westchester Lagoon in a line of townhouses, three stories including a garage, kitchen/dining and bedrooms on three floors. Jack had left it to his son Johnny in his will and it was where they all camped out when they were in town. Johnny was currently enrolled in his first year of college at the University of Alaska Fairbanks. She called him from the townhouse.

"Kate! Dang, Van and I were beginning to think you were dead."

"Not the first time I've heard that since I came down from the mountains."

The relief in his answering laugh was plain to hear and she felt a slight twinge of guilt at having left him—and so many others—hanging as to news of her whereabouts. "George said he sent you my note."

"He did. Only reason I didn't come home looking for you." A pause. "You shouldn't have taken off that way, Kate. Frightened the living hell out of everyone."

There was no answer she could give that would make sense to an immortal, invincible eighteen-year-old, so she made none. After a moment he said, "Good you're home, though."

"Actually, I'm in Anchorage, at the townhouse."

"What? Why?"

She told him. He was silent for a few moments. "Well, I'd offer to help but I'm only two-thirds of the way through Justice 202."

Her turn to laugh. Justice 202 longform was *Introduction to Criminal Investigation and Interviewing*. "How well I remember. You managing to stay awake in class?"

"Barely. When I start to doze off I think about Len and Virgil and Louis. Or any of your cases. Wakes me right the hell up."

"Yeah. How's Van?"

"She's good. She's great, actually. Kind of lucked out there."

"So did she."

She could practically hear his blush bounce off the satellite. They talked a little more and then Kate hung up and liberated the Forester from the garage.

The office was in the Carr-Gottstein building downtown across from the old courthouse. Fancy digs for a Park rat made good, Kate thought as she passed beneath the statue of the whale kicking the whalers out of their boat as they tried and failed to harpoon him. There was a metaphor in there somewhere, and a pretty Alaskan one at that.

She exited the elevator on the seventh floor and walked down the hall to the door that identified the business only by brass numbers indicating the address of the suite. She opened the door to behold Agrifina Fancyboy in all her glory. A fresh-faced Yupik from western Alaska, Agrifina had watched one too many Lauren Bacall movies on satellite television growing up and in her professional persona as Kurt's assistant had cultivated an intimidating style of dress, accessorized with a paralyzing poise. She looked up from the computer into which she was inputting information at the speed of light. "Ms. Shugak."

Kate didn't bother saying "Kate, Agrifina, please," because Agrifina had ignored her the first dozen times she'd said it so why keep trying. "Ms. Fancyboy. Is he available?"

"I believe so but allow me to ask." Agrifina rose from her ergonomic yet elegant chair, probably designed by Versace, and paused for a moment to allow for the full force effect of her two-piece gray suit with an asymmetric lapel, probably made from the finest wool shorn from sheep with only the finest of pedigrees on the South Island of New Zealand. As she turned to knock on Kurt's door Kate noticed that her stockings had acquired seams. Maybe that was a thing now. She couldn't bring herself to look twice at Agrifina's heels, which appeared to have gotten an inch higher since the last time Kate had been in the office. Kate wriggled grateful toes inside her Asics, although she really wished they'd make them in black instead of bubblegum pink and neon green.

"Kate!" Kurt exploded out of his office and gave Kate a hug that raised her right up off the floor. It seemed to have become a meme. He set her down again without letting go. "We all thought you were dead!"

"People keep saying that."

Kurt looked around. He was the first one to do so since she had come down from Canyon Hot Springs. Not Auntie Vi, not even Bobby and Dinah, no one had so much as given a sideways look at the current gaping black hole that walked next to Kate every moment of every day.

"She's not with me," Kate said.

Kurt grimaced. "Sorry."

"Can I talk to you for a minute?"

"You absolutely can." Kurt let her go. "Could you bring us some coffee, honey?"

Inside his office Kate raised an eyebrow. "'Honey?'"

His grin was the very personification of shit-eating. "We might be an item now."

"'Might?'"

He squirmed in his chair. "Are, I guess." He ran a hand through his hair, messing up a perfect cut that Kate would bet large had been orchestrated by the little demon of orderliness channeling the Fifties in the outer office. "I don't really know what happened. We were working late one night, and—"

"Stop. Stop right there. That's need to know and I don't, oh god how I don't."

His grin softened. "She's really something, Kate." His

voice softened on the words and he might even have gone a little dreamy around the eyes.

She'd busted Kurt for selling bear gall bladders to Chinese buyers, and then hired him when they both wound up in Anchorage at the same time and she needed a grunt for leg work. The job had evolved into her being his silent partner in Pletnikof Investigations, which in two years itself had grown into one of the go-to firms in Alaska for employee vetting. He also did some investigative work for civil and criminal lawyers and was always on tap for whatever Kate threw at him. She only wished there were more Park rats like Kurt.

"So." He cocked an eyebrow. "You look a little pissed."

She worked her jaw back and forth to loosen it up. "A woman came into the Park looking for an AWOL husband. Last night she hired me to find him, sometime after which she lit out up the Step road on my four-wheeler. This morning her body was found about a mile up said road from the village. So, yeah, I am a little pissed."

Kurt's eyebrows went up. He sat back in his chair and made a come-on motion with his hand, and she told him the saga of Fergus and Sylvia McDonald. He listened with a gathering frown. "So she's dead, possibly by foul means, and he's missing."

"Yeah."

"You want a workup on both of them?"

"As much as you can as fast as you can. She wrote me a retainer check." Kate pulled it out of her jacket pocket and handed it over. "Let's put Pletnikof to work for her."

He read it and whistled. "Full pay? She really wanted him found."

"Looks like it."

He cocked his head. "But?"

"He was tarryhooting off in the Bush, Kurt. Maybe he found something."

"Maybe something found him. Maybe a grizzly who mistook him for a pre-nap snack?"

"Maybe. Maybe something else." She shifted in her chair. "Got a feeling, is all."

"I'll back your feelings against anyone else's hard evidence any day. Got anything for me to start on?"

"Her driver's license number." She scribbled the number on a tablet he shoved across, along with the mailing address that had also been on the license when she got a quick glimpse of it that morning. "Right now, could you find me their home address?"

Kurt, who in the fullness of his employment as Pletnikof, PI had discovered a heretofore unknown talent for skimming the cream off the Internet with a few keystrokes, squared his shoulders and hunched over his laptop with a determined look in his eye. By the time Agrifina had come in with mugs full of the best coffee Kate had ever had, hers perfectly doctored to her taste, and a plate of homemade lemon sugar cookies crisply brown at the edges, Kurt had an address for her.

"That was quick."

He raised an eyebrow. "Facebook."

She sighed. "I can't tell if you're that smart or everyone else is that dumb."

He scribbled it down and handed it to her.

Her own eyebrows went up this time. "Nice neighborhood."

Kurt grinned. "But—"

They said together, "—I wouldn't want to live there."

Sylvia and Fergus McDonald had lived above Potter Marsh in one of the McMansions that had popped up there like very large, very expensive mushrooms after Big Oil came in in the Eighties. Over ninety percent of the subdivision's residents either worked directly for Conoco, Shell or Alyeska, and ninety-nine percent of those who voted were registered Republicans only because if they voted Libertarian they couldn't win.

The McDonalds' home had less pretension than some, with only four bedrooms and five bathrooms and a three-car garage. The worst that could be said was that their view excluded Redoubt even on a clear day. Nevertheless, Kate thought, geologists must make serious coin.

Kate made a pass up the street and turned around, parking half a block up on the opposite side. It was eleven in the morning and the street was quiet, all the worker bees off to their nine-to-fives and the kiddies off to school. The lawns in front of each house were squared off with military precision and none of the very few trees permitted by covenant were old enough to vote, let alone drink. Apart from a beige sedan parked down the hill there were no cars in evidence. There was probably a covenant about that, too.

She pulled on a pair of thin vinyl examination gloves, tugged an UAF Nanooks ball cap low over her forehead and got out of the Forester, closing the door gently behind her, and walked up the street to the McDonalds' house with an every-right-to-be-here stride. She turned onto the slate path that led up to the door and kept a steady pace when she saw that the door was slightly open. She went up one side of the steps and ghosted across the porch to the side opposite the hinges and leaned forward to listen. From inside came a faint rustling, the scrape of a drawer.

Could be a serviceman, a housekeeper, even a relative, but there were no lights on that Kate could see. Most break-and-grab guys left doors open for quick egress once the job was done, and most of them left the lights off while at work, too, the better not to attract the wrong kind of attention.

She gave the door the barest of touches with the knuckles of one hand and it swung wide without a sound. New construction or good construction, or both. There was no protest from inside and she slipped over the sill and crouched at the end of a table against the left wall. A clear glass bowl sat on the table half-filled with change, keys, tie tack backs and push pins. On the floor next to the table sat a beat-up brass spittoon right out of a saloon in a John Wayne western.

The hallway stretched the length of the house, a large archway on the right, two doors on the left and ending in a kitchen. It appeared that the McDonalds had fallen into the clutches of a decorator because all the walls were painted in different primary colors. The ceiling, mercifully, was white but the colors combined with the mahogany laminate floors created such a dark atmosphere that Kate wouldn't have been surprised to bump into the Minotaur.

A quick glance through the archway revealed a large living room overfilled with dark leather furniture and glass tables in steel frames. The facing wall was lime green. The rustling sounds seemed to be coming from the first door on the left, which was also slightly open. Kate crept around the table and peeked in.

It was an office, in the process of being thoroughly trashed by a large man in jeans and a Chicago Bulls windbreaker, his head encased in a black balaclava that made him look like a member of ISIL. Subtle.

All the drawers were out of the large desk, paper scattered over the floor, and the man was in the process of pulling the books out of a floor-to-ceiling bookcase one row at a time, making so much noise now that Kate could have shouted at him and he probably wouldn't have heard her. It pained her to see books so misused, and she pondered the possibility of going to their rescue.

The top row of books were gone, the second, the third, he had to bend a little to run an arm behind the fourth row and sweep them all onto the floor. The pile was growing and he wasn't finding anything and it wasn't improving his temper. "Fuck!"

He kicked at the books and his back foot slid out from under him and he fell hard on his back, his head bouncing once off the floor. "Fuck! Fuck! Fuck!" He scrambled to his hands and knees and Kate pulled back a little too hastily and stepped into the spittoon, which gave an almighty clang when she tried to kick it off and it banged against the wall.

"The fuck?" The door to the office slammed back against the wall and the man in the balaclava ran into and very nearly right over the top of her. Kate tumbled into an almost picture perfect backward somersault and miraculously ended up on her feet facing the burglar. The bad news was that her left foot had retained the spittoon. It clanged loudly when she landed.

"Fuck!" He jumped at her, to hit her, to shove her out of his way? It wasn't clear. Who the hell knew how, she got her feet under her in horse stance, spittoon and all, and grabbed the hard right he was swinging in her direction in her right hand. She kept on pulling him through his punch, turning in place as she did without shifting her weight. It pulled him off balance and she helped by hitting him hard on his right shoulder joint with the flat of her left hand. He completely lost his balance then and went stumbling past her, unfortunately right through the open front door. She tried to shake off the spittoon but it wouldn't shake and she gave up and went after him, clang, step, clang, step. He careened down the front stairs but he'd recovered his balance by then and he hotfooted it down the slate path, building speed out to the sidewalk and down the hill to the beige four-door she'd seen on the way in. He hadn't locked the door to it, either, and the engine had started before he had the door closed and he was moving down the hill before Kate gained the sidewalk, clang, step, clang, step, clang, step. He'd dirtied the plate, the bastard. She should have noticed that before.

Still, she felt pretty good. A little lightheaded, maybe, but good. The guy had had at least a foot and a hundred pounds on her and she was still standing and without a scratch. Moses Alakuyak would have been proud of her form, and she'd done it all on her own, too, without any backup, even if she had been hampered by a spittoon. Not bad.

Before that unaccustomed lack of backup began to weigh on her more heavily than it already did she extricated her left foot from said spittoon and went back into the house for a quick, methodical sweep. None of the other rooms had been touched, just the office, so she took another quick look outside to make sure no one else had arrived to toss the house and went to assess the damage.

The paperwork was the usual: bills, bank statements, mortgage paperwork. The McDonalds' brokerage account indicated that Fergus and Sylvia must have started saving in their cradles, or, again, geology paid a lot better than investigating. There was a drawer full of tax folders going back a dozen years, each subsequent year showing a steady increase in income, but on the face of the amounts shown nothing so glaring as to indicate criminal activity. There was a thank you card from a young relative in Tennessee for a graduation check the previous June.

There wasn't a computer. Not a laptop, a desktop, or a tablet. Odd. She tried to remember if Sylvia had had one in her room. Might have been a laptop in the outside pocket of her little suitcase, as she might have seen no reason to get it out. The Park had full cell coverage now. People could and did access everything on their phones.

She pawed through the books. They were mostly nonfiction, a lot on climate change by Brian Fagan, modern politics from Jared Diamond to Robert Kaplan, American history from the Founding Fathers to a recent biography of Bill Clinton. Also present was every single book ever written about the Klondike Gold Rush, from bibles like Pierre Berton's *Klondike* to self-published chapbooks by various members of the Alaska Miners Association. Fergus McDonald evidently lived his job.

As witness the shelf full of rock samples in the living room; the one non-decorator-inspired display in the entire house, so far as Kate could tell. Well, other than the spittoon. Copper from Montana, silver from Idaho, many gemstones from Colorado including a tiny, beautiful tourmaline geode that looked like a slice of crystal watermelon. All had hand-written tags denoting dates and states. A personal collection, then, Fergus at leisure with his rock hammer.

There were a few old metal gold pans and a new plastic

one, bright blue, and that was about all of interest to be found in this curiously anonymous residence. The only evidence of Sylvia's existence was the full closet in the master bedroom upstairs and the collection of cosmetics and hair product in the bathroom. The garage was empty but for a cord of wood stacked against one wall and a pair of bikes hanging from the ceiling.

When she'd asked the night before Sylvia had said she'd worked as a secretary at the Suulutaq offices in town. There were no pay stubs in the desk but the bank statements showed automatic deposits for each McDonald twice a month. Kate compared a brokerage statement with a bank statement from the same month and it showed no transfers between accounts, so the brokerage account had to be funded from some source other than their salaries. There was no indication of the account from which funds were deposited into the brokerage account.

She did a second sweep and then left the house, toeing the door not quite closed behind her, and walked at a steady pace up the hill to the Forester. It turned over at the first ask and she drove smoothly down the hill, passing the Anchorage police department cruiser going in the opposite direction with Nick Luther in the passenger seat. She kept her hat on and her head down and hoped he hadn't spotted her. No lights and sirens in the rear-view, and she turned onto Rabbit Creek Road and punched the button for the radio. Instead, the last CD that someone, probably her, had put in came on. Jimmy Buffett.

Jimmy Buffett was responsible for her and Jack, or that was their origin story and she was sticking to it. Once, just hearing the first verse of "Happily Ever After" could send her into a blue funk with no end in sight. Now, it made her smile at the memory. He'd had a beard when she met him, which he'd shaved off when they'd been investigating a mass murderer and some profiler had said all mass murderers had beards. Jack had wanted to buy Buffett a beer in the worst way and about died when he'd heard the singer had been in the state and actually performed in Dutch Harbor. "What if the day you met him was the one day a year he was an asshole?" Kate had said. "Everyone has an asshole day, Jack. Better to admire from afar and keep your illusions intact. Love the song, not the singer."

Retaliation for this heresy had followed swiftly and comprehensively and lengthily. Kate found herself smiling at that memory, too. She'd been lucky to have Jack in her life, and she would always be grateful he had given her Johnny, even if it had taken her a while to realize it.

She was hungry so she stopped at the Lucky Wishbone for a Mom All-Dark and drove out to Point Woronzof, where a young couple were trysting in the front seat of a pickup. Kate parked at the other end of the lot and concentrated on the other view, which took in Susitna, Foraker, Denali and the Talkeetna Mountains all the way around to the Chugach. Between Kate and mountains the Knik Arm, sludgy with brash ice, moved steadily south on an outgoing tide.

Kate switched over to the radio to catch the end of the noon news and opened her takeout. As luck would have it, the first item up featured the Bannister Foundation, the brainchild of Erland Bannister, eighty-one years young as the reporter coyly put it, grandson of Stampeders, heir to an Alaska empire built on banking, transportation, coal, and, of course, oil. A man with a tragic past, who as a teenager had lost his father in an attempted burglary of their home, the murderer never caught. His sister Victoria, convicted of murder and attempted murder of her two sons, although she had later been released under circumstances that were still murky. His daughter, Charlotte, killed in her own home. His nephew Oliver, tried and imprisoned for fraud and racketeering and assault. Bannister himself wrongfully convicted of attempted murder, his verdict vacated after a year in prison. In spite of these multiple personal tragedies, a man who went on to become a giant of Alaskan industry.

He had, the reporter announced breathlessly, liquidated his vast empire at substantial profit in the year following his release from prison, and had invested half of the proceeds in the Bannister Foundation, the newly created non-profit arm of the newly incorporated Bannister Inc. People could only speculate the capital held by Bannister Inc. but the Foundation's holdings were reported to be in excess of $500 million dollars. What was the Bannister Foundation? The reporter was happy to elucidate, and the list of good works the Foundation supported went on, and on, and on; everything from international non-profits like Doctors Without Borders and Heifer International to national charities like United Way, the Humane Society, and the Alzheimer's Foundation of America to local concerns like Bean's Cafe, the Brother Francis Shelter and, unbelievably, the Anchorage Planned Parenthood clinic. Kate would have thought the last thing Erland would have been interested in backing was an organization that supported women having power over their own bodies.

She waited to hear that Erland had written a six-zeroed check to the ACLU, but no. Instead, it appeared that Bannister, Inc. would be stepping in to take up some of the slack where the state, being broke due to decreasing oil stocks and the current price per barrel of oil, had withdrawn support. For example, the legislature had stopped giving tax credits to the film industry. Erland Bannister thought that was a crying shame—they even played a clip of him saying so at an Anchorage Chamber of Commerce luncheon—that the state of Alaska had gotten out of the movie business. Fifty-Three North Productions was created on his say-so to match funds with Outside producers in an attempt to build a homegrown industry, as witness that zenith of quality television programming, *Surviving Alaska*, Alaska's newest reality TV show. In the last six months Fifty-Three North and its investors had employed over a hundred Alaskans and spent almost $5 million in support services. There was even a rumor, the reporter said even more breathlessly, that major Hollywood film producers had invested in this enterprise, including some big-name film stars, although no specific names had been revealed as yet.

Kate could think of one name right off the bat. Her hand felt warm and she looked down to see that she had crushed a bag of very fine french fries in a clenched fist. Appetite gone, she got out of the car and tossed the rest of her lunch in the trash can. The young couple's tryst had ended and there was a flurry of clothing being reassembled. She walked a little way down the Coastal Trail, looking at the view of downtown Anchorage, tall shining buildings reflecting the peaks of the Chugach Mountains behind them. Most of them had been built by oil. Most, but not all.

"And 'There's never a law of God or man runs north of Fifty-Three,'" she said out loud. She wondered if the reporter had asked Erland where he'd gotten the name for his film company. Rudyard Kipling was always good for a world-building epigram, especially if it was a white male world, and they didn't come any whiter and maler than Erland Bannister. There was a law of Bannister and it did run north of the fifty-three.

She got back into the Forester and googled the Suulutaq Mine on her phone. It showed up under Global Harvest's website and she pressed the phone icon. When they answered she said in her crispest, most efficient voice, "Yes, could you put me through to a Mr. Fergus McDonald, please?"

No pause at all. "Mr. McDonald doesn't work in Anchorage, ma'am, but I can put you through to our geology department."

"Thank you."

Click, click and a second voice came on the line. "Geology, Magnus Campbell."

"Mr. Campbell, hello. I was looking for a Mr. Fergus McDonald."

A bit of a pause this time. "Mac's at the mine this shift."

"No, he isn't, Mr. Campbell." She took a chance that the news of Sylvia McDonald's death had yet to reach his office. "I'm a private investigator, and I've been retained by his wife to find him. I was wondering if we could talk."

"Sylvia hired a private investigator?"

"I'd really like to talk to you about your co-worker. May I come to your office?"

"Jesus! No! Don't come here—stay the hell away from the office."

Kate, beginning to enjoy herself, said, "Well, I suppose I could ask my questions on the phone, but I'd really rather meet with you in person if you can find the time. I'm just a few blocks from Suulutaq—" a lie "—and it would be no bother."

"Fuck no! No," he said, calming himself with an obvious effort. "Uh, I haven't had lunch. Could you meet me?"

Kate eyed the garbage can. "As it happens I haven't had lunch, either. I'd be happy to meet you. Somewhere downtown, convenient to your offices? Perhaps Club Paris?"

"No! Not downtown!"

Kate grinned at the windshield. "Where would you suggest? I'm easy." Just not cheap.

"Southside Bistro. I'll be there in half an hour. How will I know you?"

"I'll find you," Kate said. "Thank you, Mr. Campbell, it's very kind of you to take the time."

She hung up and googled Global Harvest. Like most major concerns nowadays, they had an employee page, listed alphabetically by department. Under Exploration and then Geology she found names, job titles and headshots. Campbell was thin and blond with watery blue eyes in a narrow face that depended down into a chin that nearly reached the top button of his shirt. Scandahoovian without a doubt, or Scots. Same difference.

She called Brillo next, who said, "I heard you were dead."

"That is the word on the street," she said. "Can you tell me anything about those bones I found?"

"Jesus, Shugak, I just got 'em."

"Can you tell me how long they've been there?"

"What am I now, a fucking seer? They've been picked clean and stripped of everything edible, and they're pretty soft from long exposure."

"How long?"

An impatient huff. "Five years minimum, be my guess, and only my guess."

Kate felt an easing of the tightness in her breast that had been there since Juna had limped into Canyon Hot Springs. "Male or female?"

"Can't tell. No whole arm or leg bones and no pelvic bones at all. It'll take a while to assemble what vertebrae survived all those chewy little fuckers out on the tundra. Is it true you found 'em on your property?"

"Not personally, no. A bunch of runners came through and one of them fell on them." Wouldn't it be wonderful if they were the bones of an old prospector chancing his luck in the Quilaks during the Stampede. "When do you think you'll know more?"

"I got no goddamn idea, Shugak, and since you gifted me with another fucking body this morning—Jesus, you're like the fucking grim reaper—and since the fucking gang bangers in Fairview have declared war on the fucking gang bangers in Mountain View the lab is pretty fucking full already, it's going to be a while before I do so don't hold your fucking breath."

He hung up on her. She was pretty sure he enjoyed doing it, too.

But he'd lifted a weight from her shoulders. Despite their obvious age, she had been terrified that the bones had been the remains of Jennifer Mack or Ryan Christianson or both. It wouldn't have been the first time the Quilaks had claimed blood tribute from those who dared to cross from Alaska into Canada. But Jennifer and Ryan had eloped over the mountains just four months before, so these bones could not possibly belong to them.

Kate, who had been the principal architect of their elopement, had a vested interest in their continued survival. Their families, friends and the rest of the Park had been persuaded to believe that they were dead. If it was ever discovered otherwise, they might be shortly thereafter.

Secrets. She kept too many. Sometimes the sheer weight of all of them made her feel like one of the black and midnight hags.

She drove to Southside Bistro to meet her date. It was an upscale restaurant in a business mall, bustling with upscale diners in business attire sitting at tables with linen tablecloths. Fortunately this was still Alaska and no one looked twice at her jeans. Magnus Campbell was in jeans himself, topped with a white oxford shirt and a gray tweed sports jacket whose patch pockets were pulled sadly out of shape, as if they had been loaded and unloaded with rock samples over its life. "Mr. Campbell?"

He cleared his throat. "Ms.—Shooter?" He got to his feet and knocked over his water glass. Their waiter appeared and whisked away the detritus, mopped up the water, reset Campbell's place, and awarded them both with menus as if he were handing over a Nobel Peace Prize before taking himself off to grace the next table but one with his presence.

"Guy's got style," Kate said. Campbell sat down again, very nearly upsetting his second glass of water. She extended a hand. "Kate Shugak." When he put his hand in hers she held on and leaned forward a little, to where his hand was almost brushing the front of her T-shirt. She smiled at him.

Helplessly, he smiled back. When she saw his pupils start to dilate she released his hand with a show of reluctance and let her eyes fall to his lips for a moment. They were lips, nothing to write home about, but he didn't have to know that. "I do appreciate your taking the time."

He looked like Mowgli being hypnotized by Kaa. The two impeccably tailored, stylishly coifed women sitting at the next table looked on with wondering eyes, but as any red-blooded man could have told them it wasn't the T-shirt or the jeans, it was the woman in them, and Magnus Campbell was the very last thing from immune. The waiter, hastening to the aid of a fellow male clearly in need, reappeared to take their drink and food orders and vanished again. It didn't do a thing to break the mood.

Campbell cleared his throat, unconsciously leaning forward as Kate leaned back. "Ms.—"

"Shugak," Kate said. "But call me Kate. If I may call you Magnus."

He cleared his throat, evidently something of a nervous tic. "Of course." He sounded a little hoarse. "Are you really a private investigator?"

"I really am." She smiled.

He cleared his throat again. He could barely meet her eyes. "And Sylvia McDonald hired you to look for Mac?"

"Yes. She flew into Suulutaq yesterday. He wasn't at the mine and they told her he'd taken off for the weekend on Saturday. Then she checked in at the nearest village. He wasn't there, either, and he hadn't been seen." She let her eyes wander over his face again. "Have you heard from him?"

His "No" came out as a high squeak. He flushed and cleared his throat. "No, I haven't."

But he dropped his eyes and looked about as guilty as someone could get without standing in front of a judge. Kate's voice turned coaxing. "You must have spoken frequently. You're both geologists, after all." She smiled. "Such an interesting job, I've often thought, and so vital to the state." She might have fluttered her eyelashes. "We can't pull it out of the ground until you geologists find it for us."

"Oh, brother," one of the women said as the other woman rolled her eyes, but it worked, if working meant Kate spent the entirety of a bowl of really excellent mussels and a hunk of fresh-baked parmesan bread listening to Campbell wax rhapsodic about aggregate and core sampling and the fire assay process and the proportion of gold to copper which commonly occurred together but not with molybdenum, one of the things that made the Suulutaq discovery so very special. Fergus McDonald's name cropped up now and then, and from all this dough rose the tidbit of information that Magnus and Mac had last spoken the previous Saturday, or the last day before Mac left the Suulutaq mine to go on walkabout. It was the same day Fergus and Sylvia had last spoken, too.

When asked, Magnus was ready and willing to tell her all about Fergus McDonald as an excellent geologist and a long-time friend. Over the past ten years they'd worked together at mines all across the United States and even one in Papua New Guinea. "Not my favorite job," he said, making a face. "Too hot, and the natives didn't seem to care much for us, to the point where they stationed government soldiers around the town and the mine for our protection. Not to mention the taipans."

"What's a taipan?"

"A poisonous snake. They're common there."

Kate shuddered and it wasn't a pretend shudder. "One of the benefits of living in Alaska. No snakes."

He brightened. "But we did very well there, indeed."

"Indeed?" Kate said invitingly, smiling deep into his eyes.

It took a moment before he remembered what he'd just said. He blushed again, cleared his throat again, and was saved again when the waiter swooped in with the check.

Only it wasn't the check. The waiter lowered his voice to a deferential murmur. "The gentleman in the corner booth has paid for your meal." He divided a smile between the two of them, bent a look of pity on the geologist, and whisked off.

Kate looked beyond Magnus Campbell's shoulder, who was looking for their mysterious benefactor in the exact opposite direction their server had indicated.

Erland Bannister was looking back at her.

She looked back at Magnus and smiled again. "How nice. An old friend. I'll have to go over and say hello. I'll be in town for a few more days, Magnus, maybe even a week. Should we, perhaps, exchange phone numbers?"

Campbell dropped his phone twice and Kate said, "Why don't you just tell me your phone number and I'll text you." He did and she input his phone number and sent him a smiley face emoticon. Predictably, he blushed again, and texted back

^h8s iz mAgn7s

Really, it was like taking candy from a baby, and she should feel ashamed of herself, and she would. Later. She sent him on his delirious way with a light kiss on his cheek that hit really close to his mouth, and turned back to look across the crowded room at Erland. He wasn't alone, although the woman with him had her back to Kate so all she could see was a lot of fine white-blond hair done up in an elegant twist. Something about that hair rang a distant bell in her mind and she frowned.

Erland's smile widened and he beckoned.

This would not end well. Kate threaded her way through the tables, aware eyes were following her déclassé self over to the best table in the room with one of the most powerful men in Alaska seated at it. As Kate approached the table the blonde turned and didn't smile. "Kate."

It took all of Kate's considerable willpower to answer with any kind of civility. "Jane."

"Yes," Erland said, manifesting a vast surprise, "you two know each other, don't you?" He smiled. "Alaska is such a small state, really."

Like the fucker didn't already know Jane Morgan was Jack Morgan's ex-wife and Johnny Morgan's egg donor. "We do," Kate said, but she didn't say how nice it was to see Jane, and Jane didn't say how nice it was to see Kate, and in the meantime frost formed on the wine glasses.

She didn't ask what the two of them were doing there together—some of the items Kate had found in Jane's drawers during a bit of harmless B&E a few years back could give her a good guess—but Erland told her anyway. "Jane's working for the Bannister Foundation nowadays."

"How nice for you both," Kate said. "I just came over to thank you for lunch."

"It was my very great pleasure," Erland said, even bowing a little in place, although it felt more to Kate like the drawing of a sword. "I'm glad to see you in health. I had heard that you had been hurt in, um, the line of duty." His eyes glittered. "If line of duty is the correct term for a private investigator."

Kate smiled. It wasn't the same smile that had ensorceled Magnus Campbell by a mile, but then Magnus Campbell hadn't made her job title sound like "two-bit whore," either. "I hear you are doing great things these days, Erland. You've turned into a real philanthropist."

He gave an airy wave with a liver-spotted hand that was so thin it was almost translucent. "I do what I can, now that all the fuss over my little problem is past."

"'Your little problem.'" Kate's brow wrinkled and then smoothed. "Oh, of course, you mean your conviction and imprisonment for assault, kidnapping, attempted murder. And other assorted felonies. I'm afraid I've lost count."

Erland's eyes narrowed when Kate raised her voice enough to be heard at nearby tables. There was a brief silence all around, ears straining for more. "A decision that was vacated by the state Supreme Court, as you well know."

"Yes," she said kindly, "unfortunately the courts are not quite as reliable as one could hope for. Such a shame. Well. I must be off. No, no, don't get up."

He hadn't been going to, of course, and Kate realized that the rest of him was as thin as his hand, and that that hand was shaking where it lay on the table. He followed her eyes and put his hand in his lap. "I expect we'll meet again soon," he said. "Jane and I will be visiting the Park quite often, now that I have interests there."

"Yes, I heard. A reality television show, isn't it? Trust you to aim for class every time, Erland." She bestowed a valedictory smile on the both of them—Jane had not spoken one further word—and left the restaurant. She got into the Forester and drove to the other side of the business park, parking in front of the post office without turning off the engine. She rolled down her window and took a series of long, deep breaths. After a while her heart rate slowed and her blood pressure returned to normal. Two women pushing strollers jogged past, the babies barely visible beneath the packing material piled over them. Ordinary citizens came and went, checking their mail, mailing packages.

Whatever skills she had to offer, Erland had hired Jane Morgan to get to Kate, no doubt of that. So she wouldn't be got to. It wasn't like they were moving to the Park, however many "interests" Erland had there. Erland living permanently in Niniltna, she'd like to see that. And he was eighty-two now, according to the radio, and looked it. They had met for the first time three years ago when his daughter had hired her to get her mom and Erland's sister out of jail. Then he had been a handsome, vital man, exuding power and the often irresistible personal magnetism that comes with it. Now, he was so thin he looked almost emaciated, and that shaking hand. Parkinson's, maybe? She wondered what the life expectancy was from diagnosis. She'd have to look it up. Might be cheering. The thought surprised a laugh out of her, and she half turned in her seat to say, "I am definitely not—" and then stopped herself, because no one was sitting there to hear her.

Her phone rang then and she snatched it up without looking at who was calling. "Hello?"

"Hi, Kate, this is Gavin Mortimer. I was just checking in to see if—"

"No ID on the bones yet, Gavin," Kate said and hung up before he could say anything else. Her phone rang again immediately. "What the FUCK do you want from me! I told you there's no ID yet! They aren't fucking miracle workers down at the lab! Maybe if you idiots in Anchorage ever voted for a goddamn tax they could hire some more people!"

There was a short, sharp silence. "It IS you!"

She looked at her phone and put it back up to her ear. "Brendan?"

"Who the hell else would it be! You're in town and you didn't call me first thing! What's wrong with you?"

"Nothing." She took a deep breath and let it out. "Nothing, now."

"Good to hear that from the source, is all I'm saying. Jesus, Kate, I—"

"—heard I was dead?"

"Well... yeah."

"As it happens, I'm not."

"Good to know." She heard him swallow and say in a different voice, "Goddamn good to know."

She smiled into the phone.

"Is Jim with you?"

"No. I'm on my own."

"Dinner?" he said, sounding even more cheerful.

"Have you ever known me to turn down a free meal?"

"Who says I'm buying?"

The two joggers with strollers went by in the other direction. "Hey, do me a favor and dinner's on me."

"Oh?" His voice filled with suspicion, mostly mock but not entirely because he'd known her a long time. "And what favor would that be?"

"A guy went missing in the Park during an orienteering race four years ago. Could you see what's on file about that?"

"What the hell is orienteering?"

"Near as I can figure, it's jogging in the Bush with a compass."

"What's wrong with GPS?"

"Will you do it?"

"Sure, fine, whatever. What's his name?"

"Barney Aronson. And thanks, Brendan."

"Yeah, yeah, just bring your wallet. Everything I drink Robert Parker will have rated a hundred points before it gets to the table."

"You realize I have no idea who Robert Parker is."

"And you have to wear something other than jeans."

"What!"

When he stopped laughing he told her where and when, cussed her out again for not calling him, and they hung up.

Nine

FRIDAY, NOVEMBER 4
The Park

J IM DROVE STRAIGHT HOME FROM BOBBY'S, strapped on a set of wireless earphones, turned the volume up to nine and put the Stones on his phone. It was exactly the beat necessary to split and stack firewood and since he was aiming for total physical exhaustion so he could crash and burn that night there was no one better to lead the way than the perpetually peripatetic Mick Jagger. The blue-gray sky, the gray temperature, the gray landscape (which wasn't really gray but felt like it with all the bare-branched trees and shrubs looking grimly determined to survive another year in spite of everything an Alaskan winter could throw at them), all of it combined for a gray mood.

The upside was she had come down out of the mountains.

The downside was she hadn't come home. Never mind the found remains or the missing man or the dead woman or the case she had apparently taken on before she'd been back a full day, she hadn't even bothered to let him know she was back before she was gone again.

He added what he had split so far to the stack of firewood that was threatening to engulf the entire west wall of the hangar, roof to ground. He exercised great care to stack it evenly, neatly, and nonviolently.

It wasn't like he figured she'd ever forgive him. After the first blind panic following her disappearance, when he'd finally realized where she'd gone, he'd understood and from somewhere found the self-control to leave her be. But he missed her. God almighty, how he missed her. It was infuriating. Coffee and watching the sun rise over the Quilaks in the morning was somehow diminished alone. Working, together or apart, during the days, not knowing if she'd be there when he got home but knowing she would always at least end her day there after she'd tied up her latest case. The attempts to outdo each other in the kitchen. The evenings on the couch in front of the fire, legs tangled as they read. The warm weight of her next to him in bed when he woke in the night. The laughter, even the fights, the loving—"Yes, all right," he said, or maybe yelled or possibly bellowed to the gray sky, "I said the fucking L word, you gonna revoke my fucking man card?!"

The firmament provided no answer, which only proved there was no god, goddammit.

He slammed another round of wood in the splitter and threw the switch. Stack and repeat.

Theirs wasn't what you could call a traditional

relationship. He'd had the needle for her from long before Jack died, and then he'd suffered through her near miss with—what the hell was the guy's name, the childhood sweetheart? Edgar? Edwin? Ethelred?—and then when she finally condescended to sleep with him he was determined to keep it at just that, sex and nothing more. And then the next thing he knew he'd moved into her house. Suckered him right in, make no mistake about it, the female was deadlier than the male, and the worst thing was he had liked it. Kate and Johnny and that goddamn dog were the closest he'd ever come to having a real, live-in family. A family that actually liked him. And he got laid on a regular basis without having to work for it and it was the best sex he'd ever had when he'd been afraid everything would get old fast and he'd want to move on. Hell, he'd meant to move on, it had been his MO since puberty, but Kate Shugak had a gravitational well he hadn't been able to climb out of. Or wanted to, truth to tell. He didn't know which was scarier.

He should have known when he'd been last in California and his ex had indicated a willingness to start things up again, and he hadn't. He fucking hadn't, and he fucking should have known then. When they have you by the balls your heart and mind will follow. No question Kate Shugak had Jim Chopin by his balls. Oh the embarrassment.

He tried to mourn for the old careful-never-to-get-more-than-laid Jim. He really did try. Mostly all he could drum up was an echoing ache of loneliness. Kate and the dog were gone and Johnny was in Fairbanks and here he was, rattling around in a house that got creakier and lonelier and colder by the day. And by the night. Especially the bed. Once waking up alone had been his preference.

He split more rounds and stacked them. He was having to stretch now to reach the top of the pile.

Hadn't he been a good man? (Well, after he got her shot.) Hadn't he? He'd left her alone for four fucking months. He hadn't written her so much as a fucking note, or even asked for the smallest sign that she was alive or, much as he wanted to, headed up into the mountains after her. He sneered at the round of wood he picked up. No, he'd been a good boy and minded his manners and hadn't intruded where he was very obviously not wanted. Or needed.

Every moment of daylight that he could spare away from the airstrip since July had been spent combing the entire homestead with a rented excavator with a claw on one end and a blade on the other, knocking down and stacking beetle kill and pulling stumps and building slash piles that burned for days. He never touched a pile of beetle kill until he had crawled over and under it, dreading and hoping to find Mutt. By fall there wasn't one of the hundred and sixty acres he hadn't been over on foot at least twice. He hadn't found her but no one, not even Kate, could say he hadn't tried.

So if he was such a good man, where was his reward? Where the hell was she? Not here, that was for damn sure, and not even in fucking Niniltna, although she'd been there, oh yes she had, but she sure hadn't bothered to stick around long enough to see him.

And now he was terrified, practically fucking paralyzed with fear that he'd never see her again, ever.

Two wedges of wood fell from the splitter and he picked them up and hurled them, one after the other, at the wall of the hangar with all his strength. They hit hard and fell to the ground, taking half of the top row of firewood with them and leaving two dents side by side in the brand new aluminum siding.

He stood there, glaring at the dents, and was startled when someone poked him. He turned to see Howie Katelnikof. He stared at him for a long time before he turned off the splitter and removed his headset. "I'll give you this, Howie, you got some serious balls showing up here."

Howie, as skinny and greasy-haired as ever, had new, improbably white teeth he had dressed up with a new mustache, a wisp of black straggling down both sides of his mouth like twin centipedes. They moved when he talked. It was a little disconcerting. He shuffled in place and looked everywhere but at Jim.

Jim waited. When Howie didn't say anything Jim said, "Was there something you wanted, Howie? After which I can take immense pleasure in telling you to fuck off?"

"I figured you weren't doing anything..." Howie's voice trailed away as he looked beyond Jim and becoming aware of the airstrip, the hangar, the generator shed, and the pile of uncut logs that was beginning to rival the height of

Tower II of the Hotel Captain Cook in Anchorage. He cleared his throat and shuffled his feet some more and wisely let that thought die a natural death.

"As it happens I am busy here, Howie. What do you want?"

"I'm scared somebody's after me."

Jim gave Howie a long, incredulous stare and burst out laughing. It was the last reaction either one of them expected, but he laughed loud enough to make his ears ring, hard enough to make him bend over and lean his hands on his knees, long enough to bring tears to his eyes. "Oh, Howie," he said finally, straightening up and catching his breath. "Who knew you'd bring me the best news I've had all year."

Howie looked panicked. "I'm not kidding, Jim!"

"I don't care, Howie."

"But I could—they could—"

Knowing he shouldn't, Jim said, "Who are they?"

"There's these two guys in the Park. Big guys, mean-looking bastards with prison tats and everything!"

Unimpressed, Jim set a round of wood in the splitter and threw the switch. Barely bothering to make his voice heard above the engine, he said, "If you're all that scared, why don't you talk to your producer? Seems they've got a vested interest in keeping you healthy."

But Howie, the little weasel, had ears like a weasel, too. "Jesus, Jim! I can't tell them I was bootlegging!"

Bootlegging. Color Jim surprised. "Why not?" He tossed the splits and picked up another round. "They could write it into the show. Swashbuckling frontier entrepreneur, prospect of violence. Work some sex into it and they'd probably come in their pants at the very thought."

"Jim."

To Jim's surprise, Howie actually had the guts to step next to him and turn off the splitter. He had thought that Howie's main purpose in life was to stay out of arm's reach of anyone who might wish him harm, which included just about everyone in the Park except Willard. "Jim," he said, staring all the way up at Jim's six feet four inches from his four foot eleven and managing not to look too pitiful as he did so, also a surprise. "First off, these guys aren't fooling around. Martin's already disappeared."

"Martin? Martin Shugak?"

Howie nodded vigorously. He did, now that Jim had cause to examine him more closely, look really and truly frightened. Kind of like a rat in a corner facing down a whole bunch of cats. Or two, anyway. "Martin was in on it with you?"

Howie swallowed. "Well, you know, after you put Ken Halvorsen out of business, booze in the Park kind of dried up. Besides, the elders are talking about making Niniltna dry again, and not everyone wants to drive fifty miles out to Bernie's for a shot and a beer."

"So you and Martin saw a demand and supplied it."

"What? Well, yeah, people wanted booze and there wasn't any, and so...you know how much you can make on a pint of Windsor Canadian? I mean, not as much as a place you have to fly into but still. And then there are all those villages on the river, and well, Martin has a boat, so..."

Martin Shugak was one of Kate Shugak's many cousins. He was worth about as much as Howie Katelnikof, but still, he was one of Kate's cousins. She would have gone looking for him had she been here. Which she wasn't. "You think these two goons disappeared him?"

"They were looking for him, Jim. Either they disappeared him or he saw them coming and disappeared himself. And if they made him talk first they'll know I was his partner." He was almost sniveling now. "You gotta help me."

"Jesus, Howie. If there were a gold medal in fucking up I'd award it to you personally. Who do these goons work for?" Howie's eyes slid away and Jim snorted. "Your supplier? And, oh, let me take a wild guess, you've stiffed them on their money?"

Howie looked down at his feet, one boot digging a hole in the dirt. "Well, no, not really, except maybe I guess they might think so, but really it wasn't our fault."

"I know, Howie. It's never your fault." Jim's voice was so understanding that Howie looked up, startled. When he saw Jim's expression his face went a dull red. He looked up at the roof of the hangar and started bouncing nervously in place.

"So your supplier fronted you a plane- or a truckload of booze, you took delivery without paying for it—later you'll have to tell me how you did that because it sure sounds a neat trick—and your supplier, understandably peeved, has sent two men in to either get his dough or take it out of yours and your trusty partner Martin's hides. Does that about sum things up?"

Howie bounced harder.

"Lovely," Jim said. "And they may or may not have already, uh, schooled Martin. And you want me to make everything all better."

Howie's familiar whine came back full force. "Geez, Jim, it's not like I'm asking you to take them out or anything." He let the suggestion lie there for a moment, and then for a moment longer. When Jim didn't pick it up he cleared his throat and shuffled his feet and said hastily, "Just, you know, maybe talk to them. You've got that whole scary ass trooper thing going on."

Jim's answer was fast and hard. "Not anymore."

Howie snorted. "Yeah, right. Look, just maybe let them know someone's watching. Mention that there are twenty million acres in the Park and people go missing here all the time." He remembered Martin and swallowed. "Hey, you could tell them about that body they found up at Canyon Hot Springs. Nobody even knows how long it was there, right?" He pursed his lips and considered. "But, you know, don't mention my name or anything."

Jim pulled up in front of Auntie Vi's B&B and sat in the cab of his pickup with the engine off for a few moments.

He was not looking forward to this but he was damn sick and tired of splitting and stacking firewood, and it seemed that the Amazing Reappearing and Disappearing Kate Shugak had given him some nervous energy to work off.

If he couldn't see her, talk to her, touch her, maybe he could help someone for her. He steeled himself and went inside.

Auntie Vi was at her kitchen table. Auntie Joy and Auntie Balasha were with her. None of them looked happy to see him. "She was here," Auntie Vi said, her expression fierce. "Where you?"

He took a calming breath. "I don't know what you thought I could have done if I had been here."

"Stop her!"

He could feel the red creeping up his neck and tried to will it back. "Have you met Kate Shugak, auntie?"

She wasn't listening and he was subjected to the same tirade she had unloaded on him at the homestead. He knew that much of it was built-up worry over the Suulutaq mine suspending operations and sorrow over the death of one of their own and even anxiety over the election— as women and women of color and Alaska Native women of color there was a lot on the line for them. Auntie Balasha punctuated every statement with an emphatic nod and Auntie Joy looked as if she was going to burst into tears. All he could do was wait until Auntie Vi ran out of steam, which she did do eventually and ended up staring at him with angry, wounded eyes. Jim understood that it was his penis that was specifically under fire here. He took a deep breath and gentled his voice. "I'm sorry, auntie." He put a comforting hand on her shoulder and was shocked at how frail she felt. He looked around the table. For the first time the aunties, who had seemed well nigh immortal just four months ago, looked old, and, even more frightening, tired. "I know you're upset," he said, "and I'm sorry for it. She'll probably be back in a day or so. She never stays there long, you know that."

Auntie Vi let his hand rest on her shoulder for perhaps a second and a half before shrugging it off. "What you want."

"I'm looking for Martin."

"Why?"

Jim debated with himself how much to say. "Howie was looking for him."

"Howie?" Auntie Vi looked at Auntie Balasha, who looked at Auntie Joy. All three of them looked at him with vast skepticism. "You help Howie find Martin."

Jim chose his words carefully. "Howie is worried that something might have happened to Martin because he hasn't seen him around for a few days. It's probably nothing, but he asked me to see if I could find him. Martin."

Auntie Vi snorted.

That seemed to be the general consensus. No help forthcoming here, which left one other place to go in town. If he had been reluctant to walk up the steps to Auntie Vi's B&B he was doubly disinclined to knock on Bobby's door.

The door to the A-frame swung wide, Bobby on the other side. He stood for a long moment, inspecting Jim from head to toe and back again. Behind him Dinah said, "Hey, Jim."

"Dinah." He mustered up a smile.

"Come on in. I just put on a fresh pot." This earned her a hard look from Bobby. She raised an eyebrow. That was all, but Bobby scowled and fell back a step. Jim walked into the house and sat down at the counter. Nobody said anything while Dinah poured out three mugs and set out the fixings and a plate of peanut butter cookies. They drank and ate and the silence gathered like a dark cloud. Dinah looked back and forth between the two men and slapped the counter. "Oh for heaven's sake. Will you two knock it off?"

Eyes on his coffee Jim said, "He has a right to be angry at me, Dinah." He gave a half laugh that could have sounded like a sob to an impartial observer. "Pretty much everyone does."

Dinah leaned across the counter and this time she smacked the side of his head. Then she smacked Bobby.

Both men reared back.

"The hell?"

"Dinah!"

She glared at them both with equal disfavor. "So, okay, that happened. Get over it, both of you." Bobby snorted and Dinah leveled a finger at him. "Especially you. She's alive. She's healthy. You've seen her, you've talked to her, you know this to be true."

"Nice somebody has." It wasn't quite a mumble.

"And you," Dinah said to Jim, "you're as bad as he is and have less to get over."

"Less! I nearly got her killed!"

"No, you moron, Ken Halvorsen nearly got her killed and you took him down afterward, and I repeat, she's FINE. She's ALL GOOD. Get OVER yourselves and move ON. She has."

"All the way to Anchorage." Try as he would, it did come out sounding as if Jim were pouting.

Dinah rolled her eyes. "Like she'll be there a nanosecond longer than she has to be. She's on a case, Jim. It's how she earns her living." She gave him a pointed look. "Not everyone we know can afford to just up and quit their job."

Jim set his teeth. He wasn't going into that with anyone. Except maybe Kate. And she wasn't here. "Have you seen Martin around lately?"

"Martin?" Bobby said. "Martin Shugak?" Jim nodded. "No, and why would I want to?"

Jim debated with himself over how much to say. "Howie stopped by the homestead. He seems to think Martin is in trouble."

"Howie!" Bobby hooted. "Howie's asking you for help in getting Martin out of trouble? Seriously?" He threw back his head and laughed. "Man, I thought I'd heard everything." He stopped suddenly in mid-laugh.

"What?" Jim said.

Bobby looked at Dinah. "Remember Ace and Deuce?"

"I do."

Bobby said, "I was out at the Roadhouse the other night. Saw a couple of guys there, strangers. Big bruisers, covered in tats, both right out of the cast of *Oz*. Kept to themselves, but Bernie said they were asking around about Martin."

But by the time they got to the Roadhouse, Ace and Deuce were nowhere to be found, and Martin Shugak was still MIA.

Like other people he could name. "Damn."

Bernie stroked his chin. "Well…"

Jim and Bobby looked at him, alerted by something in his voice. "What?"

"After my conversation with Bobby that evening, I made sure I bussed Ace and Deuce's table when they left."

Jim felt a smile begin to creep across his face. "You didn't. You did not."

"I did." Bernie's hand dropped below the counter and reappeared holding a Ziploc bag. It contained a dirty pint glass. "Ace's. The guy with the mullet. The bald guy was drinking bottled water and took the bottle with him when they left."

"That's why you were carrying it that weird-ass way," Bobby said, remembering. He looked at Bernie with an expression that was almost respect.

Jim accepted the bag and held it up to admire. "I could kiss you, man."

"Don't get all mushy on me, Chopin." Bernie ran a hand down his ponytail and fussed with the front of his T-shirt. "Although anyone could see the attraction."

"Bobby said they're renting a cabin?" Bernie nodded. "Can we go see?"

But there was nothing in the cabin other than a couple of unmade beds. Ace and Deuce were traveling light. "How did they get here? Drive? Fly?"

"I think they had a pickup, old beater, green. Had to have been Alaska plates or I would have noticed." Before Jim could ask he shook his head. "Sorry. Didn't get the number."

Ten

FRIDAY, NOVEMBER 4
Anchorage

B RENDAN WAS GRINNING AT SOMETHING on his phone when Kate slid into the chair opposite him at Orso's. He'd scored a table in a corner, out of the eyesight of most of the other diners and out of the traffic pattern of the staff, which wasn't surprising, since the state of the front of his tie testified to how at home he felt here. He looked up and his face lit. "Kate!"

The megahertz of the bellow confounded all his efforts at privacy as every head in the place turned to look at them. "Hey, Brendan."

He got up and she endured the now expected bone-crushing hug, staggering a little when he let her go. He was beaming all over his broad, good-natured face. "Kate," he said. "Kate."

"That is my name." It was impossible in the face of that welcome not to smile back.

"God damn, it's good to see you, Kate." He looked at her in silence for a moment and then said in a surprised voice, "You look good. Better than good. You look like Ann Nzingha. You know. If you were black."

"And if I was a warrior queen."

"And lived in Africa," he said. "But still."

"Thank you."

He smiled and released her hand finally. "Sit, sit."

She sat opposite him and nodded at his phone. "What was so funny?"

"What? Oh," he said, and chuckled. "God told a couple of guys in Georgia to blow up HAARP."

HAARP was an aurora research facility in interior Alaska run by the University of Alaska. "Really. What did HAARP ever do to them?"

"Evidently it was threatening to control their minds."

"Presupposing the existence of such."

He nodded. "All evidence to the contrary." He swiped the screen and handed her the phone. "Check out the trophy shot."

"Geez," Kate said.

"Yeah, enough ammo there to invade Lithuania. Well. Liechtenstein, anyway. Plus a bunch of meth and dope. I know, I'm astonished, too."

She handed the phone back. "How close did they get?"

He grinned. "They never got out of Georgia." She laughed, and he said, "I admit, I prefer my evil villains to be on the low side of the I.Q. spectrum."

"Let's just hope they didn't procreate."

"Amen to that." He sat back and looked at her with satisfaction. "I'm not going to ask how you've been, or what you've been up to. You look good enough to eat and that's enough for me. I was pretty scared there for a while."

"Me, too."

He gave the empty space next to her chair an involuntary look. "And—"

"Did you find anything out about Barney Aronson?" she said.

His mouth twisted but he let it go. "Went out on a scheduled run, with company, four years ago and never came back. Day job, master mechanic at Continental Motors, working on Subarus. Married, no children. A half million dollar life insurance policy, even though rumor had it he and his wife didn't like each other much. She remarried, sold their house and bought a condo."

"Really? He's only been missing for four years. Don't you have to wait seven years before someone can be declared legally dead?"

He shook his head. "There's a statute for petition and inquiry. Basically if you can convince a district judge or magistrate that there are reasonable grounds to presume death, they can summon a six-member jury to examine the evidence and have him or her declared dead."

"Huh. Anything else?"

"Nope. I looked up this group he belonged to. They go running around the backwoods with nothing but a compass and a bottle of water. On purpose. It amazes me he's the only one they've lost so far." Their salads came. "You're seeing hinky everywhere," he said, "and no surprise when practically the first person you meet when you come out of the mountains winds up dead."

"Murdered."

"You're sure?"

"Pretty sure." She told him the details.

"Huh." He ate some salad. "You're feeling like it's cause and effect."

"She hires me and ends up dead twelve hours later? Kinda hard not to feel like the Angel of Death."

It wasn't like he could deny it with any conviction so he didn't bother trying. "You'll figure it out."

"It's what I do." And she didn't smile when she said it.

Their meals came. Auntie Vi's cookies the night before, oatmeal this morning, the mussels at lunch, this seafood mac and cheese, everything she put in her mouth tasted like heaven one bite at a time. Mortality added its own spice, evidently.

They shared a piece of chocolate cake that transported her back to the original cacao plant in Brazil and lingered over coffee heavily laced with cream as the restaurant emptied out around them. Brendan was the longest-serving DA in Anchorage, the go-to guy when you need to cut a deal or prosecute a case to the point that no one on the defense team had a square inch of skin left to them, beginning with the accused. He shared all the gossip current in the office and Kate listened and nodded and smiled when it seemed called for, all the while thinking of Sylvia's body crumpled by the side of the Step road, and of the pile of bones that had lain on Old Sam's homestead in the mountains, unregarded, for years. It was such a lonely way to die.

Brendan shifted in his chair. "We've pretty much closed the joint down."

But something in the way he said it caught her attention. "Brendan?"

He looked shifty as only an experienced ADA could. "We should probably go so they can go home."

"Brendan."

"I don't know if you're ready to hear this, Kate."

"Pretend I am."

He sighed. "On your own head be it." He leaned forward and dropped his voice. "Erland Bannister just put out a press release announcing that the Bannister Foundation would be fully funding the construction of the Samuel Dementieff Memorial Museum in Niniltna."

Kate sat very still, absorbing the words.

The silence stretched out until Brendan couldn't stand it anymore. "Kate?"

It seemed like a long time before she spoke and when she did it was in a calm, measured tone that betrayed nothing of the feeling boiling beneath. "Here's a guy I never met until three years ago, and now he's all up in my business, in my family, in my home." She took a deep breath and let it out, and summoned up a smile. "I find it...irritating."

"I can only imagine," he said, and hesitated.

She noticed. "Out with it."

"You heard about Jane Morgan?"

She nodded. "I actually saw them at lunch." She told him about it.

He was silent for a moment or two. "Well," he said finally, "there is one upside."

"Enlighten me, do."

"You're bound to outlive him." He waggled his eyebrows. "Assuming you can stay out of the hospital yourself from now on. As a favor to your friends. I'll cop to some bias here."

She thought back to lunch earlier that day, and how unexpectedly elderly Erland had appeared. "Is he ill?"

He shrugged. "There are rumors, but at his age there are bound to be. I do know he's tried to reach out to his nephew and his sister."

"And?"

"And neither will have anything to do with him. Of course, Oliver's hoping for early release on good behavior, so he's bound not to. Victoria..."

"How is she?"

He shrugged. "Still in remission. Still running the family business."

"Max Maxwell still working for her?"

He grinned. "He and I had dinner at Club Paris last month."

She smiled. "Did you wind up under the table?"

"No, because only a moron tries to match martinis with that guy. He may be older than god but he can still hold his liquor."

"I'll have to give him a call." Actually, not a bad idea, she thought, and tucked it away for later.

He sat back, eyes never leaving her. "You're taking this pretty calmly. I figured poking a grizzly in the eye with a sharp stick would be nothing to it."

"One thing at a time," she said.

That sounded ominous, and like time for a change of subject. "Did you get the books?"

She nodded. "George sent them in with a load of two-by-fours, and thanks for that. Why three Cleopatra biographies, by the way?"

He grinned. "She was an interesting woman. You're an interesting woman. I figured you could relate."

"I don't have a pearl or I'd whistle up a glass of vinegar."

He leered. "Be worth it for a trip up the Nile with you, babe."

Saturday, November 5

A hand slid deliciously down her spine. She arched her back, legs parting eagerly to wrap around—

A car door slammed and someone shouted something

and Kate was yanked rudely from sleep into the darkness of an Arctic winter morning, aroused and annoyed about it.

For the last four months her body had been fully concentrated on healing itself and nothing else. Convincing her inner organs to settle down from the trauma of having been so rudely disarranged by bullet and scalpel, keeping her food down, moving without pain, sleeping without nightmares, and regaining her physical strength, she had bent all her formidable powers of concentration on becoming the Kate Shugak she had been before Ken Halvorsen had shot her. She would settle for nothing less, and allow no time for anything else, not other people, not other concerns and certainly not sex.

It wasn't that she didn't enjoy sex, and it sure wasn't that she didn't enjoy it with Jim Chopin, but it had been four months and she felt a little, what, gun shy? She had tested her body repeatedly over the healing process, in tearing down Old Sam's cabin, in building another, and in continual hikes into the surrounding terrain, much of it vertical and all of it at an altitude that forced her body to work that much harder.

So now that she had regained her health it appeared that her subconscious had decided that it was time to include something else. Great. She should have expected it, and she probably would have had she given it any thought. Her college roommate had once told her, "The body must be cleaned and fucked regularly." Kate had been shocked at such frank speech, until she met a man who knew what the hell he was doing, after which she thought her roommate might know what she was talking about after all.

She shifted restlessly and threw off the covers to cool down. The clock on the nightstand read 7:30 a.m., late for her, but then Brendan had kept her out past her bedtime. She got up and went to the bathroom. The overhead light was bright and unforgiving, illuminating every blemish on the face and body of the woman staring back at her, beginning with the scar the size and shape of a quarter between and below her breasts. Dead center, was what they called that. She raised her chin, her hand going to her throat. The scar bisecting it pre-dated the new scar by nearly a decade and over time it had faded from red to silver to a pale olive and had reduced in size from a rope of abused tissue to a thread. The effect was still felt, though, whenever she spoke, a rough husk of sound somewhere between Tom Waits and the crunch of gravel beneath monster-truck tires, although that, too, had moderated over time. Jim had told her once she was starting to sound like Scarlett Johansson, with a soupçon of Darth Vader.

It was only normal that as she regained her health her sex drive would wake back up, too. Hence the dream. Human. Natural. Nothing more to it.

Dropping her hand, she looked the rest of herself over with a critical eye. Five feet tall, a hundred and twenty pounds, a thick cap of short black hair that this time Dinah had cut to fall in wisps around her face so that she was almost stylin'. Almond-shaped eyes with a hint of Asia around the fold that tilted up slightly at the outer corners, high, flat cheekbones, a short nose and a wide, full-lipped mouth that revealed a perfect set of white, straight teeth when she smiled, courtesy of both her parents and, she was pretty sure, a Filipino ancestor not too far back there somewhere.

There was no mirror at the cabin and her body's reflection surprised her. It wasn't that she looked like Thor or anything but the heavy lifting required in the demolition of the old cabin and the building of the new one had added muscle to her arms and legs. Her shoulders seemed squarer, somehow, her breasts higher—not bad for thirty-nine-year-old breasts—and her waist oddly smaller, which made her— she turned sideways to check—yes, she had something of an hourglass figure going on these days and if her eyes did not deceive her there were dimples on her ass where ne'er had dimples been seen before. She didn't think. She'd have to ask Jim.

Or not.

She put that thought firmly back into the cage from which it had slyly escaped and dressed in jeans that felt snugger around the thigh and a T-shirt that was manifestly tighter around the bust. She went down to the kitchen to make oatmeal with all the fixings. She poured another cup of coffee and opened the drapes in the living room to watch the light come slowly back into the sky. Six more weeks until the winter solstice, when they would start gaining daylight again. Kate's favorite day of the year was

January 1, the day on which Alaskans were rewarded for surviving the holidays by a gain of half an hour of daylight a week by the end of the month. It was almost like the first day of spring.

The sky looked more gray than blue this morning and she brought up the weather app on her phone. Snow, maybe two to four inches was in the forecast, but then it had said that the day before and the day before that it had forecast rain. She left her mug in the kitchen and suited up in a shirt, a sweater, leggings and a jacket, a knit cap and tennis shoes and mittens and went out for a walk, following the Coastal Trail around the lagoon and under the railroad tracks and out onto Knik Arm. Light on the southern horizon outlined Susitna and illuminated the broad current of ice moving steadily down Cook Inlet on the outgoing tide.

She alternated walking and running all the way out to Point Woronzof and back again, seeing only a skijorer being towed by two black labs. The labs were so overjoyed by the presence of another human being on the trail that they both jumped at Kate as she passed, yanking their owner off his feet and into the ditch on the beach side. She waded through the mêlée to give him a hand up. "Thanks," he said, unhooking one ski from around his left ear and the other from behind his back. He gave her an interested look, evidently in the belief that turning himself into a human Tinker Toy made him attractive to the opposite sex. She was off down the trail the next second, having contrived to touch neither dog during the encounter.

She felt good, physically. Mentally, emotionally, the jury was still out and it was fine with her if they stayed out for the foreseeable future. Her boot camp method of healing hadn't left a lot of time for anything else, and truth be told she had welcomed the singularity of purpose. Her attention had been much divided over the past nine years. The scars were evidence of just two attempts on her life. There had been more, including that homicidal jackass on the boat and the undignified experience of being clocked and dumped into an actual dump, inside an actual garbage bag.

She wondered how many more lives she had left, and then she wondered if she was doubting her immortality. Forty was the age for that, so she'd heard, so she had a year to get used to it.

Her phone dinged. A text message. She read it, pocketed her phone again and picked up the pace. She got back to the townhouse, showered, dressed, and called Brillo, who sighed heavily when he recognized the voice on the other end of the satellite. "Either her head hit something hard or something hard hit her head. The bodies are stacking up like cordwood around here, Shugak. Jesus, try to be patient, wouldja? I said I'd call you if and when I knew anything more and I will. Now lemme alone to get some goddamn work done."

She clicked off and thought about all the trees she had looked at by the side of the road where they'd found Sylvia. All of them were too far away from Sylvia's body and she had found no blood or brain matter on any of them.

Her phone beeped and whistled. She read the screen and sighed. "Gavin."

"Oh, hi, Kate. I hope it isn't too early to call. I was just wondering if—"

"No, Gavin, no ID on those bones yet."

She hung up on whatever Gavin Mortimer was about to say next. Her phone rang again, this time with the prologue to "City of Angels". She answered. "Kurt."

"Hey, Kate. I got some info on the McDonalds."

"Go."

"They've been all over North America, Canada, and the US, and one time even in New Guinea, working in resource extraction. She always works in the office, him always in the field. They buy in, too, they've got an investment portfolio worth about a million bucks—you and I are definitely in the wrong line of work—most of it invested in natural resource companies. Copper in Montana, gold in California, silver in Colorado, copper again in Arizona but the company went bust. They still own stock in it, though, oddly enough. Near as I can figure it they go to work for the company, check it out, and then buy stock and never sell it. And they never spend more than two or three years in one place."

"Restless."

"Yeah, actually, that might be true. So far I haven't picked up a whiff of any kind of shenanigans, like they're clearing out the safe on their way out. One thing, though."

"Which is?"

"Sylvia was a CPA."

"You're kidding."

"Nope. Foster School of Business, U-Dub. Where they met, I think, because he was at Earth and Space Sciences at U-Dub at the same time, working on his graduate degree."

"Family?"

"No children, on purpose, I think, at least I can't find any bills for fertility clinics."

"Parents? Siblings?"

"Both only children, both orphans. Might have been something they had in common."

"Huh." They listened to each other breathe for a while.

Kate said, "What's a CPA doing working as a secretary?"

"Excellent question, Shugak. You could almost be a PI yourself."

"You'd clean up if you took that show on the road, Pletnikof. And?"

"And I took a quick run back at all their places of work. There is no there there, Kate. Not a whiff of anyone doing anything wrong. Still, I suppose if you were looking to estimate the financial health of the company you were working for, you could do worse than be a CPA in a secretarial position and a geologist on the ground."

"Who was her boss at Suulutaq?"

"Bruce O'Malley."

"O'Malley? Wait, isn't he the—"

"President and CEO of Suulutaq? Why, yes, Kate, I believe he is." The shit-eating grin came clearly over the airwaves.

"Well, now." Kate sat back in her chair. "So that's a thing."

"I thought so."

She sat in silence for a while after they'd hung up.

Two people put themselves through school, marry and travel North America, with a side trip to New Guinea according to Magnus Campbell, serially investigating the health of mineral resource extraction companies, investing accordingly and doing well by themselves as a result. Nothing wrong with that on the face of it, it was a Kodak moment of the American dream. Inevitably their attention turns northwards, to Alaska, the biggest pot of literal gold at the end of any mining rainbow. They go to work for Suulutaq Mine, the second-largest deposit of gold—and copper—ever discovered on the planet, and maybe the first when they got done exploring it.

Where the American dream screeches to a halt, when one of them goes missing and the other is found dead, possibly murdered, which in itself argued against the viability of the first.

Fergus McDonald, with a rock hammer, in the Park. What had he found? He'd found something, all right, and she'd bet it had had something to do with the envelope that had disappeared from Sylvia McDonald's handbag.

She checked the time and called Magnus Campbell at his office, only to be forwarded to an efficient secretarial type who informed her that Mr. Campbell had not come in that day. She thanked her and called his house, Campbell one of the last humans left with a land line. The phone picked up on the third ring. A man's voice said, "Hello?" and nothing else, and it was the nothing else that activated her spidey sense.

"Where the hell are you, Hank?" she said. "I've been waiting outside Walmart for ninety fucking minutes with two full carts, and so far three different guys have tried to pick me up, and I swear to god the fourth guy to come by—"

"Ma'am. Ma'am. MA'AM."

She huffed out a breath. "Since when do you ma'am me, you moron?"

"I'm afraid you've got the wrong number."

"What? No, I—" She pulled the phone away from her face and counted to three. "Oh, sir, I'm sorry, I guess I do. I beg your pardon, I didn't mean to—I'm just so—I'll let you go now."

She clicked off and counted again. When the man on the other end hadn't hit star sixty-nine in ten seconds she heaved a sigh of relief, blocked the number and headed for the garage.

Magnus Campbell had lived in a one-bedroom apartment in a nine-plex on Jefferson in Spenard, and when Kate got there it was surrounded by police cars. She was waved through by a uniformed officer and parked a couple of blocks down. She walked back up the street to loiter at the back of the gathering crowd and waited for someone else to ask what happened. Obligingly a newer arrival did and three different people tried to tell him at once, human beings always happy to spread bad news.

"Home invasion."

"Somebody broke into this dude's apartment and he caught 'em at it and they had a fight and he's, like, dead, man!"

"Totally!"

"Who was it, anybody know?"

A round of shrugs. "Some dude."

And then Nick Luther slid by, riding shotgun in an APD cruiser. Kate pulled her head into the collar of her coat like a turtle and walked away with deliberate slowness.

The Park, Anchorage

George had an early flight into Anchorage that morning. Jim got the last seat at the last minute and avoided George's eyes as he shelled out the fare George extorted out of anyone flying west. The only time in the last decade he'd had to pay for a flight was when he'd gone Outside for his father's funeral. He asked George if Martin had flown out of the Park recently. George said that since Martin still owed him for the last three flights he'd been on George wouldn't allow Martin within spitting distance of one of his aircraft. Martin was well aware of that, so no.

They landed at the Lake Hood strip instead of Merrill, most of the passengers Suulutaq employees who were flying Outside for their two weeks off. Jim hiked over to Ted

International and rented an SUV. He drove straight to the townhouse and spent far too long knocking on the door with no answer. He peered through the window and saw the mug on the coffee table. There was no window on the garage door so he couldn't tell if the Forester was there or not.

He climbed back in the SUV and called Kurt. The woman who answered the phone sounded like Doris Day at her shirtiest with Rock Hudson but finally put him through.

"Kurt, it's Jim Chopin."

"I heard. What's up?"

"I'm in town. Where's Kate?"

A short silence. "She's in town, too."

"I know that. Is she staying at the townhouse?"

"She didn't say, but that is usually where she stays when she's in town."

Jim felt his temper rise. "So you've seen her."

"Yes."

"She happen to mention how long she'll be here?"

Jim heard the creak of a chair. "She's on a case."

"The missing geologist and his dead wife?"

"You know I can't tell you that, Jim."

"You won't, you mean."

"She will hurt me if I do."

Fair enough. "She have her phone with her?"

"Why don't you call her and find out?"

"Thanks, Kurt. You've been so helpful. Really." He hung up.

Displaying what he felt was praiseworthy self-restraint, he had not attempted to call. He hadn't even texted. She'd come down out of the mountains, she knew where he was, she would have called him if she'd wanted to talk to him.

"Fuck." He opened the text app.

I'm in town. Call me.

There was no immediate response.

He tapped in a number and gathered together the tatters of his self-control. "Hey, Brendan. It's Jim, Jim Chopin."

"As I live and breathe, Jim Chopin, Chopper Jim, the Father of the Park, come to call. Or just call, in this case."

"Yeah," Jim said, trying not to think about the time he'd walked into the townhouse to find Kate and Brendan all cozied up together over drinks in front of the fire. "I'm in town. I haven't caught up to Kate yet. Have you seen her?"

"Why, yes, I have."

"You know where she is now?"

"Nope," Brendan said cheerfully, and didn't add, "and I wouldn't tell you if I did" but the subtext was clear. There might also have been a "Neener, neener" tagged on there somewhere.

"Thanks anyway," Jim said and hung up. That fucker Brendan for sure had seen Kate a lot more recently than Jim had.

He looked at the ditty bag he'd brought with him. There

was no point in calling Brillo, who had only ever tolerated him when he brought along Kate and Mutt. Who else? Fred Gamble had retired this spring and moved Outside. He thought a little harder and remembered Kate's trip to Newenham the previous January. He tapped in a number.

"Federal Bureau of Investigation."

"I wonder if you could put me in touch with a particular agent," he said. "Not one necessarily stationed in Alaska."

It appeared that the FBI was good for more than subverting elections even if it was just finding one of its own agents. He hadn't been waiting five minutes after he'd hung up when his phone rang. "Sergeant Chopin?"

"Agent Mason? Thanks for calling back so promptly."

"I, ah, recognized your name in association with someone else I have met previously in Alaska."

"Yeah, and I know which someone else, and first thing I'd better tell you is that it's no longer Sergeant Chopin. I used the title to get past reception."

"Ah." A pause. "I did know that, actually."

A trap, into which amazingly he had not fallen. "My point is that I have no law enforcement standing whatsoever to ask any favors of the FBI."

"Point granted, but, ah, now I'm curious."

Jim opened his grip and pulled out the glass Bernie had given him. "I've got a glass with fingerprints on it. I was hoping you could lift them and run them for me."

Another brief silence, during which he imagined Agent Mason, whom he'd never met, stroking a properly square

FBI chin with meditative fingers. "What, ah, precisely would this be in aid of?"

"There's a guy missing in the Park. The fingerprints belong to one of two, well, people of interest, shall we say, in his disappearance. They aren't locals. The Park is—"

"I'm, ah, familiar with the Park, Mr. Chopin."

"These two men stood out enough to engage the interest of some friends of mine, one of whom served one of them a drink in this glass." Jim waited. This would work or it wouldn't.

"Where, ah, are you at present, Mr. Chopin?"

"Anchorage."

"Ah, Anchorage, excellent. Do you know where the FBI office is there?"

"I do."

"Go there. Someone will meet you in the lobby."

Click.

So he drove to the faux-brick fortress on 6th Avenue and negotiated the defensive perimeter of bollards, a moat evidently being impractical, at least for the moment. He was met on the civilian side of security by an efficient prepubescent with hair pulled so tightly back into a bun her eyes were mere slits. She accepted the Ziploc bag and its contents with the air of one who had been on the receiving end of much worse in her day, and invited Jim to leave forthwith. He did so.

Since he was downtown he dropped in at Bean's Cafe and the Brother Francis shelter and since it was just getting light out took a cruise down Minnesota and through Spenard where a lot of homeless people hung out. At the light at Northern Lights he waved over a guy with a cardboard sign that said "Veteran, Will Work for Food" in black Marksalot. The guy, a Yupik with a runny nose, shook his head at Jim's question. Jim gave him a twenty and repeated the exercise at Northern Lights and C. No word of Martin Shugak anywhere.

He wondered what it would be like to be broke and on the streets, and then he wondered what the history books were going to say about this era in American history, when the rich got richer and the middle class disappeared and the poor moved into the streets. Who was it who said that nations were judged on how they treated their least advantaged citizens? Really, at this point the best favor the Baby Boomer generation could do for their nation was to die off as rapidly as possible.

His stomach growled so he ended the internal rant and went to Jackie's in Spenard and had fried spam and eggs with rice. Breakfast of champions. He went up to the counter to pay and an emaciated, pock-marked man with dreadful teeth dressed in a grimy leather duster was harassing the woman sitting next to him, who was dressed like Julia Roberts in *Pretty Woman* before the makeover. Evidently she hadn't worked hard enough the night before to suit him. She looked miserable and so did everyone else within earshot. "Keep it," Jim said to the server, and turned to grab the pimp by the ear and haul him to his feet.

"Hey! What the fuck, you fucking fucker—"

A sad commentary on the quality of his education and the subsequent limits it appeared to have placed on his vocabulary. "Shut up," Jim said and dragged him by the ear out the door. Behind him he heard it close on cheering and applause. He proceeded to kick the pimp's ass across the parking lot, step, kick, step, kick, easily disarming the guy when he finally managed to get out his piece, a Lorcin .25, perfect size for shoving down his pants, although given the relative size of pants and pistol harder to get out, let alone find. Jim ejected the magazine and the round in the chamber and threw the handgun up on top of the roof of the facing strip mall. He pocketed the ammo and kicked the guy back across the lot. "Where's your car, asshole?"

The pimp, grizzling down his chin, pointed out a black Lincoln Town Car that looked brand spanking new. "That's mine."

Jim sighed. "Of course it is." He took the keys away from the pimp, beeped the car open, checked beneath the seat and in the glove compartment for a backup piece, and tossed him into his car and his keys after him.

The guy was literally trembling with rage. "Who the fuck do you think you are, you fucking—"

"Uh-uh," Jim said, wagging a finger at him. The pimp jammed the keys into the ignition and let a heavy foot on the gas slam his door shut as he peeled out of the lot. Jim walked back to the restaurant and stuck his head inside. "You got enough money to get home, lady?"

A wizened old geezer in what looked like an original Alaskan tuxedo said, "She does now," and slapped a fifty on the counter next to her. He gave Jim an approving nod.

Jim nodded back and left.

Who knew how liberating taking off the uniform would be?

He went back to the condo. Still no one home but her neighbor said, "She left about half an hour ago."

Of course she had. He got back in the SUV and stewed for a while, and then called one of the people on his list who had airplanes for sale. This one was bigstick, who had given him the link to the Texas website on airstrips. He was home and he told Jim to come the hell on over, it was turning into a goddamn party. He sounded like the old geezer at Jackie's had looked and when he opened the door to his Airports Heights home Jim was only off by about ten years. This guy was Jim's own height or taller, with a shock of white hair and blue eyes lost in creases put there by laughter or squinting into the sun, or both. "You the guy who called?"

"Yes, sir, Jim Cho—"

"Well, come the hell on in, Jim."

The door opened onto the living room which appeared remarkably full of other men and one woman, slight, brunette, pretty, who flashed him a smile and offered him a beer. "No, thank you."

"Something wrong with the beer we serve in this establishment?" bigstick said.

"No, sir. I just think I might be flying later today."

"Oh, you do, do you?" bigstick gave him an appraising glance before turning to address the horde, all of whom appeared to be having second thoughts on accepting their beers. "All right, get 'em out."

Everyone got out their wallets. Jim did, too.

"Let's see 'em."

Everyone got out their driver's licenses. Jim did, too. He was standing right next to bigstick so he showed his first. His host snorted. "You been here, what, twenty years?"

Jim had no idea how bigstick knew this but felt on the whole the better part of valor was to agree. "Yessir."

His driver's license was waved away and he put it back in his wallet and put his wallet back in his pocket. He was starting to enjoy himself.

The crowd resolved into five men other than his host, who examined all their licenses carefully. When he was done he gave what could only be described as a triumphant smile and produced his own. "Mine's only four numbers long, the rest of you yahoos got five and six." He snorted. "Bunch a cheechakoes."

Jim hid a grin.

His host fixed the room with a paralyzing eye. "I got one plane for sale, at one price, and I ain't dickering. Who wants it?"

Three of the younger men tried in a chorus to get bigstick down on his price and were booted from the house unceremoniously. The fourth man got mad and stomped out. The last guy stayed, stubborn. bigstick looked at Jim. "Well?"

"You had it listed for $559,000," Jim said. "Let me take a look at her, take her up. If she's as sweet as you say I'll take you to my bank and get you a cashier's check today."

The other guy—no one had yet howdied or shook—looked at bigstick. "I'll give you ten grand more."

bigstick scowled. "I told you, goddammit, no dickering, I set a price and that's it," and by damn if he didn't open the door and invite the guy out.

bigstick closed the door behind him and looked at Jim. "I got her parked at Merrill. You got a license?"

Jim was smart enough to produce his pilot's license this time. The woman had been the only one to sit down during the entire to-do. She winked at Jim from the couch as they left.

They went out to Merrill Field. It was from bigstick's pilot's log that Jim finally learned his name, Robert Weisner, "And don't goddammit call me Bob. The name's Robert. Ro-bert. Get it?"

Jim got it. The Stationair looked brand new, white with blue and gold stripes in a sort of wavy pattern interrupted by the tail numbers, a custom job that must have cost some bucks. The engine started at a touch and purred like a kitten full of his mama's milk. Jim flew left seat and they took her down to Homer, ninety-plus air miles south. They did a few touch-and-goes in turn with the Air National Guard Herc that flew in there every day for practice whose crew seemed delighted to have company, and then Robert had Jim do three full stop landings. The Homer airport was a long strip of paved bog that rolled like a giant-sized washboard and the first time Jim gave the struts a pretty thorough testing. Robert grunted. "Take her around again."

Jim did two more full stops, six landings in all, each landing smoother than the previous one as he became attuned to where the gear was relative to where his ass was, the sensitivity of the controls and the power of the engine. It was blowing twelve west southwest, big white clouds scudding across the sky, and the view of the Spit and Kachemak Bay was spectacular.

After the third full stop landing Robert grunted again. "Let's go home."

They landed back at Merrill at one p.m. and taxied to Robert's tiedown. Jim kept everything running and waited for the verdict, which was not long in coming. "Well, I spose you won't ding er up too bad if I sell her to you."

Jim called a mechanic he knew over at Spernak, got clearance from the tower and taxied over. The mechanic poked around the insides and ran a few tests and gave Jim a thumbs up. Jim tipped him a hundred and turned to Robert, who was grinning. "No flies on you, youngster," he said genially.

They drove to Alaska USA, who did the title search while they were standing there because Robert knew the loan officer and transferred a small fortune from Jim's account into Robert's. They drove back to Merrill, where Jim took formal possession of one airplane, an electronics package that seemed to include every state of the art ATON that had been invented up to yesterday, all the handbooks that came with them plus the ones for the aircraft which together filled a wetlock box right up to the top, along with six Bluetooth headsets that looked brand new, and so, according to the paperwork, was an Aircraft Spruce E.L.T. 406 with GPS. Weisner unscrewed the baggage panel so Jim could verify the emergency locator transmitter's existence and the wires leading to the test switch on the panel and the external antenna.

She was, in fact, an aircraft cherry in every respect. "Robert, I gotta ask," Jim said. "How can you bear to part with her?"

"You met my wife?"

Jim thought of the slender brunette back at the house. "Uh, sorta."

"We're dragging up, heading south for warmer climes."

Jim put an already affectionate hand on the side of 18 Kilo Oscar. "This baby sure would have given you a cushy ride Outside."

Robert looked a little sad. "That she would have." He said no more, and Jim was wise enough to leave that where it lay.

Robert drove him back to the house to pick up his rental and he drove back to Spernak and taxied 18 Kilo Oscar over to gas her up for the first time, topping off both tanks even though Robert had been classy enough not to run the fuel down to the last drop before he sold her. He taxied back to Spernak and negotiated a couple of hours' parking with the manager, who displayed noticeable drool. Jim had another thought and asked him if he'd given a Martin Shugak a ride to or from the Park and the manager checked his computer and came up nil. If Jim hadn't just bought the perfect aircraft he might feel a little downcast about that.

Jim drove back to the condo. Still no Kate and she hadn't responded to his text. Fine. He drove out to International to turn in the rental and was waiting for a cab to show up when his phone rang. To his astonishment it was Agent Mason.

"Yes, Mr. Chopin. My associate in Anchorage lifted the prints from the glass and faxed them to me. I, ah, ran them through NCIC and came up with a match."

"Jesus." Jim went back into the warm and sat down. "When it's business as usual it takes you guys six months, and when it's a rush it takes at least four weeks. What the hell?"

"Yes, well…" Mason hesitated. "I don't know if I told you, Mr. Chopin, but I'm something of a special agent without, ah, portfolio. Currently, as it, ah, happens, I'm in Chicago, working a racketeering case that has to do with the Outfit. You've heard of them?"

"Vaguely. The mob for Chicago."

"Yes, ah, well. The prints on your glass belong to Carmine DiFronzo, a known associate." FBI-speak for two-bit hood. "Although one gathers not the smartest bulb in the DiFronzo box, who was given a job strictly as a favor to his father, a distant cousin of the current boss. Said cousin is also a known associate. You said there were two men?"

Jim found himself sitting bolt upright. The mob was in the Park? "Yes. Two."

"Ah. Yes. Well, DiFronzo is often seen in the company of two other gentlemen of interest, Milton Spilotro and Dante Accardo. Accardo was away for a while on a little matter of assault and battery and other, ah, supplementary concerns, but DiFronzo is almost never out of Spilotro's sight."

"Spilotro is DiFronzo's babysitter."

"Ah, possibly. Probably. Both men have been in and out of juvie and prison since they didn't graduate from grade school, B&E, armed robbery, assault and battery, Spilotro was once arrested for rape but she was a prostitute so that went away fast. The locals like him for a couple of murders but neither were civilians and one gets a general, ah, feeling of relief that someone took out the trash." A pause. "I made a few calls. Neither of them have been seen in Chicago in the last month."

"For crissake."

"I'd very much like to know what they're doing in Alaska, Mr. Chopin."

"And in the Park," Jim said, the numbness beginning to wear off. "Especially in the Park. So would I. Do you have mug shots?"

"I'll text them to you. This number work?"

"Yes." A cab pulled up outside the glass and he waved at it. "I've got to go, Agent Mason, I don't have lights at my airstrip yet and I want to make it home before twilight."

"I quite understand. I'll inform the, ah, local authorities there in Anchorage, shall I?"

"I'd appreciate it." Jim hesitated.

"Perhaps without specifically naming my, ah, CI."

"I appreciate your discretion, Special Agent Mason, and I can't thank you enough for your help."

"Their files were literally on my desk, Mr. Chopin. Sometimes you get lucky."

They hung up and Jim cabbed it back to Merrill in a daze.

Only there to discover that, yes, sometimes you did get lucky, and then sometimes that luck ran out. Chick Noyukpuk, coming off what appeared to be a monumental bender, was looking for a ride home and, of course, he was too broke to buy a ticket on Spernak, for which the manager looked indecently joyous. Jim looked from Chick to the pure, pristine, brand new treasure that was 18 Kilo Oscar and with reluctance told him to get in.

Halfway there Chick, in the middle of a tall tale involving a piece of heavy equipment he'd lost in a bog somewhere between Ahtna and Tonsina after shaking off heavy law enforcement pursuit, began sweating profusely and announced that he was going to barf.

Jim made him do it into his own boot.

Eleven

SATURDAY, NOVEMBER 5
Anchorage, The Park

KATE RETURNED TO THE TOWNHOUSE A little shaken. First Sylvia McDonald, then Magnus Campbell. And Fergus McDonald, whose disappearance appeared to have kicked off what was now feeling like a cascade of events, was still missing.

Absorbed in speculation, she was inside before she realized that Jim wasn't parked outside waiting for her. She looked again at his text.

I'm in town. Call me.

Her finger hovered over the call back button when the phone beeped and whistled, startling her so that she almost dropped it. It was Kurt. Mostly, it wasn't Jim. "Hey, Kurt."

"Kate, I've gotten a look at the McDonalds' Visa card. Two cards, same account, they both charged everything for the miles, had automatic payments set up for all their utilities."

"How did you even do that, Pletnikof?"

"Girl, please. One odd charge popped up just last month—a one-time payment to a guy named Commodore Lippy."

"Sounds like someone who commanded a destroyer at the Battle of Manila Bay."

"I know, right, but it turns out the guy's an independent assayer."

A brief silence. "Really."

"Really. I called, said I had a sample for him to look at, he said he worked out of his home and he'd be there all day. I'll text you the address." Her phone dinged. "Kate, you know how paranoid gold miners are."

"I do."

"Assayers are even more so, mostly because they know too much about too many claims and they're always afraid someone's going to bust in and demand they give it all up at the point of a gun."

Kate sighed. "You know, Kurt, if this turns out to be some kind of pissing contest between rival claims I will not be a happy camper."

"I hear you."

"Something else. Magnus Campbell was killed this morning in a home invasion."

There was a brief silence. "Jesus, Kate."

"Yeah, I know."

"It has to be connected."

"I know, Kurt."

"You need to be careful."

"I always am."

He snorted. "Jim called this morning. He's in town."

"Yeah. He texted me."

"Uh-huh. You overnighting again?"

"I think I'll head for home this afternoon."

"Good." There was a wealth of meaning in the single word. It was evident that Kurt thought Kate needed someone to have her back. At this point she didn't disagree, but before Ken Halvorsen she'd never felt the lack. "Call me if you find anything else."

"Wilco."

She called Max Maxwell next. "Girl!" he said, like he always did whenever they spoke, reminding her of Old Sam, who used to call her the same thing. "You in town?"

"Only momentarily, so don't even think about scoring one of your ten-martini lunches off me this trip."

He laughed, a reassuringly robust sound. They'd lost too many old farts lately and the ex-Territorial Policeman was one of her favorites. "Quick question. You know Commodore Lippy?"

"The assayer? Sure, we've both been around for a while. Although I've been around longer than him."

"Of course you have. What can you tell me?"

"He's got the same poker up his butt about his business they all do, but he's a good guy."

"Will he talk to me if I show up on his doorstep?"

"He might. He might even let you inside." And then

he laughed in a way that Kate knew from experience meant he knew something she didn't and he wasn't going to share.

The address Kurt sent her to was a one-story log cabin on Lois Drive between Turnagain and Spenard that looked old enough to have been built by Vitus Bering, if he'd ever stepped foot on shore. The logs were so weatherstained they were almost black in color, although they gleamed with log oil, and the green asphalt shingles on the roof were newer than everything else by at least a century. It was set back from the street on a large lot, surrounded by an eight-foot-high chain-link fence, which could have been there to protect the enormous raspberry patch between fence and house from the moose. Kate didn't think so, especially when she went through the gate and walked up to the front door. It was as solidly built as the rest of the house, with one very small, thick-paned glass window. There was a button next to the door. Kate pushed it, and while she waited spotted the two cameras almost hidden beneath the eaves of the overhanging roof.

"Whaddya want?"

She looked up to see one eye and a nose mashed against the tiny window and took an involuntary step back. "Commodore Lippy?"

"Who wants to know?"

She tried to make herself seem as small and as unmenacing as possible. "My name is Kate Shugak, sir. I—"

"Did you say Shugak?"

"Yessir."

"Any relation to Ekaterina?"

"My grandmother."

A bolt was drawn back, another, a third, and there was the sound of a key in a deadbolt. The door opened to reveal a bulky man of medium height with very little hair left. All of it was white and combed very carefully straight back from a face rippling with wrinkles. A pair of blue eyes as sharp as any Kate had met examined her from head to toe. "You're Stephan's daughter, then."

"Why, yes. Did you know him, sir?"

"Him and your mother, too, but I knew your grandmother better. Come inside."

She did so, wondering what "better" meant in this context and if it was the reason for Max's laughter.

He offered her coffee and a chair. The cabin reminded her of the one her father had built on their homestead, with the addition of two rooms in the back, the bathroom, and the bedroom. The kitchen, dining, and living area occupied the front of the house, minimally but comfortably furnished. Two rows of vinyl records filled up a shelf unit on top of which sat a turntable between two enormous speakers that looked to have been around since the Ames Brothers. She smiled. "Haven't seen one of those in a while."

"Yeah, everyone's downloading now." He laughed at her expression. "What, because I'm a vinyl guy I can't know about iTunes?" He fished around in a pocket and pulled out an iPhone. "A hundred and twenty-eight gigs and most of it's music."

"Fair enough," Kate said. There was no sign of what Commodore Lippy did for a living, not even so much as a year-old copy of the *Prospecting and Mining Journal*. "How did you know my grandmother, sir?"

"I did some prospecting in the Park back in the Fifties and Sixties," he said. "Spent some time in Niniltna. Your grandma was the go-to person for permits for everything up to and including taking a leak in those parts. This was before ANILCA and the Park Service taking over every damn thing, of course."

Treading carefully, she said, "When did you give up prospecting for assaying?"

He looked at her for a long moment, and snapped his fingers. "It was your guy who called earlier."

She neither confirmed nor denied.

He leaned back in his chair. "I owe your grandmother enough that I'm not drop-kicking you out the door, although that may be all you get. So what do you want, Kate Shugak?"

"Fergus McDonald," she said.

His expression didn't change.

"He's gone missing in the Park."

Still nothing.

"And his wife was killed, possibly murdered, and a friend of theirs was killed this morning here in Anchorage in a home invasion."

He grinned. "You here to warn me I'm in danger of my life?"

Anyone looking at that grin would have run, not walked

in the other direction. Kate maintained what she hoped was a neutral expression. "You could be, I suppose. If you were and if my visit put you on your guard, then you'd owe me, wouldn't you?"

He looked at her for a speculative moment, and burst out laughing. "You are Ekaterina's granddaughter, no question. All right, Kate Shugak. Follow me."

He walked them back through his bedroom, a utilitarian room with a bed and a nightstand and a door through the rear wall, as substantial in size and heft as the front door. It led directly into an outbuilding much newer in construction than the cabin, at least on the inside. Counters ran around three walls arranged neatly with many tools —Kate recognized a pair of tongs and that was about it— and a large electric crucible situated beneath a stainless-steel hood like the ones over restaurant stoves. There was a sprinkler system that was newer than the drop ceiling from which it protruded. There were no windows but there was a camera in every corner near the ceiling matching the ones on the front of the house.

He saw her noticing them. "Ain't Costco grand?" he said. "So you got me, Kate Shugak. Yes, I'm an assayer."

On the fourth wall, the one next to the door, there was a desk with a laptop, a wire basket half full of paperwork and a standup file with an assortment of mailing envelopes in it, including ones for USPS Express Mail. "There was a charge on Fergus McDonald's Visa card to you last month. Did you assay a sample for him?"

Nothing.

"And did you then express mail that assay to him at his home address? Because his wife had one of those envelopes—" she pointed "—in her purse when I met her in the Park."

"Answer your own question, then."

"I can't. It wasn't on her body."

He shrugged.

"Look, Mr. Lippy, two people are dead and one is missing, and that missing person is a Suulutaq geologist known for going exploring with his rock hammer in hand. He had business with you recently. Did he send you a sample of something he found in the Park?" Still nothing. Kate gave him her last shot. "Didn't you say you owed Emaa?"

This time she didn't try to fill the following silence. After a bit Lippy said "Aw hell" and pushed the chair in front of the desk to one side. He peeled back the bamboo mat beneath, revealing the door of a safe sunk into the concrete slab of the floor. He glanced up at her. "Back off."

She backed off and pretended to be absorbed in the contents of a little wooden case on one of the counters. It contained a small, thin square of flat black stone and six glass apothecary bottles. One was marked nitric acid and another hydrochloric acid. An old-fashioned assayer's kit. Old Sam had had one.

"Here," Lippy said, and she turned to see him holding out a envelope. "Hold out your hand." She did and he tipped the contents of the envelope into it. "Those are the samples Fergus McDonald left with me four weeks ago."

She rolled the rocks around in her palm. They were the size of big marbles, roundish and rough with a lot of granite running through them. She caught a few sparkles. She raised her eyebrows. "Looks like every bit of fool's gold I've ever seen."

"Oh, it's the real thing all right," Lippy said.

She stood very still, staring at him. "Where did he find it?"

Lippy laughed and took the rocks back. "That would be the question now, wouldn't it, Kate Shugak? No one who hires my services has any obligation to tell me where they found their ore samples. And I think a lot better of their intelligence if they don't."

And that was all he would say, although he did let her take pictures of the rocks with her phone before he put them back in the safe. And then he ushered her back into the house and out his front door, and he did not say she should drop by the next time she was in town, although she might do that anyway. She liked him.

Besides, she knew a miner in the Park. If Fergus "Mac" McDonald had found that gold-bearing rock anywhere in the Park, Clarence Bocee might know where.

She dropped the Forester at the townhouse and cabbed it to Merrill and caught a ride home with George. This time he put her firmly in the shotgun seat.

"Thanks for getting all the supplies into Canyon Hot Springs, George. And for the loan of the sat phone."

He shrugged. "You paid for it." He gave her a sidelong glance. "You know what they've been saying in the Park?"

"That I'm dead? Yeah, I heard. Greatly exaggerated, yadda yadda." She hooked a thumb over her shoulder. "Full plane. I figured things would have slowed down a little when the EIS statement came out."

"They did, briefly." He shrugged. "Then they started up again."

"What's that about?"

"Who knows?" He grinned. "I just cash the checks."

She leaned her head against the window and slept the rest of the way back to Niniltna, disembarking stiffly to walk down the hill to Auntie Vi's. It was coming on dusk a few minutes earlier than it had when she left. She trudged up the steps and opened the door. "Auntie?"

"Katya?"

Her phone beeped and whistled before she had time to toe off her shoes. It was Gavin Mortimer, again. "No, Gavin," she said. "Not in the eight hours since you last called."

He apologized and hung up, and for the first time she wondered why he was so anxious for the identification. Aronson had been missing for four years. She called Kurt. "One more thing, Kurt—get me some background information on Aronson's heirs, will you?"

"He didn't leave much, Kate, and what he did his wife got."

"No children, right?"

"No, no kids."

"Huh. Well, just make one more pass at him, okay? Humor me."

"Sure. Call you later."

"Thanks."

She hung up her coat and walked into the kitchen, where Auntie Vi was rolling lumpia. She nodded at the chair opposite her. Kate washed her hands and pushed up her sleeves and got to work. A spoonful of filling made of some fried crumbled meat and chopped vegetables and bean sprouts was spooned into a thin pastry prone to tearing, was rolled and the resulting tubes stacked in a baking pan lined with waxed paper. The first layer was soon finished, another sheet of wax paper and they started on the second.

"You back to stay now?"

"Probably. I don't know."

"You find who kill that lady?"

"I'm still looking."

"You see Jim?"

"Not yet."

Auntie Vi made a sound like she was spitting. "Ay de mi, Katya, you one spineless girl."

Kate paused in mid-roll and stared across the table. "Pretty good talk from a woman who was trying to get me to dump him for a good Native boy."

They rolled more lumpia.

"If you stay we can finally have potlatch for Edna."

Kate didn't say anything. Lumpia froze well.

"She was coming home from berry picking."

"I heard." Kate might have seen Auntie Vi's lips tremble if she looked up, so she didn't look up.

"Not the worst way to die, on the way home from picking berries."

"No."

"She always put too much spice in her blueberry jam."

Kate knew better than to have any comment on the matter. The aunties could criticize each other all they wanted. They would annihilate anyone outside the Gang of Four who dared to do so, even Kate.

They rolled more lumpia.

"I miss that dog," Auntie Vi said.

They filled the pan and started on another.

Twelve

SUNDAY, NOVEMBER 6
The Park

—SMOOTH HIP FIRM BENEATH HIS HAND. HE rolled over, pushing his knee between—

And then a thunder of knocking caused him to lurch up out of sleep, his erection an irritated thrust against his belly. "Fuck," he said.

If only. He'd spent the last four months at hard labor, falling into bed every night too exhausted for wet dreams, and all Kate Shugak had to do was show up back in the Park for his libido to start lunging off its chain.

Another round of knocking, this time demanding enough to make something rattle in a kitchen cupboard. He scrubbed his hands against his head in an attempt to get his brain started and tossed the covers to one side. The digital readout on the nightstand read 7:00, and he cursed his way into a pair of sweatpants and pulled a sweatshirt over his head on his way down the stairs. He hit the light switch next to the door at the same time he yanked it open. "What!"

Bobby Clark glared back at him. "You got coffee or what?"

For at least five seconds Jim thought longingly about slamming the door in Bobby's face and going back to bed. Instead, he turned and headed for the kitchen, there to make his sentiments known by using extreme vigor in filling the carafe with water, to the point that it was a wonder it didn't break when he slammed it home in the coffee maker. He measured out the coffee, adding an extra heaping spoonful in the hopes that the resulting brew would dissolve the enamel on Bobby's teeth and hit the switch. He heard Bobby unzip his coat and his imperceptibly halting step as he moved to sit down at the table on the other side of the passthrough. Jim brought out sugar and half and half and spoons and slammed them down. He returned to the kitchen and willed the coffee maker to work faster, and when it obeyed pulled the carafe and let it drain directly into the mugs. He carried them to the table, as good as tossed Bobby's in front of him and sat down to doctor his own. Bobby tasted his without a wince. Fucker.

They drank in silence, two big, pissed-off men, both of whom had been in love with the same woman at one time or another and between them there was always the knowledge that Bobby had got there first. Jim could really give a shit so long as he got there last, but nevertheless Bobby was always a little proprietary when it came to Kate Shugak and more than a little suspicious of Jim's staying power.

Jim drained his mug, reached over to take Bobby's out of his hand without asking and got up to refill them. This time he brought back what was left of Auntie Vi's fry bread, nuked in the microwave and served with melted butter and powdered sugar. The two men dipped and ate and finished their second mugs. This time Jim held out his hand for Bobby's mug instead of snatching it.

Jim put on another pot and returned to the table. By now the light was coming up behind the Quilaks, illuminating the blades of the still dark peaks in sharply etched relief. The land outside the floor-to-ceiling windows fell gradually away from the cabin to the southeast and then down to the Kanuyaq River, making the view on a morning such as this nothing less than staggering.

"Glad to see the end of that gray overcast," Jim said. When all else failed, in Alaska you could always talk about the weather.

Bobby grunted.

Or not. Jim looked out the window again, this time in the direction of the yard, where Halvorsen had breathed his last in July.

Bobby followed his gaze. "He shot Kate."

"Yeah." It occurred to Jim that he was sitting across from another man who had killed.

Bobby read the thought on his face. "The difference is I was drafted. You volunteered."

"How does that make it different?"

"I didn't want to go, I didn't want to be there, all I

wanted was to do my thirteen months and fifteen days and go home alive, and I was willing to kill anything that got in the way of that. My weapon was never out of my reach, eating, sleeping, fucking, didn't matter, it was right there. I only wish I'd managed to take out a couple officers while I was killing my way home because you'd rather have the VC at your back than some of them."

Jim didn't think he was kidding.

Bobby gestured. "Whereas you, you willingly put yourself in the line of fire, to serve and protect. You wore the weapon, sure, but I never saw you pull it. You went home every night. Trust me, it's different." He paused, watching his fingers turn his mug in a circle. "I been up to the post half a dozen times since I saw those two yahoos at Bernie's. Nick wasn't there and neither was that child playing trooper dress-up and that new dispatcher doesn't know shit."

"Those guys still camping out in Bernie's cabin?"

"Far as I know."

"Wanna go see if they're there this morning?"

A grin split Bobby's face. "Sure. I'll drive."

An answering grin spread across Jim's. "No need. Grab your coat and follow me."

Bobby stopped dead when he saw the strip. "Dude. Seriously. How long?"

"Three thousand feet."

"Jesus. What are you thinking of buying, a Herc?"

Jim laughed. "Not hardly, but if I need an excavator or a D-8, I want to be able to rent one and have it hauled in."

Bobby eyed him. "So, retirement not taking you out of the Park."

"Not up to me," Jim said.

They were at the hangar now and Bobby kept any inevitable reflections about the permanence of the airstrip and all its mod cons to himself. Jim unlocked the padlock and flipped back the hasp and slid the doors open.

Bobby drew in a breath of pure delight. "Oh, my dear lord above. The station wagon of the air." He circled 18 Kilo Oscar with a worshipful eye and a caressing hand. "She's a beauty, Jim. When—"

"Yesterday."

He recounted the events and Bobby laughed. "Gotta love those old farts. You flew her home after?"

"Merrill to touchdown in an hour and a half." At Bobby's look he shrugged. "I was pushing it a little, I admit. Wanted to beat twilight and just barely made it. I had Chick Noyukpuk with me so I buzzed Mandy's place and she ran over on her four-wheeler and parked at the far end and left her headlights on. Didn't really need it but you know, helpful. I still have to put a reflector board up at either end."

Bobby tore his eyes from 18 Kilo Oscar long enough to survey their surroundings. "I remember now. Your father died last year."

"Yeah."

"You said he'd left you an inheritance."

Jim shrugged.

"Yeah." Bobby took a deep breath. "Well, you going to show me what this baby can do?"

The strip at the Roadhouse was usually hard-packed snow in the winter but now it was just dead grass left over from summer. The sun still hadn't fully risen but there was enough light to land. Bernie poked his head out of his front door when Jim cut the engine. "Nice ride, Chopin."

"Thanks."

"Bar doesn't open until noon."

"Ace and Deuce still around?" Bobby said.

Bernie gestured at the row of tiny cabins behind the Roadhouse, just out of earshot of the airstrip that fronted Bernie's house. "Same cabin as yesterday. You packing?"

Jim and Bobby looked at each other. Bernie rolled his eyes. "Wait there."

Five minutes later Bernie trotted out carrying two long guns, one a rifle, the other a shotgun. He tossed the rifle to Bobby, who caught it and checked the magazine. He looked up and laughed at Jim's expression. "Don't worry, Chopin, we got your back."

In the end it proved unnecessary. The cabin was still empty, although today the few toiletries in the bathroom were gone.

"Any idea when they left?"

"No. Damn it."

"Were they in the bar last night?" Jim said.

"Yes. No. Hell, I don't know. It was Saturday night, and Shitting Seagull came up the river for his annual visit and things got a little enthusiastic."

The Cordova harbormaster was an eccentric individual who reserved transient parking for alien spaceships only he could see, but he was more than pleased to regale Park rats with tales of his more exotic visitors. Niniltna simply emptied out when Shitting Seagull came to call at the Roadhouse.

"All the other cabins full?"

"Yeah."

"Want to knock on some doors?"

"No."

They did anyway, but their only reward was getting to see Dulcey Kineen naked and that only for a brief moment until Albert Balluta yanked her back inside. The interview was conducted in shouts through a firmly closed door, and they didn't remember Ace and Deuce any more than any of the rest of those sleeping off the night before did.

"Well, hell," Bernie said. "If I'd known they'd gone I could've rented out their cabin."

"Was Martin Shugak here last night?" Jim said.

Bernie shook his head. "Didn't see him." He stopped. "Wait a minute."

"What?"

"Gull said he saw smoke coming out of one of the cabins at Potlatch when he was going by. He stopped and yelled but no one showed, so he just kept on."

"I thought I heard Scott Ukatish had pulled out of Potlatch."

"You did. He moved to Cordova. That's why Gull was surprised to see smoke."

Jim thought about that. Potlatch was some distance from the populated areas but still in the Park and on the river. And it wouldn't be known to Outsiders or for that matter many Alaskans. "Want to take a ride down the river?"

"Yes," Bobby said.

"Hell, yeah," Bernie said.

Potlatch wasn't even twenty-five miles from the Roadhouse as the crow flies and they were circling over the tiny jumble of weathered gray houses twenty minutes later. Indeed there was a plume of smoke coming from the largest of them.

"That's Scott's place?"

"Yeah."

They circled low and slow, or as slow as 18 Kilo Oscar would allow, and Jim picked out the faint trace of an airstrip running east–west in back of the buildings. He came down to about ten feet and ran the length of it. It looked frozen hard and free of obstacles except for a few tufts of pea grass. It might even be long enough. He pulled up, turned and began his approach as slowly as possible. He touched down at the extreme eastern end and rolled out to within ten feet of the western end.

"You gonna be able to get out of here again?" Bobby said.

"Might have to leave one of you behind."

"Great."

The cold cut like a knife and their breaths steamed in the air. There was always a price to pay for good winter weather and it always came in the below freezing area of the thermometer. Dead grass crunched beneath their feet as they went single file between two small houses, the slightly larger one with the smoke plume coming out of the stack on the right.

A man with a rifle held in front of him stood at Scott Ukatish's front door. Been hard to miss the sound of their landing. "Who are you and what do you want?"

"Hold on there, friend," Jim said, hands raised. "We saw the smoke, and we know Scott's in Cordova."

"I know. He sold me this place last summer."

"Didn't know he'd put it on the market."

"He didn't. I was on a rafting trip down the river. I saw this place and stopped in. He told me he was leaving and I bought it."

"Been living here ever since?"

"I have."

The guy was tall and lanky and had a face that had spent a long time outdoors, thick-skinned with a permanent tan. Somewhere between his late thirties and early forties. His hair was dark and short and badly cut, like he'd been doing it himself without a mirror. He was wearing a plaid shirt worn at the elbows over a pair of Carhartt's that were the very definition of broke in. He definitely wasn't Martin Shugak.

"You live here alone…?"

"Yeah. I like my peace." His rifle was an AR-15 that looked new but not brand new. "You're disturbing it."

"A guy named Martin Shugak drop by here recently?"

"Never heard of him." He gestured with the rifle. "Goodbye."

The man went back inside and closed the door before all the heat got out but not before Jim got a glimpse of the interior. It looked clean and neat, with a full bookcase made of fresh pine two-by-twelves that extended over an entire wall and a tiny wood stove with a busy fire burning brightly behind a glass door.

The door shut firmly in their faces.

"Here's your hat, what's your hurry," Bobby said.

Jim led the way back to the airstrip and they climbed in and donned their headsets. The engine again started at a touch—Robert Weisner was already assuming a godlike aura in Jim's fond memory—and 18 Kilo Oscar made a graceful ascent into her natural habitat with runway to spare. He climbed to five thousand feet and looked south and west. It was clear all the way to Prince William Sound and then some. "Want to go to Cordova?"

Bobby, riding shotgun, gave him a look beneath lowered brows. From the back Bernie said, "You don't like it that he didn't give us his name."

"Just getting a feel for my new airplane," Jim said, and put her nose on south southwest.

SUNDAY, NOVEMBER 6
The Park

The next morning Kate went to breakfast with her defenses up, but Auntie Vi seemed less inclined to attack. A good night's sleep helped almost anything and it seemed they had both had one. Sourdough pancakes and eggs and sausage patties consumed over conversation no more toxic than "Please pass the syrup" completed the cure. Kate leaned back in her chair, nursing a second cup of coffee and looked through the kitchen window at Quilak peaks drenched in alpenglow. Given enough time, most might be right once again with the world. The Park had its own curative properties.

Most. Not all. Which was more than anyone had any right to expect.

"Auntie, is Clarence Bocee still around?"

Auntie Vi snorted. "Clarence! That—that—" there followed an Aleut word that Kate didn't know but sounded pretty reprehensible "—rock hound! You stay away from him, Katya!"

"He used to work with Mac Devlin, didn't he?"

Another snort, equal in indignation. "Greedy carpetbaggers, both of them, boomers, make money and take it out of state."

"You mean like Global Harvest, auntie?"

Global Harvest being the parent company for the Suulutaq Mine, which had bought Auntie Vi's bed-and-breakfast and hired her to run it for them.

Auntie Vi reared up, affronted. "I live here! I spend money here! I pay Amelia Totemoff and Grace Kvasnikof to work here and they live here, too!"

"I'm sorry, auntie," Kate said, and she was. Auntie Vi deserved better than having her niece snipe at her. "So is Clarence still living in that cabin out past Bobby's?"

This produced another rant about good girls chasing after bad men, which Kate bore meekly. She could have explained but she didn't think it would do any good. Auntie Vi wasn't in a listening mood.

She put on every article of clothing she had with her and set out, her breath smoking the air, driving through a Niniltna coated with frost. Every limb of every tree, evergreen and deciduous alike, looked as if they had been carved from white quartz. Every house and cabin was frosted with a thick layer of crusty white rime, their windows scrolled with ice flowers. Smoke curled from every chimney in slow motion, gray wisps that hung in the still air like phantoms.

It looked like an illustration by J.R.R. Tolkien crossed with a painting by Thomas Kinkade. With maybe some Disney thrown in, and on the whole so sweet it was a little nauseating. A dog barked as Kate went by, another, and then another, and soon every dog in the village was setting up a howl that seemed to wash over the frozen river and back again and up into the foothills to echo off the peaks of the Quilaks, themselves icy scimitars drawn against the morning.

If it didn't snow soon, and a lot, next year's fire season was going to be an interesting one, to say the least.

The wooden bridge over Squaw Candy Creek was frozen in place and the ATV tires bumped over it with barely a rumble. Half a mile down the road there was a turnoff on the river side, from which a narrow trail led to a cabin perched precariously near the river's edge. The yard was filled with bits and pieces of heavy equipment, excavator claws and buckets, grader blades, dozer tracks. Part or all of a gold dredge was stacked in pieces, and the only thing in the yard higher than it was the stack of firewood piled next to the cabin.

She wound through the debris in the yard and killed the engine. Cabins commonly bore the racks of caribou and moose above their doors. This one was outlined in gold pans fixed to the wall with a single bolt through their centers. None of the pans had ever seen an Amazon buy link and Kate suspected some of them dated back to the Stampede. Wall art, Park style.

The door opened and a head poked out and squinted at her. "Kate?"

"Clarence."

"I heard you were dead."

"I heard that, too. You got a minute?"

"Sure." He ushered her inside, did an arm sweep of the seat of a recliner only slightly younger than the cabin, and waved her into it. "Want some tea? I just brewed up some samovar."

Nothing sourdoughs liked more than some samovar tea, and Kate accepted the mug with pleasure and inhaled the spicy citrus aroma with near orgasmic enjoyment.

"Ah—"

She looked up to see Clarence holding up a bottle of Grand Marnier. "Gah," she said, "no, and I mean no thank you." She watched him tilt it toward his mug. "You're not."

"I am," he said, and did so, a healthy glug.

"God, Clarence, that's like swearing on Sunday in a born-again Baptist church. You just don't do that. And geez, it's only ten-thirty in the morning."

"It's five o'clock somewhere," he said, and took a defiant swallow.

The interior of the cabin was like a thousand others in the Park, one square room with a sleeping loft. There was a wood stove for heat and a Coleman two-burner for cooking, a sink that drained into a five-gallon bucket with marine blue paint still flaking from it, and built-in plywood shelves sagging beneath the weight of canned and dry goods. There were some books, most in the Alaskan-minerals-and-where-to-find-them genre but also including anything ever written by David Weber and Johnny Ringo, and many more magazines, all to do with mining. A galvanized steel tub hung on one wall of unfinished two-by-twelves, big enough for Clarence to bathe in if he didn't mind his knees around his ears while he did so. A washboard hung next to it.

Clarence didn't look as if he'd made use of the tub for either himself or his clothes in recent memory. A few years or a decade older than Kate, it was hard to tell, his sandy hair was thinning and scraggled down the back of his neck and his brown eyes were a little bloodshot. His skin looked like he'd been eating out of cans for a while and not green beans or spinach, either. He wore tattered jeans and a faded plaid shirt, and she could see his left heel through a large hole in his sock. One lone pair of gnawed-looking Sorels sat next to the door beneath a Carhartt's jacket that had aged from its original brown to a kind of glacial gray.

Portrait of an unsuccessful gold miner. Still, not necess-arily an unhappy one. Clarence probably owned his cabin and the property it stood on free and clear. The Kanuyaq ran right outside his kitchen window and was full of salmon in summertime. In spring a herd of caribou might wander down out of the Quilak foothills to fill up their tanks on the grass on the other side of the river, and there was always a moose or two wandering by. Kate had seen the chest freezer on the porch outside. There might be a garden in the yard somewhere between the blades and the tracks. Even if there wasn't there were always fiddlehead ferns and dandelion greens and berries of every kind to pick wild and eat and freeze for winter. A subsistence lifestyle didn't have to cost a lot, especially if you were single and without kids. And for gold miners, family was always secondary to the allure of Au-79. It didn't look like Clarence even had a dog.

Her eyes came back around to Clarence, who was regarding her with the usual interest of a male Park rat within five feet of a woman of even marginal nubility for the first time in too long. "You're looking good, Kate."

"Thanks, Clarence." She didn't add "You, too" because it would only encourage him. "I was hoping you could do me a favor."

He brightened, because this sounded like a deal he might be able to parley into other goods and especially services. "Absolutely."

She pulled up the photo app on her phone. "I've got a few pictures of some ore samples. Any idea where they came from?"

He scrolled through the photos. "Huh."

Kate sipped her tea and waited.

Clarence felt around in the magazine stand next to his chair for a pair of reading glasses and perched them on the very tip of his nose and scrolled through the photos again. Any awareness that a female was within range had completely vanished from his consciousness, but then gold miners were like that, too.

Kate enjoyed her tea and berated herself silently for not stopping in to the Kobuk Coffee Company while she'd been in Anchorage.

He looked up, frowning. "It's hard to tell from just a photo. Any chance I can see the actual samples?"

"I'm afraid not."

He accepted this without a blink because he wouldn't have shown his samples to anyone else, either. He sat back and pushed his glasses up on his forehead so he could massage his eyes. "If I had to guess, I'd say these came from somewhere near the Suulutaq."

Kate put her mug down slowly. "Really."

He leaned forward and pointed. "See that line of copper? For all the hoohaw about the Suulutaq being the second-biggest gold mine in the world, there is even more copper there than gold."

"You don't look all that convinced," she said.

He shrugged and handed her phone back. "Like I said. If I had to guess."

"Yeah. Well, thanks, Clarence. I appreciate it." She pocketed the phone and pulled out a pint jar of nagoonberry jelly. "Auntie Vi put this up this fall. One of her best batches, I think."

"Wow." He handled the jar with proper reverence. "Nagoonberry. Man, I never get any of this stuff unless it's a potlatch or something and I'm first in line. Tell her thanks for me, Kate."

"You bet," Kate said, but she wouldn't. She only hoped Auntie Vi wasn't keeping count of the jars in her pantry.

She drove up to the airstrip.

George was loading a plane for the Suulutaq and she wangled the last seat. It was a full flight, again odd for a mine that had, it felt like only moments before, been on the verge of shutting down before it ever opened up. When they touched down at the mine she spotted three core drills at work up on the plateau, and there were lights on in every window of the two-story modular building that was mine headquarters. Inside, Vernon Truax was at his desk, a fifty-ish man thickening around the middle with large-knuckled hands and a broad, bluff face. "Kate Shugak," he said without getting up. After all, she was no longer the chair of the Niniltna Native Association and thus worthy of no particular courtesy.

"Vern," she said. "Things looking busy around here."

"Why shouldn't they?"

"Well. There was that whole thing about your EIS."

He waved it away. "We're expecting some major changes with the new administration coming in. And have you seen the price of copper lately? Not to mention gold?" He grinned, and it was a tight, triumphant grin, the grin of a guy who lived and breathed big business and saw nothing but good times and black bottom lines ahead. "Was there something you wanted? I'm kind of busy here."

"Your field geologist still missing?"

He frowned. "How'd you hear about that?"

"His wife hired me to find him."

"She's dead."

"Yeah, but she wrote me a check for a retainer and I haven't run it out yet."

He snorted. "Yeah, whatever, and no, Mac still hasn't shown up. And before you ask, I don't know where he is."

"He a good worker?"

"Yeah," Truax said, a little grudgingly Kate thought. "He showed up, did his job. Never any problem with his work."

Kate had heard more heartfelt encomiums. "He ever go missing like this before?"

"No. Well, he took off whenever he had some downtime. He'd go hiking up in the hills or fly into Niniltna."

"Did he say what he was doing?"

"He wasn't real social, Kate."

"He have any friends here he might have talked to?"

"Like I said. He wasn't real social. He'd roomed alone, ate alone."

"Get along with his co-workers?"

Truax shrugged. "Never heard any complaints. He always showed up when the core samples came out of the ground, and he put in his time on the subsurface map we're making of the discovery." He grinned again. "We might not be the second-largest gold mine in the world anymore."

"Nobody was mad at him? He hadn't made any enemies?"

"He'd had to have had actual conversations with his co-workers first, I would think."

She would think so, too. She pulled up the photo app on her phone and handed it to him.

"What's this?"

"Pictures of some ore samples. I was wondering if you could tell me if they came from the Suulutaq."

"They better not have." He scrolled through them a lot quicker than Clarence had and handed it back to her. "Nope."

"No? You're sure?"

He heaved himself up out of his chair walked over to a tall metal cabinet. "Take a look."

She followed his pointing finger to see shelves holding rows of cylindrical core samples. "Your samples?"

He nodded. "Cores, not rocks, of course, but you can see the difference. There is more copper in the Suulutaq than there is gold, and not forgetting the molybdenum. Those photos show way more gold." He closed the cabinet again. "Your samples don't look like anything we've ever pulled out of the ground around here, and I've been here since the beginning."

"Did Fergus McDonald have an office here?"

"A desk, not an office."

"Mind if I take a look?"

"Sure." He walked her upstairs to a collection of cubicles, stopping at one. There was a picture of Sylvia tacked to the wall over the desk and some pens and paper clips in the center drawer. "No computer?"

"He had a company-issued laptop. He must have taken it with him."

She looked in the side drawers. One held a collection of rocks that looked like they'd been tossed in whenever McDonald came into the building and emptied out his pockets. Unlike the samples she had seen in the McDonalds' living room in Anchorage, no attempt had been made to catalogue them by location or date found.

She closed the last drawer and felt the mine

superintendent's firm hand on her elbow. He ushered her to the front door and left her there. "Thanks for stopping by."

"Thanks for your help."

They exchanged insincere smiles and she headed for the airstrip, where she was able to catch George on his return flight. This time she was riding shotgun, but he took one look at her face and concentrated on flying the plane. It was infinitely safer.

They landed back in Niniltna and as Kate was getting out Kurt called. "A USPS express mail charge just popped up on Sylvia's Visa. She sent something to her husband care of general delivery in Niniltna the same day she flew there."

"What? Why? Why wouldn't she just bring it with her?"

"Because it was an online order to be sent from the business in New York City."

"What business?"

"A dealer in rare manuscripts. Schuyler's Rare Finds. Before you ask I already called and they were closed. Did she have it on her?"

Kate remembered the express mail envelope she'd seen in Sylvia's room at Auntie Vi's. "She did the night before. She didn't when we found her body." She looked across the airstrip at the post office, a one-room addition to a small clapboard house. "I'll call you back."

Cheryl Jeppsen, the Niniltna postmistress, greeted Kate with what was by now the standard look of surprise. "Kate, you're back. I'd heard—"

"Yeah, I know, you thought I was dead."

Cheryl managed to summon up an affronted look. "Certainly not. I heard that silly rumor and I told people it was silly when I heard it. I knew you were fine. If anyone was going to be fine in those mountains it would be Kate Shugak, I told them."

"Thanks, Cheryl." Kate's gratitude was as genuine as Cheryl's denial. "Listen, you remember Sylvia McDonald?"

Cheryl's face collapsed into a well-crafted expression of sorrow. "Oh my, yes, I heard about that poor woman." She affected a shudder. "I saw Nick load her body on the airplane to take it to town. Horrible, just horrible." Her protuberant eyes focused on Kate with an avid expression. "I noticed you flew in with the body. Did you find it?"

"She was my client." Kate went on rapidly before Cheryl could pelt her with the questions she could plainly see trembling at the tip of her tongue. "I've just learned that her husband, Fergus McDonald, was sent an express mail. It was sent care of general delivery, to this post office. I'm pretty sure she picked it up the day she arrived. Did you give it to her?"

"Why, yes. She was such a pretty little thing. You could tell George and the boys thought so, too, their tongues were hanging out down to the ground watching her walk across the strip." Cheryl tittered, and then sobered. "Oh. I... I hope I didn't do anything wrong. She had identification, she could prove she was his wife and I thought..."

"Do you still have the slip on file here?"

"I can't afford to lose this job, Kate," Cheryl said, looking twenty years older from one moment to the next. "Please don't call the postal inspectors on me. One more complaint, and—"

"Cheryl. Do you still have the slip on file here?"

"Of course." Cheryl scurried around the dutch door and Kate heard the sounds of a drawer opening and a flutter of paper. There was an aircraft on final into the strip outside, too.

"Here it is," Cheryl said, reappearing, flushed, holding the form in her hand.

The writing on the label was cramped and illegible, and the label itself was crumpled. She could make out the date stamp, the day before Sylvia McDonald had flown to Niniltna, the From: Schuyler Rare Finds, and the To: Fergus McDonald. Contents could have been book, or maybe brochure? It was too badly creased to decipher. "Did she say what it was?"

Cheryl shook her head. "She said her husband was meant to have picked it up before she got here."

"Could you tell what it was?"

The postmistress screwed up her face in thought. "It felt kind of like a blue book, you know, the exam books they give you in high school? Only bigger, and made of stiffer paper.'

Kate handed the slip back. "Okay, thanks, Cheryl. I appreciate it."

"Kate?"

Kate, lost in her own thoughts, looked up. "Yes?"

Cheryl was actually wringing her hands now. "You won't..."

Cheryl Jeppsen had fallen out of a bad marriage into one of the few good year-round jobs Niniltna had. She might be an inveterate gossip, she might hold back someone's mail a day or two if she was peeved at them, she might even hand over mail to one person that was addressed to someone else. But she was, in that inimitable phrase of Sharyn McCrumb, one man away from welfare, or as in this case one job, and Kate would not be the person who shoved her over that line. "I won't, Cheryl. Thanks again, you really helped me out."

She stepped outside, pulling the door closed behind her, and watched a Cessna 206, white with blue and gold stripes and the tail number 18 Kilo Oscar roll out of its landing and taxi over to her side of the strip.

The engine shut down and the prop stopped turning and the pilot stepped out.

It was Jim.

Thirteen

SUNDAY, NOVEMBER 6
The Park

S HE WAS DISTANTLY CONSCIOUS OF OTHER
people getting out of the plane but she couldn't summon
up the wherewithal to identify them, say hi or even care
who they were. All of her attention had been taken hostage
by the presence of the man standing off the nose of the
unfamiliar aircraft.

He looked good. God, did he look good. His shoulders
seemed broader, his hips slimmer, his legs longer, his hair
blonder and his goddamn eyes bluer. He wasn't even in
uniform, but the bomber jacket and the Levi's did fine as a
showcase. She found her eyes drifting down to the button
on the fly on his jeans and she yanked them back up to
his face.

It was comforting to see that he was as dumbstruck by
her appearance as she was by his. His eyes roved over her
from head to toe and it felt as if her down jacket and jeans

were melting right off her body and for just a second she was more than okay with that.

He said nothing. The only sound was their breath, the only movement the clouds it formed in the cold air. Her heart was pounding so loudly in her ears she wasn't sure if she could have heard him if he had spoken. This was ridiculous. She pulled herself together and tried for a smile, although the expression felt stiff on her lips. "You look like you've seen a ghost." Try as she would the words came out shaky.

He took a deep breath. "The last time I saw you you were unconscious on a hospital bed and I had your blood all over my clothes. Give me a minute." His voice was deep, resonant, the words maybe a little shaky themselves.

One of the two figures who had climbed out of the plane after Jim came forward. "Hey, babe." She was engulfed in a bear hug.

"Bobby," she said, and the world returned to real time. Over his shoulder she saw Bernie, who gave her a little wave. "Bernie. Hi."

"Good to see you, Kate."

"Backatcha."

Bobby held her by the shoulders for a close inspection. "Come home with? Dinah and Katya would be very happy to see you."

She gave Jim a fleeting glance. "Uh. I was going to go out to the homestead."

He snorted and said just loudly enough for her to hear him, "About time."

She felt the heat begin to creep up her neck and was glad she was wearing all of her winter clothes, including the thin white wool scarf that came up to her chin.

"Okay then, see you later." Bobby looked at Jim. "Tell her what we've been up to, asshat."

"Will do, dipshit."

"See you, Kate, Jim."

"Bye, Bernie."

Kate and Jim were left to stare at each other some more. Finally, she nodded at her ATV. "Well. I should get going if I want to make it home before dark."

"You could," he said. "Or." He jerked his head at the airplane. "We could fly."

The 206 touched down at the end of the runway and eased to a smooth stop in front of the hangar. Jim killed the engine and got out to open the hangar doors and Kate recovered enough to help him push the tail around and back the Cessna inside. He gave her the dollar-and-a-quarter tour over the rest of it, not forgetting to point out the weather station. "You can install the app on your phone and log in with my account. I paid for two users."

She handed him her phone without comment and walked back out onto the runway in front of the hangar, hands stuffed into her pockets, surveying the complex from the ground as she had from the air before they landed.

The hangar was perpendicular to the runway, the evergreens and the undergrowth were trimmed back to an evenly respectful distance, and everything was so neat—she squinted. "What's that?"

He came up and handed her her phone. "What?" He followed her pointing finger to the two dimples in the side of the otherwise pristine hangar wall. "Oh. That." He might have shuffled his feet a little. "I dropped a piece of wood."

She looked at him. "Gravity generally works down, not up."

He looked away. "Yeah, well, maybe I dropped two."

He was clearly uncomfortable and she decided to table it. For now. "You did all this this summer?"

"Summer and fall."

"All by yourself?"

"God no. I had some guys come in from Ahtna to knock out a bunch of trees and blade the place level. I hired help to assemble the hangar and the sheds, and I had an electrician from Ahtna come out and wire the place to code. I hired the entire senior class to limb and buck the trees."

"They cut the firewood, too?"

"No. No, I've been on that."

She ran her eyes over him again. "Well, no wonder."

He looked away. There might have been a little color in his cheeks. "Kept me busy." He looked back. "And you?"

"I tore down Old Sam's cabin and built a new one." He didn't say anything. "Did you know? How did you know?"

"Well, when you're standing in line at the post office, waiting to pick up your packages, and a semi delivers two pallets of freight, most of it building materials, and George Perry shows up in a high-altitude helo to haul them east, not south as you might expect if he were taking them to Suulutaq…" His voice trailed away. "George didn't say a word but I doubt it was much of a secret to anyone in the Park." He smiled a little. "I mean, Cheryl Jeppsen had a front row seat."

She smiled a little, too, and looked up to see him looking at her mouth. Their eyes met.

He took a deep gulp of air. "Help me close up and we can get out of the cold."

The house looked much the same. Kate's steps slowed when they came into the yard and she moved even more slowly up the stairs, casting an involuntary look behind her. The clearing was much the same, a semi-circle of buildings, the old cache still sturdy on its long legs, the greenhouse, the house, the garage and shop, even the old outhouse was still upright and functional because you never knew when your septic might blow out and in the Bush it was all about backup.

If Kate's eyes clung briefly to the spot where Mutt had lain after she was shot Jim didn't say he'd noticed, because he was smart like that.

She stepped inside and sniffed the air. "Did you spill some Clorox?"

He looked shifty. "Why would you think that?"

She shed her outer gear and went straight to the kitchen

and got out the flour, salt and yeast. He watched her for a moment and then went to build a fire in the fireplace and refill the woodbox. When he was done she had the dough on to rise and had gone to investigate the contents of the chest freezer on the back deck. She returned with a package of moose ribs and opened it up to let them thaw in the sink.

The tension in the air had lessened some by the time these homely tasks were completed. She made coffee. He got a beer. They sat down on opposite ends of the couch. The sun sank into the southeast and the fire crackled on the hearth.

"So." He rolled the bottle between his hands. "Bobby said you're on a case."

"Yeah." Silently she thanked him for the segue from the personal to the professional, and told him about Sylvia McDonald, and Fergus McDonald, and then Magnus Campbell. After which she paused and said, picking her way delicately through the words, "I, ah, got your text."

"Good to know. When you didn't answer, I wondered."

He didn't ask her why she hadn't replied. "Did you go to town to pick up your new airplane? Which is a very nice airplane indeed, if I didn't say so before."

"Thanks." He told her about his adventures with bigstick and she laughed, and that husky, partly broken sound nearly undid him then and there. "And I was looking for Martin." He took a swig of beer. "A little bit, anyway."

She lowered her mug. "Martin? Martin Shugak?"

He nodded. "Howie Katelnikof dropped by."

She stared at him. "Voluntarily?"

He quirked an eyebrow. "He's in fear of his life, evidently. There's some muscle for hire been asking questions about—" he took a deep breath "—Ken Halvorsen and Martin Shugak."

She got there immediately. "Was Martin running for Ken?"

"Looks like maybe."

"Oh." She rolled her eyes. "Oh, of course, and Howie, too, which is why he's scared."

"Yeah, he's afraid the muscle was sent by Halvorsen's supplier." He shrugged. "Maybe Halvorsen missed a payment, but Halvorsen's dead—" he managed to say this without a quiver "—and Halvorsen must have told them that Martin was working for him so Martin is next on their list, and while he didn't say so, I'm sure Howie, the little weasel, is afraid they're going to catch Martin and persuade Martin to give him up."

"Have you seen said muscle?"

"No, but Bernie has, up close and personal. They were at the Roadhouse, staying in one of the cabins and drinking in the bar. He waited on them." He paused. "And he gave me a glass he'd served beer in to one of them."

"No way."

"Way. He didn't like the look of them, he said, not enough to not take their money, but—"

"Certainly not."

"—but enough so that he thought law enforcement might maybe come sniffing around after them. They were pretty rough-looking according to him and Bobby, who saw them, too. Lot of tats."

"Prison tats?"

"He thought maybe so. Anyway, he gave me the glass and I brought it into town with me."

Kate groaned. "You didn't hand it into the lab, did you?"

"God no. Never see or hear of it again. No, I called that FBI agent you met last year in Newenham."

"James Mason?"

"Yeah." He told her about handing over the glass to the FBI and Mason's subsequent call back, and flying out to Bernie's that morning only to find the muscle gone.

She pursed her lips in a long, silent whistle. "Wow. The mob in the Park."

He felt bound to say it. "Not particularly heavy hitters, mob-wise."

"No, but still." Her brow creased. "What the hell, Jim. The mob's getting back into bootlegging? I thought that went out with Prohibition."

"Yeah, so did I."

Her eyes narrowed. "You think they're here for some other reason?"

He sighed and finished his beer. "If so, I can't imagine what that reason would be." He hesitated. "Something else. Erland Bannister has been around. A lot. George says he's in and out of Niniltna two, three times a month. Hell, I saw his G II overhead I don't know how many times while I was working on the strip and the hangar."

"I ran into Erland in Anchorage." She told him.

He didn't try to hide his wince.

"Not all downside." Her smile was lop-sided. "At least he bought me lunch."

They were silent for a while. They'd both stretched out on the couch, legs lying next to each other's but barely touching.

"So you didn't find Martin in Anchorage."

"Hide nor hair."

"So he's probably still in the Park."

"Probably."

They were silent for a few moments. "Where were you coming back from, today?"

"Cordova. When we flew out to Bernie's he said Shitting Seagull came in for his annual toot and said he'd seen smoke rising from one of the houses at Potlatch. I thought it might be Martin so we flew down to take a look, but it wasn't."

"Scott Ukatish still there?"

"No. Some guy who said Scott sold him his house. He wasn't, shall we say, welcoming. Didn't even give us his name." He shrugged. "Bugged me. Bernie said Gull said Scott had moved to Cordova. The weather was holding so we flew on down. Found Scott in the Cordova House." A smile spread across his face.

"What?"

"He was barkeeping. And he was dressed to the nines."

"What, he'd ironed his jeans?"

"Oh, no. I'm talking more like a leather mini-skirt over fishnet stockings and four-inch heels."

Kate blinked. "Really."

"Said he'd lost a bet."

"But?"

"But I couldn't help but notice how well those heels fit."

"Well," Kate said, "to each his own. How's Cordova taking it?"

"Oh, you know that town, they're pretty much up for anything. And when we talked to him he said he did sell his house to, quote, some guy, unquote, five years ago."

"Scott stayed through last summer, though, didn't he?" Kate had reason to know, and two excellent reasons to forget.

"He said the guy he sold it to was gone a lot and was okay with Scott living there until he moved in full time."

"He remember the guy's name?"

"All Scott cared about was that the check cleared. At any rate the guy wasn't Martin, and he did legitimately buy Scott's house. So we came on home." He tired of fiddling with the empty beer bottle and set it on the floor. "I noticed there was no smoke coming from Potlatch on the way back."

She smiled. "Once a cop."

And boom, there was the elephant in the room. He raised his head and looked at her. Her eyes widened at his expression. "I'm sorry, Kate. I'm so awful, goddamned sorry, I can't even begin to tell you."

"Jim—"

"I should have shot him the moment he walked into

the clearing. He was carrying a weapon. He threatened you, and I'm standing there with my finger on my own trigger and can't even pull it until he shoots Mutt and then you and then..." He scrunched his eyes closed. "I'd always been able to talk them out of shooting before. It never— but it's not like they don't train us—"

"Hush," she said.

"I'm so sorry, Kate. I looked for her. Everywhere. I searched every square foot of this homestead out to the corner markers, first on the ATV and then on foot. I spent days at it, searching the homestead and beyond. I didn't— she wasn't—I never found her. Not even a trace of her. I'm so sorry."

"Hey." He opened his eyes to find that she was kneeling next to him, and that she had one hand on the back of his neck and the other on his knee. "There is nothing to be sorry for."

"The hell there isn't."

He moved to get up and she pulled him back. "No." Her voice was stern in a way he had never heard it before, in a way that forced his attention. "Is that why you quit?"

"I never shot anyone before, Kate. I've never had to. Hell, I've barely ever drawn my weapon on the job. And then the one time I should have..."

"Quitting make it all better?"

He whipped his head around, his expression fierce. She did not back down. "As a better detective than either of us once said, 'Remorse is the ultimate in self-abuse.' You can be sorry if you want to, Jim, but I'm telling you there is no reason for you to be."

"But—"

"You know why Ken was here? He was here because of me, because I killed his cousin." She waved away his protest. "As good as, yes, I did, and it wasn't because his cousin was trying to kill me, although I have no doubt he would have if I'd let him get the drop on me. No, I was there for my mom and my dad, and every other drunk he enabled with his bootlegging. I was there for revenge, and I got it. Ken came here for the exact same reason. It took nine years, but what goes around comes around is only a cliché because it's true."

"I still should have shot him when he walked into the clearing holding that rifle."

"Okay. You should have shot him sooner, but you did get him later, and you got me to Ahtna General in time to save my life." She leaned forward and kissed him.

His voice was ragged. "This better not be because you're in any way sorry for me, Kate."

She pulled back and looked at him, and burst out laughing. She laughed so hard she had tears in her eyes. And then she leaned forward and kissed him again, tears of laughter still gathered on her eyelashes.

He sat very still, all his attention on the full red lips pressed into his. It couldn't be this easy, it just couldn't be. After a moment her tongue came out and teased his mouth open. He hauled her into his lap, one hand knotted in her hair, the other clamped around her waist. Dimly he heard her gasp and the hell with that, he was busy. He was starving for her and he kissed her just like that. She might have groaned, maybe, he didn't know and didn't care. He heard pinging sounds on the floor and realized he'd ripped off her shirt without bothering to unbutton it and the T-shirt underneath was over her head and off and she wasn't wearing a bra and jesus, the feel of her breasts in his hands, the taste of her nipples on his tongue, he was dizzy, it was like he'd never been there before.

He raised his head and managed to say, "Let me just apologize in advance for the lack of foreplay."

"In a hurry?"

"Yes."

"Good. Me too."

That was all he needed to hear. He jerked her jeans and underwear down and off and tossed them somewhere and pushed his hand between her legs and, oh my fucking god, she was already wet for him but there was no point in not making sure and he pushed her down on the couch and shoved her legs apart and attacked her with his mouth. She screamed, yes, she did, and her body arched like a bow, head and heels only touching the couch, thighs quivering on either side of his face. He pulled back and fumbled at his fly and found she was there before him, and then her hand was on him and they rolled off the couch onto the floor and he was inside her. There was a moment in there somewhere, a moment when they paused, staring into each other's eyes, motionless in that most intimate of embraces. No word was said and it didn't last long before they moved on to more important business but they both felt somehow as if a promise had been made.

Late in the night Kate woke up in bed, Jim asleep next to her, with only a confused series of memories as to how they'd gotten there, beginning on the floor next to the couch and continuing on the stairs and hadn't they tried to take a shower at some point and made it only as far as the bathroom floor? She had no idea what time it was as they'd knocked the clock off the nightstand, and how many times the sun might have risen and set, and—oh hell, she'd forgotten about the bread.

She slipped from beneath the covers and pulled on the first thing that came to hand, Jim's T-shirt. It reached her knees, better than a nightgown, and she went quietly downstairs to find the bread had almost but not quite risen over the edges of the bowl. She'd just punched it down and covered it again and had moved the moose ribs from the sink into the refrigerator when Jim came around the corner from the living room. He was naked, all hard muscle and long bone with no hint of softness anywhere.

With a slight shock she realized drool was pooling in her mouth. Could she be so shallow that she could allow herself to be seduced on looks alone? Evidently she could because without thinking about it she went down on her knees. He stood it for as long as he could before he yanked her up by her hair and plopped her down on the counter and had her hard and fast and loud right next to the bread.

She only hoped they didn't frighten the yeast.

Fourteen

TUESDAY, NOVEMBER 8
Kate's homestead

"YOU WERE NERVOUS."

"Hmmm?"

"You were nervous." He was watching her wake up, his head propped up on one hand. "That's why you didn't come straight home. You were nervous about this."

She closed her eyes again and stretched, reveling in the soreness she felt pretty much everywhere. "Maybe I was. A little."

"Why?"

"It hurt. The healing. A lot. For a while there I didn't think it was ever going to stop hurting."

He reached and touched the scar between her breasts with one gentle finger. She shivered. "You thought I would hurt you more?"

She smiled. "The unaccustomed exercise, maybe. And I think, too—"

"What?"

She opened her eyes to meet his. "I might have felt a little, I don't know, shy? It had been a while."

"Are you blushing?" He leaned in. "You are. Kate Shugak is blushing. I didn't know such a thing was possible."

"Jerk." She shoved him flat with both hands against his chest and climbed over him to head for the bathroom and the shower. When she came out again she could hear him banging around downstairs in the kitchen. Her stomach gave a loud growl and she pulled on clean underwear and jeans and a white T-shirt, combed her wet hair and padded downstairs on her bare feet.

He was laying out strips of bacon in their biggest cast-iron frying pan. "Hungry?"

"Starving. I missed dinner."

Their eyes met, and they both laughed.

"I'll fry up the whole pound then," he said.

"Oh, yeah, baby. Talk to me. Just like that." She turned on the oven, punched down the bread, shaped it into loaves before pouring herself a mug full of coffee. There was even half-and-half in the fridge. No truer sign of affection.

She sipped and gave a luxurious sigh. There was nothing like a night's—interrupted—sleep in your own bed followed by coffee from your own coffee maker.

"You need to go into town today?"

"Why?"

"Election day. To vote."

She looked at him. "It's Tuesday?"

The shark's grin was back and, boy, was it smug. "It is."

"I missed dinner twice?"

"We both did, it is Tuesday, and it's election day."

"Oh. Right."

"I'm whelmed by your enthusiasm."

"So am I. We've got one candidate who declares bankruptcy so he doesn't have to pay his bills, games the system so he doesn't have to pay his taxes, feels free to assault any woman any time anywhere, is BFF's with a KGB thug and who jokes about using nuclear weapons. And in the opposite corner, ladies and gentlemen, his opponent, the only candidate he could possibly beat. Politics pretty much broken in this country. We can only hope it doesn't break the country, too."

"Uh-huh. You gonna go vote?"

She sighed. "I have to. If I don't Emaa will rise up from the dead and smite me down where I stand." She deepened her voice and put her consonants way in the back of her throat. "'There were times when our people couldn't vote at all, Katya. You have a voice. It is your duty to use it in respect of their memory.'"

"Jesus." He shuddered. "Don't do that. It's like Ekaterina's standing right here."

"What I'm talking about." A phone rang. "Yours or mine?"

He gave her a look. "I don't have R2-D2 as a ringtone."

"More fool you." She found her phone under the table where it must have landed when Jim yanked her pants off, and by then it had gone to voicemail.

It was Kurt and she saw that he had already left her two messages. She called back. "Kurt? Hey, sorry, I—what?" She met Jim's eyes through the passthrough and grinned, a wide, satisfied grin. "I was up late. I slept in this morning. Okay, two mornings. So sue me." She listened. "Hey, wait a minute, okay? I'm going to put you on speaker."

She came into the kitchen. "Jim's here, too."

"Hey, Kurt."

"Oh. Ah. Hey. Hi, Jim. So…you found her."

"Uh-huh."

"Right. Yeah. Uh. Ouch! Quit that! Okay. Okay, I called the book guy in New York yesterday and he wouldn't tell me anything. So I called him again this morning at six a.m. our time, I'll have you know, which is ten a.m. their time and when his shop opens. His name is Brent Schuyler, pronounced Sky-lur, and he sounds about eleventy-hundred years old."

A female voice said something in the background. "Okay, yeah, all right, geez, sorry. Actually, Fina called him, and she actually sweet-talked him into telling us what was in the package."

Jim raised his spatula in salute. "Yay, Fina."

"Yup, that's my girl." There were kissy face sounds.

"Yeah, yeah, get a room. What was it? What did he send?"

"Get ready for the weirdest part of this whole crazy mess, Kate. It was a prospectus for the Kanuyaq Mine."

Kate stared at the phone.

"Kate?"

She exchanged a mystified glance with Jim. "Yeah, we're here. The Kanuyaq Mine?"

"Yup."

"The defunct Kanuyaq Mine? The copper mine the owners abandoned eighty years ago and pulled up the rails of the railroad behind them as they left?"

"That's the one." Kurt waited. "Kate?"

"Yeah, we're here. First of all, what is a prospectus, exactly?"

"I asked him that. Babe, stop that! Fina asked him, I mean. It's a formal legal document that is filed with the Securities and Exchange Commission that lays out the details of a prospective investment opportunity."

"So the backers of the Kanuyaq Mine wrote a brochure that tells all their rich friends, hey, we found a shitload of copper in the ground up here, buy a share and we'll double your money when we get it out."

"Pretty much."

"Did whathisname have another of those prospectuses?"

"I knew you'd ask that. He said no. He said he can keep a lookout for another one but he's only ever seen this one in fifty years in the rare-document business and he's not hopeful."

"Would the SEC have a copy?"

"Mr. Schuyler says probably not. The Kanuyaq went into operation in, what, 1907? The SEC's only been around since 1934."

"Maybe the University of Alaska has one in its archives.

Or maybe the Department of Natural Resources has an archive of its own in Juneau."

"I can ask."

"Do, please, and right away." Kate had that urgent feeling she always got when a case was beginning to break, and that she knew from experience presaged the moment when everything began to tumble out of control, where detection met chaos theory. That was usually when people got hurt, although this time everyone who could get hurt was missing or already dead. On a sudden inspiration she said, "Hey, and if you tap out on finding a prospectus, see if you can find any document that lists the original shareholders in the Kanuyaq."

"Geez, Kate, you're talking more than a century ago."

"I know. It's a long shot but it might explain Fergus McDonald's disappearance and why someone killed his wife and his friend."

"What are you thinking?"

"I don't know yet, but see if you can find a list, okay?"

A sigh. "Sure. I suppose this is right away, too?"

"The sooner the better. Thanks, Kurt."

She hung up and started to say something to Jim when her phone rang again. She looked at the screen. "This guy again? Seriously?"

"Who?" Jim said.

She said into her phone, "Gavin, I'm thinking you just can't wait to see me naked again."

"What?" Gavin said.

"What!" Jim said.

"Look, I told you, there is no ID yet on the body and that I'd call you when there was. If you call me one more time, I won't." She hung up and turned to Jim. "How do you feel about taking the Cessna up to the Step?"

He stared at her for a long moment, and then swiped the phone out of her hand and pulled up the weather app.

The honking big high hanging over Alaska showed no signs as yet of going anywhere and Jim took off hot into a clear, calm blue sky and reset the altimeter for the elevation of the Step. The sun hovered not far above the horizon for its brief daily appearance and the Park rolled away beneath them in a vast, frosted expanse. Ahead, the Quilaks stood to attention, sabers raised to discourage anyone foolhardy enough to attempt boarding. The Step, an enormous natural ledge as big as any one of the individual mountains but with a lot more level ground, coalesced out of the metamorphic wall. Jim did a fly-by and then came around in a broad bank and set the 206 down in a runway paint job.

"Nice," Kate said.

"Thanks." He sounded offhand but she knew better.

They taxied to the main building, a modular similar to the building that housed the Suulutaq offices, just older and smaller. Dan was waiting for them at the door and all over the Cessna the instant the prop stopped rotating. "Man, oh man, oh man. Jim, Jesus, what a beauty. Look at her, she looks goddamn new. What a cherry! When did you get her? Why haven't I had a ride in her yet? When can I? When you gonna let me take her up?"

"Saturday, that's why, some day, and never."

"Yeah, yeah, I get it, she's new, you don't want any mitts but yours on her. That'll change."

"No, it won't."

"Well, at least gimme a ride. Come on, Jim."

"What are you, ten? Get away from my baby, O'Brian."

Ranger Dan tore his eyes away from his newfound love. "Kate!"

"Yeah. I'm here, too. How 'bout that."

"Kate!" The chief ranger picked her up off the ground and whirled her around and set her back down to give her a thorough look over. "Damn, you look good."

"Don't sound so surprised."

"Yeah, well—" The ranger looked at Jim and thought better of what he was going to say. "Come on in, I'll buy you a cup of coffee."

They sat down in the little mess over espresso drinks from the fancy machine on the counter—"The federal gummint ante up for something as unnecessary as an espresso machine? Oh, hell no. We did a whip-around and paid for it ourselves"—and Dan said, "So what's up? Not that I'm not happy to see you, Kate."

Jim rolled his eyes and occupied himself with his Americano.

"Tell me about the Kanuyaq Mine."

He blinked. "Sorry. The Kanuyaq Mine?"

"Yeah, the defunct copper mine four miles from Niniltna. I know that much already. Tell me why someone would be interested in having a look at the original prospectus."

The chief ranger looked baffled. "I don't have a clue. They shut her down partly because all the easy ore was gone and partly because the price of copper tanked during the Depression. It's just a tourist destination nowadays and there aren't that many tourists interested in an old mine, especially given what it costs to get there. Cheaper to go to Denali. Mostly we just try to discourage kids going up there and getting their necks broke. I can't think why— well, come on, I'll show you."

He led them down the hall to his office, one entire wall of which was given over to a densely detailed map of the Park. The northern border nearly touched the ceiling, Prince William Sound the floor, and the Canadian border in the east and the Alaska Railroad in the west each almost stretched to the adjacent walls.

"Hey. New map. What's the scale on this thing, one to one?" Kate looked for and found her homestead, a tiny square of green a little south and east of the center of the Park. On the key red was for towns, blue for bits inside the Park given over to the US Forest Service, green meant private holdings.

"Not quite," Dan said proudly. "This the gummint did pay for. I insisted, as the other one was printed pre-ANCSA and falling apart to boot. So look here." A stubby forefinger pointed at a map symbol of a rock hammer crossed with a pick axe. "There's the Kanuyaq Mine. What do you want to know about it? I mean, Jesus, that you don't already know, seeing's your people have been living here for how long?"

She stared at the square above the cracked fingernail. It was bigger than the one for her homestead, but it was green, too. "Dan..."

"What?"

"Why is that square green?" She pointed at the key. "Green means the space is privately owned."

He brought his reading glasses down from on top of his head and squinted through them. "Oh, yeah. Sure, I forgot. When they did the new map they updated all the inholdings in the Park, too."

"But it's green. That means it's privately owned."

He looked at her in surprise. "Well, yeah, Kate, but just the mine proper." She looked blank and he elaborated. "That's the original mine's footprint. It's always been privately held. Just like your homestead, it was grandfathered in when the Park was created."

Kate stared at the green square. "It's a lot bigger than my homestead."

"Five miles square, I think."

"Twenty-five square miles of private property smack in the middle of the Park," Kate said, still staring at the map. "How did I not know this?"

It was Jim who asked the more relevant question. "If the nation doesn't own the Kanuyaq Mine, who does?"

The chief ranger scratched his head. "I don't know.

I know there is some kind of agreement between the Park Service and the owners. I think we pay them a nominal fee and in return we're allowed to sell permits to operators to run tourists over the place. There's never been very many of them. I've been a little worried that with the Suulutaq mine the state would improve the road and they'd start bringing them in by the busload."

"So," Jim said, looking at Kate, "if the owners of the Kanuyaq Mine want to—"

"—they could open the mine back up and start mining copper again," Kate said.

"Or anything else they found in it," Jim said.

Kate stared at him. "Or anything else they found in it."

The brief flight to Niniltna was accomplished mostly in silence, until they touched down and R2-D2 signaled an incoming call.

"Better not be that guy who wants to see you naked calling again."

"Jim, I told you—hi, Kurt. Wow. You're kidding, really? Wait, let me put you on speaker."

"I started looking for a Kanuyaq Mine prospectus online and I fell down a rabbit hole and wound up on a page on the state website that lists every Alaska corporation's annual report. Kate, did you know that the Kanuyaq Mine is still privately owned?"

"I did know that, Kurt. I've known it for all of fifteen whole minutes."

"Good, I don't feel so dumb then. Do you know what an annual report is?"

"Pretend I do."

"Like I said, there's a list of them on the state website and guess what?"

Kate felt the hair rise on the back of her neck. "There's one for the Kanuyaq Mine?"

"How the hell did you— Yeah, but only for one year, last year."

The feeling intensified. "Can you order a copy?"

"You can click right through most of them and read them right on your phone. I'll send you the link."

"Does an annual report include a list of shareholders?"

"No, but it does include their chairman and board of directors. There are seven of them on Kanuyaq's board. You want their names?"

"Text them to me."

"Will do."

"And keep looking for a prospectus."

"Why?"

"I don't know. I just feel like it's important. I don't know why. Like an itch I can't scratch."

"I bet Jim could help you with that."

"Say goodbye, Kurt." She hung up and turned to Jim. "The McDonalds made a habit of buying into the businesses employing them and they made a good thing out of it.

According to everyone I've talked to every spare minute he had from his job at Suulutaq Fergus was out prospecting with his rock hammer. What if Fergus McDonald found gold, maybe a paystreak it would pay to develop down in the old Kanuyaq Mine?"

"And the owners caught him at it? But why kill him, why not just say thanks and pay him a finder's fee? And why kill his wife? And his friend and fellow geologist, what was his name—"

"Magnus Campbell. I don't know. Were they mining it themselves and smuggling it out of the Park and selling it illegally? And got caught? All mine owners are paranoid assholes, I don't care if it's a placer miner waist-deep in a creek or a guy in a boardroom in a fancy suit. I wouldn't put homicide past a one of them." She brooded for a moment. "But that's not it, or not all of it. Let's go talk to Auntie Vi. She's what passes for institutional memory in the Park now that Emaa's gone. She might know something useful."

They left 18 Kilo Oscar at a tie down near the post office and walked down the hill to Auntie Vi's, who took one look at the two of them and gave an explosive "Hah!"

"Is that good or bad?" Jim said out of the corner of his mouth.

"Who the hell knows?" Kate raised her voice. "Auntie,

I need to ask you something. Did you know the Kanuyaq Mine was still privately owned?"

Auntie Vi huffed out an impatient breath, but Jim could tell she was pleased Kate had come to her for help. Or perhaps just pleased she knew something Kate didn't. "Of course I know this thing, Katya," she said, intimating strongly that anyone who didn't was little better than an idiot, present company included. "Old mine never a part of the Park, the owners insist."

"Who are the owners, auntie?"

"Ay, owners I don't know. Some childrens of olden days owners."

"Who were the owners in the olden days?"

Auntie Vi gave a dismissive shrug. "Muckety-mucks with money. Never see them, they never come to the Park, never talk to the peoples. They stay Outside and cash their checks." She filled the carafe with water and thumped it into the coffee maker, and produced a plate of cookies right out of a hat. "Millionaire's shortbread. Damn sure muckety-mucks never get these. You eat."

Kate would never know why she asked her next question. "Were there any owners who lived locally, auntie?"

Auntie Vi gave her a look of scorn. "What Park rat have money then, or ever?" She slammed down three mugs and filled them and slung them onto the table. She pointed. "You sit. You eat."

They weren't thirsty and they weren't hungry but they sat and they ate. The shortbread was a layer of chocolate over gooey caramel over a shortbread crust. Kate could feel her teeth dissolving in her mouth and used the coffee to wash them clean. "Well, thanks, auntie—"

The commanding finger again. "You sit. I think."

Kate leaned forward, hopeful. "Did you remember something, auntie?"

"Maybe. Maybe I remember little something."

"What?"

Auntie Vi scowled impartially between the two of them. "I'm just a kid but I remember elders talking stories about when the mine close down, and back before to when it first opens. When they find that kanuyaq, that copper, when they are looking for moneys to dig it out, they come into the village to talk to the old elders."

By old elders she meant the villagers living in that day, or her grandparents, or possibly even her great-grandparents. Kate nodded. "Yes?"

"One elder say the mine people offer shares to the villagers."

Kate's eyes narrowed. "Really."

"Not many shares but they say they want to include local peoples." Auntie Vi snorted. "They want to buy local peoples off more like."

"Did any of the locals take them up on their offer?"

"I remember story of one only. Not local really, he come up from Kodiak way. Kalmakoff. Albert? Andrei? Alex, that name. Alex Kalmakoff. A smart man. He own the local store, Auntie Lillian say he make much money financing miners."

"I don't know any Kalmakoffs in the Park," Kate said.

"He die young. Barely fifty, I think."

"Oh. So he left no descendants?"

"Oh no, he got married up to Willy Totemoff's daughter from down Cordova way. They have a little girl before he die. Mildred. Milly, we call her."

"So Alex's shares would have gone to her?"

"I suppose."

"And did she have children?"

"One daughter. Milly Junior. MJ we call her."

Kate added up the generations in her head. "Did she have any children?"

"Again one son. Those Kalmakoffs never have many kids. Not for want of trying, my mom say that Alex Jr. chased more skirts than everybody else put together." Auntie Vi glared at Jim.

"And does he, the great-grandson of Alex Kalmakoff, does he live in the Park?"

Auntie Vi gave Kate a disgusted look. "Katya, for smart woman you very dumb. Of course he does, all his life just like you. MJ marry up with Norman."

It took Kate a moment. "Norman? Norman Shugak, auntie?"

"Yes," Auntie said testily. "Only Norman I know is Norman Shugak."

"But that means—"

Auntie Vi nodded. "MJ and Norman's son is Martin. Almost a good man, that Norman. Never understand why his son so useless."

Alerted by the quality of silence that fell following her statement, she glared impartially between the two of them. "What? What I say?"

Outside again, Jim said, "Kate, you realize that it is now possible that those two guys looking for Martin aren't looking for him because he was working for Ken Halvorsen?"

"Yes," Kate said a little numbly. "I do realize that."

He shoved his hands in his pockets and frowned. "Do you think Martin knows that?"

"I don't know. I do know we better find him before they do." Her phone rang. "Kurt! Kurt, just the man I wanted to talk to. I—"

"Wait, Kate, just wait. I found out the majority owner for the Kanuyaq Mine. It's a shell company that is owned by another shell company that is owned by another shell company, like that."

"That doesn't help me, Kurt."

"This will. I got hold of a forensic accountant I know and the guy's a magician, I think it took him like three keystrokes. Behind all the shell companies is a corporation called Maestro Ltd., which the Justice Department is investigating for tax fraud in moving all its profit-making enterprises offshore funneling through, variously, Ireland, London, the Isle of Jersey, the Bahamas, Wyoming, if you can believe that, and the Isle of Man before coming finally to rest, although who knows for how long, in good old Switzerland with the Daniel Peter Group. The Daniel Peter Group is in turn managed by Cullen and Associates. And Cullen and Associates is a legal firm representing DiFronzo, Ltd."

"DiFronzo? As in the Chicago Outfit?"

"How the hell did you know that?"

"What else?"

Kurt grumbled. "Okay, on a hunch, I ran a search for all of the people and businesses Cullen and Associates have represented over the years. Guess who else is on their client list."

There was a cold feeling growing in Kate's gut. "Erland Bannister."

"Will you STOP that!"

I expect we'll meet again soon. Jane and I will be visiting the Park quite often, now that I have interests there.

Kate had thought Erland had meant his financing of Old Sam's museum, but that wasn't it, or not all of it. "So, basically what you're telling me is that there is a good chance through various proxies Erland Bannister owns the Kanuyaq Mine."

"Yes. Well, all except for a hundred shares. They are in the name of one of the first shareholders—"

"Alex Kalamakoff?"

The legitimacy of Kate's antecedents were profaned back to the third generation but Kate wasn't listening. "Thanks, Kurt," she said, interrupting his tirade. "Really good work. Gotta go."

The ATV started reluctantly after a night sitting out in the cold in front of Auntie Vi's but it did start. On the way down the hill Kate stopped into the Niniltna Native Association to vote at the polling booth set up there for the day and came out again feeling as if her hands needed washing. Jim was waiting on the ATV. "You're not voting?"

"Already did, absentee, two weeks ago. I was afraid I wouldn't at all if I didn't do it then."

"I heard that." She climbed on in front of him.

"Where we going? You didn't say."

She looked over her shoulder and met his eyes. "If my case is all about the Kanuyaq Mine, and now it seems that your case is all about the Kanuyaq Mine, I think we should go up and take a look around. It's only four miles and a bit and we've got plenty of daylight left."

"Works for me." He put his hands on her waist as she kicked the ATV into gear. "Did anyone look for Fergus McDonald up at the Kanuyaq?"

"Not so far as I know. His wife's body was found on the Step road."

"Maybe she turned right when she should have turned left that morning?"

"Maybe. And maybe someone was watching, and followed."

It was a scenic drive through trees frosted like cake decorations. They passed five moose hunkered down beneath a stand of diamond willow waiting out the cold spell. A family of river otters slid gleefully down a frozen waterfall on Glacier Creek. Overhead a trio of ravens tag-teamed them all the way up the road. There was no other sign of life, animal or human. It was as if the Park had been frozen in place for the duration.

The road hadn't seen much traffic since the previous summer so the ride was pretty smooth and they made good time. In twenty minutes the mine was in sight. Gargantuan piles of gravel tailings sat at the edge of a wide, shallow river, looking like the carcasses of dinosaurs. At the edge of the tailings massive, faded buildings stair-stepped up the not-quite-vertical hill to the right. First in line were the old offices and a mess hall and a bunkhouse. Next to them was the reason for being there, twenty acres' worth of buildings containing the machinery of an industrial mining operation and everything needed to keep it going. Gigantic belts and shovels and shaker tables with graduated grates where the water mixed with the mined ore and shook out the good stuff in smaller and smaller sizes, and rails with metal carts that carried the day's production to the train, which would take it to Cordova and the bulk carriers waiting there. The mine itself, the source of the ore, was buried deep in the earth beneath or in back of the production buildings.

Everything worth looting had been taken before a year had passed following the closure of the mine. Extremely unsafe-looking wooden staircases led to multiple entrances behind signs that read "Danger! Do not enter!" and "No Trespassing!" affixed with Park Service seals and a phone number in case of emergencies that Jim recognized as ringing directly to Dan's cell phone. He crossed the job of chief ranger off his bucket list then and there.

Kate hadn't moved to get off the ATV. "I forgot how big this place was."

He hadn't moved, either. He was nice and warm tucked up against her. Gloves, hat and parka only went so far and it was a cold, cold day and a fast ride on a four-wheeler had only made it colder. "Where do you think he'd start?"

"McDonald? I don't know, I'm not a geologist or a mining engineer. Maybe we should go find one or the other and bring them back with us."

"Maybe not. Kate, look." He pointed over her shoulder at the barest wisp of smoke rising straight up into the air.

She killed the engine at once. "I wonder if he heard us?"

They waited, listening. A wolf howled not very far off and there was a frantic thrashing of underbrush as if something large and delicious was trying to get away from it.

"Could be a squatter," Jim said.

"Could be."

"Could be McDonald."

"I don't think so, Jim. He's been gone too long, and he was a married man, it seemed to me happily so. No way would he have been gone this long without contacting his wife."

"Wouldn't be the first time a husband used Alaska to hide out from his spouse."

"Wouldn't even be the first time this month." She got off the ATV and grinned at him. "Time to be sneaky."

"You look entirely too pleased about that."

They moved slowly and carefully up what was left of the narrow gravel road that fronted the mine buildings. It rose steadily in front of them and then went round a hairpin corner, revealing the remains of thirty small clapboard homes roosting in their own debris. Management had lived here, the mining superintendent and his deputies and their families. They'd had hot-and-cold running water and refrigerators and electric stoves, all the modern conveniences and better than what most rural Americans would have enjoyed Outside at the time. Meanwhile the hired help slept twenty to a room in the bunkhouse below, or tried to. The mine would have been plenty loud when it was in operation and it would have worked twenty-four-seven so long as there was ore to get out and money to be made. But here, rank hath or had its privileges, including at least some peace.

The smoke was rising from a miraculously still-standing chimney from the one house that was mostly intact. It was the farthest one back and close up against the side of the hill which might account for its relative state of preservation. The windows were boarded over and the porch had long since fallen down, which meant it was a big step up to the front door. Someone had tried to remedy that with a cinder block.

The wolf howled again and was answered by one of its kin. "I thought wolves mostly hunted at night. Are you armed?"

He could hear the smile in her voice when she answered. "Don't worry about it, Jim."

He kept his natural reservations to himself and followed her when she scurried over to the partial wall nearest to them and peered around it. Leap-frogging each other they moved up the incline, moving from house to ruined house as silently as possible. Although the frozen grass seemed to crunch very loudly beneath their feet, they made it as far as the unoccupied ruin next to the occupied ruin undetected. Out of breath, they leaned against a pile of rock that might once have been a foundation to catch their breath. Jim started to say something and stopped when Kate held a finger to her lips. There is nothing so still as a cold winter day and they could both clearly hear a low rumble of voices. They listened for a while, unable to make out the words but able to distinguish different voices. Kate held up two fingers. Jim held up two and then three and then two again and shrugged. She made a circle around the cabin and held up her hand flat, and before he could stop her she was making a big circle around the house with the voices. When she got back her cheeks were red with exertion and her eyes bright and he almost kissed her. "There's a pickup parked back there, green, Alaska plates."

He nodded. "Bernie said Ace and Deuce had a truck."

"No back door," she said, "and all the windows are boarded up. We can't get in the front door with any kind of advantage, and if we wait for them to come out we'll freeze solid."

"Have to make them come out to us then," he said, and like to wriggle his tail at her approving smile.

"They could be armed."

"Any sensible person would be."

"Yeah, yeah, quit whining." She looked down at the clump of dry grass they were standing in. "I've got an idea."

They pulled handfuls of the grass and shoved it beneath a pile of aging planks that was all that was left of one wall of the house they were huddling behind. There was plenty of kindling in smaller pieces of wood that was just as old and just as flammable. Kate pulled her gloves off with her teeth and fumbled out a compact emergency kit in a zipped ditty bag. She held up a tube of weatherproof matches.

He grinned and put his mouth close to her ear. She shivered at the feel of his breath on her skin and he took just a second to enjoy the knowledge that it wasn't from the cold. "I'll go around to the side of their house and get ready to charge whoever comes out first."

"And I'll take the next one from the other corner."

"And if they have guns?"

She smiled and it was a cold smile for a cold day. "Let them."

He shook his head. He didn't know quite what she was up to and it was very probably the most foolish thing he'd ever done but he was going to trust her if it killed him, maybe literally. But what the hell, nobody lived forever. He took the scenic route to his spot, keeping it low and slow, until he got to the corner of the house to the left of the door. As Kate had said, the pickup was snuggled up against the house, as close to the rear wall as the large rear-view mirrors would allow, and very nicely hidden from anyone who had no reason to look for it.

"I'm so fucking bored, Milt," one of the voices said from what felt like exactly the other side of the house wall. "Aren't you fucking bored? I'm so fucking bored."

"Shut up and deal, Carmine."

Jim looked around the corner to see Kate peering back at him, grinning. When she saw him in place she nodded and ducked back down out of sight. A few minutes later he heard a crackle, another and then he watched Kate scuttle around to the opposite corner. He didn't like it that he couldn't see her. Too much like the last four months.

They waited. The voices in the house had stopped and for a few moments Jim was afraid they'd been heard. Then someone said, "Come on, Milt. We're outta booze for crissake. Let's drive out to the Roadhouse. We can leave him here, he's not going anywhere."

Who wasn't going anywhere?

The second voice sounded weary in reply, as if he'd had to say the same thing many times before. "We'll leave when we get the go-ahead, Carmine. They still haven't told us what to do with this guy."

Jim looked over at the fire and saw a flame shoot up and in the next moment the entire pile was engulfed in flame. The scrap wood had been sitting there for a long time, deemed too rotten for salvage by foraging Park rats, and so far the season had been a dry one so it had caught fast.

Then he was startled by a loud long zingy sort of extended whine, like a tea kettle on the steam. There was a loud Crack! and something smacked into the bough of the spruce Jim was standing under. It shook itself and deposited a load of frost crystals down his neck. He jumped and tried not to swear.

"What the hell's that?" the second voice said from inside the house.

"Jesus, is someone shooting at us? Milt, someone's shooting at us!"

That was Jim's question exactly as another whine and zing and Crack! something hit the side of the house. He stood there, stunned, unable to process what was happening. Zing! Crack! Thud!

He knew that sound. He'd heard it up close and personal not four months before. It was gunfire. What the hell? Was someone shooting at them? Zing! Crack! and another tree rustled behind him. He ducked back.

And then he realized. Whoever had last lived in that derelict house must have left some live ammunition behind, and it must have been buried beneath the wall when it rotted enough to collapse. And now the fire was setting it off.

Pop! Crack! and something thudded into the house.

"Milt! Somebody's shooting at us! Do something!" There was a stumbling rumble from inside the house.

"Carmine, stay where you are!"

Jim peeked around the corner and found Kate peeking back and dropped instantly out of stealth mode. "Get back! Kate, Jesus, what's wrong with you!"

She laughed. She actually fucking laughed. He stared at her, dumbfounded. "'Help will always be given at Hogwarts to those who ask for it!'"

Zing! Pop! Zing! Pop! Crack! They both ducked back around their respective corners. At least Jim did and he hoped like hell Kate had, too.

"Holy shit! Holy fuck, Milt! Did you hear that! There's a bunch of them! Get your gun, get your gun, get your gun!"

So, maybe only one of them armed. Better to be lucky than good. He had a fleeting memory of what Agent Mason had said about the two men. Maybe Spilotro wouldn't let DiFronzo have a gun.

"Carmine, don't go out there, you might get hit! Goddammit, Carmine! Oh, you stupid goddamn bastard—"

Footsteps shook the building, which was over a hundred years old and really not up to the test of large, frightened men in a hurry. The door was yanked open and came all the way off its hinges and Zing! Crack! Thud! went another bullet into the siding.

"Fuck!" A big man fell through the doorway, one knee landing on the cinder block with a crunch loud enough to make Jim wince in sympathy.

"Fuck, ow, fuck, ow, fuck, Milt, I'm hurt, somebody shot me in the knee, I'm hurt, I'm hurt, I'm hurt!"

He was clutching his knee with his back to Jim so Jim tossed the plan of attack and barreled out around the corner and tackled the guy low. The door, evidently taking its time deciding to fall inside or outside, fell outside and on top of them, knocking them apart. Jim shrugged it off his shoulders and went after Carmine as he tried to scramble away.

They went right past Kate, who peeped around the corner of the building. Still no Milt. She didn't think he'd be roused by a woman's voice. What to do, what to do. She whirled and ran to the fire—Pop! went another exploding round, a .22 she thought, something small anyway—grabbed a piece of burning wood and ran back to the house and threw it through the now permanently open doorway.

"Fuck! Fuck! Fuck!" A very large bald man with full sleeve tattoos and more up his neck to his hairline leaped from the doorway, landed solidly past the cinder block, both legs bent. He pointed a handgun at Kate in the television-approved shooter's stance. A Glock, maybe, she wasn't ept with handguns but an automatic for sure.

His mouth dropped open. "A woman! A fucking woman! Are you fucking kidding me!"

And then a streak of gray fur shot out of the undergrowth and teeth closed over his wrist and powerful jaws clamped down and didn't let go. All that was left for him to do was drop his weapon and scream and scream and scream. He tried to pull his hand free and the teeth wouldn't let go, would only crunch down harder and the head it belonged to shook back and forth, tossing him around as if he weighed no more than a pillow. He screamed again.

Kate took a quick step forward to kick the handgun out of reach, and became aware of someone else screaming or trying to, someone whose voice was muffled, someone from inside the house.

She ran to the door and looked through the flame that was beginning to catch the floor on fire and saw her cousin, Martin Shugak, wrists and ankles duct-taped together, snot and tears streaming down his face, muffled grunts coming from behind the duct tape over his mouth. Wide terrified eyes met hers and she forgot everything else and went in after him.

"You can't go back there."

"You got anyone locked up?"

"No, but—"

"Then yes we can." Kate muscled Mullet Guy, aka Carmine DiFronzo, past an indignant Estelle Kefauver and down the hallway that led to the cells. All four stood open. She pushed him into the first one and locked him inside.

"Where's Milt?" DiFronzo took a shuddering breath and mustered up enough bravado to repeat his question. "What did you do to Milt? I wanna see Milt!"

Back in the front office she said, "Where's Cochran?"

Kefauver made a vain attempt at a bristle but it failed in the heat of Kate's glare. "There was an incident at Ahtna High and the police chief asked for help. Trooper Cochran decided he was needed there more than he was here."

Of course. Not to mention which Ahtna had a Starbuck's and Niniltna didn't. "And Sergeant Luther?"

"Still in Anchorage."

When she saw Kefauver trying not to cower Kate attempted a smile. "Call him. Tell him I've made a citizen's arrest of two men I believe may be suspects in the death of Sylvia McDonald. One is in your cells and the other is injured and being detained at the clinic where he is being treated."

"Detained? At the clinic?"

"Yes. Matt Grosdidier happened to have a pair of hand-cuffs. I don't think anyone wants to know why." Kate heard an ATV pull up outside and nodded at the phone. "You should probably call Sergeant Luther now."

"Here. Blow your nose." Kate handed DiFronzo a wad of Kleenex. She hated it when suspects sniveled.

There were many different methods of interrogation that could lead to a successful outcome. Kate had a knack for hitting on exactly the right one to extract maximum information with minimum effort. She motioned to Jim to stay out of sight but within earshot and he obeyed because he'd seen her work before. He did get out his phone and activate the recording app.

Carmine DiFronzo looked exactly like his mug shot. No one should ever look exactly like their mug shot (or their driver's license photo, either, but that was a topic for another time). Brown, brown, five-eight, five-nine. He'd looked as if he'd done weights at some point but he had long since gone to fat, although he'd refused to acknowledge this by buying his clothes one size too small. His shirt was patterned in white and gold stripes and his pants were... leather? Yup. Leather. One knee had swollen to the point that the leather around it looked like it might split and the pants were already tight to begin with. His eyes were red and his hair was cut in a mullet that devolved into mutton chops which themselves deteriorated into a permanent five o'clock shadow. Part of the mullet stood up in back like a rooster tail. It might have been cute on Alfalfa but not on a thirty-year-old man. His sleeves were rolled back to display crude tattoos, with more showing through the open collar of his shirt and on his neck. He looked unkempt and he smelled of wood smoke, tobacco smoke, marijuana smoke, sweat, and urine.

Altogether an unlovely picture, although Kate knew him at once for a man who believed himself to be utterly irresistible to women. She almost took that tack and pulled back from it at the last moment, some instinct calling on her to instead channel her inner Emaa. She crossed her arms and frowned down at him. "Well. What do you have to say for yourself, young man?"

He blew his nose again with a sound like a foghorn. "Where's Milt?"

"He's getting his arm sewn back on."

He peered up at her, still snuffling into the Kleenex. "Where'd that wolf come from, man?"

"My name," Kate said frostily, "is not 'man.' You may call me ma'am." His spine automatically straightened at her tone, and she had to hide a grin.

"You guys got wolves around here!"

"I believe that has been adequately established, Carmine."

"You're not sposed to have fucking wolves! Nobody's sposed to have fucking wolves! Wolves all sposed to be dead!"

"Nevertheless, we do have them here, alive, and, yes, one of them has bitten your . . . friend."

"Is he gonna be okay?" This came out suspiciously like a whine.

"We can only hope," Kate said with a straight face. "Now then. I'm going to ask you some questions, and I want you to answer them as completely and as truthfully as you can." She held up an admonitory finger, every inch the schoolmarm. "I must warn you, Carmine, that your . . . friend, Milton, is being questioned by my associate even as we speak." She leaned down and stared into his eyes. "We shall be comparing notes afterward, Carmine, and if your answers differ in any way from Milton's, I'm prepared to be very severe with you."

His face crumpled. "There's not sposed to be wolves anymore except like in Disney, man."

Kate held up a finger.

Carmine gulped. "Ma'am."

An hour later she returned to the front office. "Did you get hold of Nick?"

Kefauver nodded. "He's on his way back."

"Good. Tell him he's going to need to send a search party up to the mine." She hooked a thumb over her shoulder. "He'll have to take this yahoo along to show them where, but Fergus McDonald's body is up there." She looked at Jim. "Did you take notes?"

"Better." He held up his phone. "I recorded it."

She smiled at him and it was all he could do not to wag a non-existent tail.

"Can you send it to her?" Kefauver gave him her email address and he did so. "Great. Let's go home."

She stopped, her hand on the door. "Oh, and tell Nick that there will be a charge of kidnapping along with all the rest."

"Kidnapping? Who?"

"My cousin Martin. Tell Nick he's at Auntie Vi's and ready to be deposed any time Nick feels so inclined."

Fifteen

WEDNESDAY, NOVEMBER 9
Anchorage

THEY FLEW INTO ANCHORAGE THE NEXT morning at first light and took a cab to the townhouse to pick up the Subaru. They parked in front of the cabin on Lois and Jim said, "Man, it's like something out of a Robert Service poem."

They knocked at the door. The eye and nose appeared at the window. "It's Kate Shugak, Mr. Lippy. I really need to talk to you again."

The door opened. "Kate Shugak." His eyes traveled past her to give Jim a comprehensive once-over. "Cop."

"Ex," Jim said.

"Huh." Lippy looked back at Kate. "I told you I'd said everything I was going to the last time you were here."

"Yes, sir, you did, and I heard you."

"Well?"

"Fergus McDonald is dead, sir."

Commodore Lippy stood in silence for a moment, and then stepped back and beckoned them inside. "Who killed him?"

"They have two men in custody in Niniltna."

Lippy grunted. "Glad they caught 'em. Now, what is it you want from me, Kate Shugak?"

Kate clasped her hands behind her back, feeling very much as if she were at attention before a senior officer. Old farts could do that to you. "Fergus McDonald is dead. So is his wife. They had no children and so far as I can discover no living relatives. There is no confidentiality at stake here any longer, so can you tell me everything you didn't tell me when I was here on Saturday?"

A smile ghosted across his face. "Wait here." He disappeared into the back and reappeared with Fergus McDonald's ore samples cradled in his palm. He looked at them with an almost fond expression. "Thirty percent copper and related trace minerals such as malachite and azurite. Seventy percent gold."

"When did he bring it in?"

"September twenty-eighth."

Kate ran a swift calculation. "That would have been his first day back in town after the two-week shift prior to the one he disappeared during. Go on."

"I called him when I was done with the assay. He was pretty excited so he might have said more than he ought. He said he'd come across an old abandoned mine. He wasn't specific but I knew he was working up at the Suulutaq and I know, none better, just how many holes been dug in those mountains, as I dug a few of them myself. I figured he was telling the truth."

"And?"

"And he said he'd found a tunnel that started out man-made but then turned into a natural crack in the rock. He said it was a pretty tight squeeze but he followed it back and found—" He held up the samples.

"Did he say what he was going to do next?"

"Well, he wasn't going to let it just sit there, that's for sure, and I didn't blame him. I mean, have you seen the price of gold lately? Gold always rises when people are scared. And copper, it may have taken a dive during the recession like everything else, but it's coming back gangbusters now. He said he was going to try to trace the original owners of the mine. See if they'd cut him in on shares when came time to get it out, in exchange for showing them the paystreak he found."

Something in the quality of their silence made him look up from the samples. "What?"

"It's what got him killed," Kate said. "It's what got them all killed."

Her phone rang as they got into the car. It was Nick.

Even in a hospital Erland Bannister had his own suite, which contained himself, a suit, Jane Morgan, and a fourth man they both recognized from the mug shot on Jim's phone.

"Ah," Jim said, in the best Special Agent Mason fashion, "Dante Accardo, I believe."

Accardo was a big man, dressed in jeans and a Chicago Bulls windbreaker, standing against the back wall with his arms folded. Kate mentally outfitted him with a balaclava. "Hi, there," she said with a friendly wave. "We've met. At the McDonalds' house? I bet we just missed each other at Magnus Campbell's, too."

Not a muscle moved in his face. A non-sniveler. Good.

"You have no right to intrude on Mr. Bannister's privacy this way. I must ask you to leave—"

Kate looked past the suit to meet Erland's eyes. "Why don't we ask Erland who he wants to stay and who he wants to go?"

Erland lay on a hospital bed with the head raised, an oxygen cannula beneath his nose. Wires snaked from a monitor to beneath his patterned silk robe. He had aged even in the days since Kate had seen him last, his skin leeched to a pale yellow and sunken into the spaces between his bones. His eyes burned with life still, though, and he fixed them on Kate's face with what she could only describe as hunger. Of course, with only a suit and Jane Morgan and mob muscle to wait on him he was probably happy to see anybody.

His voice was anything but frail. "Let us have the room, Harrison, if you please. And Mr. Accardo, if you would."

And that voice still commanded immediate obedience because the suit made a little bow and effaced himself at once, followed by the muscle, who nodded at Kate on the way out the door. Almost a salute, Jim thought. He caught Accardo's eyes as he walked past. Nothing was said out loud but much was understood.

He heard the door shut behind him and stepped back a little, the better to let Kate have the stage. The better to watch the show.

Kate looked at Jane.

"Ah no, Kate, I think Jane should stay. Just in case I head out to that big stock exchange in the sky while you're in the room. You'll need a witness other than the ex-trooper there to say you didn't do it." He smiled, and his teeth were even more yellow than his skin, but no sharper than the bones in his face.

"Fine, so long as Jane continues to remain mute."

Jane did.

"Fine," Kate said. "We got your guys." She jerked her chin at his chest. "I'm guessing you heard, since you suffered your, ah, episode right after Milton Spilotro was allowed to make his phone call."

He coughed up a wad of phlegm Jane caught in a Kleenex that was woefully inadequate to the task. "Thank you, Ms. Morgan. I'm sorry, what two guys were you talking about, Ms. Shugak?"

There were many different methods of interrogation that could lead to a successful outcome. With Erland Bannister, it was always best to encourage him to believe that you knew more than you did. Kate found a chair and brought it to Erland's bedside. She unzipped her jacket and draped it over the back of the chair, taking care to see that it hung evenly. She sat down and crossed her legs, linking her hands together over her knee. She smiled at Erland, a little pityingly. "I didn't say there were two of them, Erland, but okay. Carmine DiFronzo and Milton Spilotro, late of the Outfit in Chicago. Along with their compatriot, Dante Accardo, the gentleman recently holding up your wall over there. All three of whom I assume are on loan to you by your partners."

"The Outfit? What a quaint name."

"It's the Mob for Chicago, as you know very well. But let that go for the moment. When did Fergus McDonald get in contact with you?"

"I'm sorry. Fergus… McDonald, did you say?"

"On one of his little spelunking adventures he went into the Kanuyaq Mine." She waved him off when he would have said something. "Don't bother, they found him, too, early this morning at the bottom of a mine shaft. The troopers just called with the news."

"What an unhappy accident. I grieve for his family. Still, there are all those signs forbidding entry." He tutted. "They're put up for everyone's safety. He should have taken them more seriously."

"I'm sure he would have, if he hadn't been shot before he fell."

"He'd been shot?" Erland sounded properly shocked.

His death's head grin reminded Kate of something or someone, she couldn't put her finger on it. "He found something, didn't he?" she said. "Gold, wasn't it?"

"But how interesting."

"Maybe enough gold there to make up for all the money you lost investing in the Suulutaq Mine when its EIS went south. Fergus McDonald contacted you sometime in the past year, we don't know quite when but don't worry, when we get the subpoenas for your phone records I'm sure we can narrow that down to specific dates. He convinced you the gold was there and that it was commercial and god knows he had a good record with that sort of thing. So you investigated, and discovered that McDonald had found gold in a defunct copper mine that by some miracle had managed to be grandfathered in as private property as the Park was formed around it. You'd have a much better chance of starting—or restarting—a mining concern on private land than you would on state or federal land, so you started buying up all of the Kanuyaq Mine shares, using shell companies to hide your interest. However did you convince the owners to sell, I wonder? Did you try and convince them you wanted to build a backwoods resort of some kind? Demetri Totemoff might have had something to say about that."

"Demetri Totemoff," he said meditatively. "Oh, of course, the proprietor of that nice little lodge east of Kuskulana."

"The very same. Still, none of the owners lived in Alaska and they wouldn't care who you put out of business." She saw a spark of triumph in Erland's eyes and said gently, "Well. None of the owners, except perhaps one."

His death's head grin faded a little. Dammit, who was it he reminded her of?

"But a year and change later, Fergus McDonald hadn't heard back from you and started getting impatient, so he went back into the mine and pulled some more samples. He took those samples to an independent assayer, who confirmed his finding. I'm guessing he called you with the results, and you realized that he was going to go public with his discovery. That was not something you wanted at all, not until you'd nailed down all the shares.

"Specifically, there were a hundred shares you still needed. It was only ten percent of the original thousand but I'm told even ten percent can make some noise if necessary in a shareholder fight. So you traced the heir and you got the Outfit to loan you some talent and you sent them looking for him." She paused. "I'm kind of surprised you had to outsource for talent, Erland. Have all the locals sworn off you? Or are all of them already in prison after working for you before?"

Erland spread his hands and looked at Jane Morgan. "I don't know what she's going on about, Ms. Morgan, do you?" He didn't bother to wait for an answer. "I will admit to seeing a business opportunity. The current, or should I say previous shareholders of the Kanuyaq Mine were quite happy with the price I offered."

"I'm sure they were. I've heard you called a lot of things, Erland, but cheap was never one of them."

He bowed his head, accepting the compliment. The Joker, maybe?

"Your problem was that as soon as Martin heard your

goons were looking for him he got scared it was about something else, so he vanished, which meant they had to hang around long enough to become memorable in the Park."

"None of this has anything to do with me," Erland said. "Certainly nothing you can prove." He made a contemptuous gesture. "The testimony of hired thugs with criminal records? Nonsense."

"Nonsense, indeed," Kate said, nodding her agreement. "Or it would have been until Fergus McDonald went missing. They were splitting their time between the mine and the Roadhouse. Did he stumble across them on one of his field trips? Perhaps he went in to get more samples?"

Erland didn't answer. Kate looked across at Jane, who remained mute and impassive and at the ready with Kleenex.

"And then Sylvia. Your guys were in the Roadhouse when she walked in looking for Fergus. That would have frightened them, so, of course, they followed her." Kate's voice hardened. "The troopers found hair and blood on the passenger-side rear-view mirror of your guys' truck. What do you want to bet they match Sylvia's?"

"They may or may not, Ms. Shugak, but it really has nothing to do with me."

"Martin told us they wanted him to sign some paper. I'm as amazed to report as you are to hear it that he refused. Were they supposed to kill him after they got his signature?"

"I expect none of this will be easy to prove, or even possible." His eyes glittered. "And none of it will stop the reopening of the Kanuyaq Mine."

"We found Sylvia's phone inside the cabin they were holding Martin Shugak in, Erland, along with the Kanuyaq Mine prospectus she'd picked up at the post office the day she arrived in Niniltna. There was a text from her husband asking her to meet him at the Kanuyaq the next morning. Funny thing, you'd think her phone would have her husband's contact info, but this message didn't. I wonder whose phone number that message came from?"

His cadaverous grin seemed permanently fixed on his face, and she clicked her fingers. "I've got it. You look just like one of The Gentlemen."

For the first time since she'd walked into the room Erland looked a little disconcerted. "What?"

"Never mind. You're probably not a Buffy fan."

For one precious moment, Erland Bannister looked truly kerflummoxed.

Kate got to her feet and retrieved her jacket, shrugging into it. "The Park Service might have something to say about reopening the Kanuyaq Mine, by the way."

Erland revived at this. "Oh, I imagine they will, quite a lot, in fact, but it will do nothing to stop Bannister, Inc." His smile widened. "You should be pleased, Kate. You were going to lose all those lovely jobs when they shut the Suulutaq down. Now with the new administration, your Park could have two mines in operation and twice as many jobs." He laughed at her expression. That laugh, too, turned into a choking fit that, sadly, did not carry him off then and there. Jane was at the ready to wipe away the gobbet of phlegm.

Kate took her time zipping up her jacket. She looked up and gave the death's head in the bed a faint smile. "Have I mentioned how glad I am that you're dying, Erland?" She turned.

"Wait! Wait, Kate, I haven't told you the best part!"

He'd switched back to her first name. This was going to sting.

"Your uncle! Old Sam!"

She froze, one hand on the door.

"Even a dying serpent can wound with a last bite, Kate," Jim said. "Let's just go."

"He killed my father! Did you know that! Yes, he broke into our house and stole from us and my father caught him and Old Sam killed him and ran! Your uncle, that old man you loved so much, a murderer!"

"Kate—"

She turned and walked back to the bed and stared down at the viperous old man. He was coughing again and the monitor was beeping rapidly, the only sound in the heavy silence that had fallen in the room. Jim saw Kate's hand drop down to her side. Her hand held flat for a moment and then curled into a fist, as if into a thick mane of gray fur.

Erland stared up at her, triumphant.

Jim went around her and stood over the bed. "You lie," he said.

"I beg your pardon?"

"You killed him," Jim said. "You were there, and it's

what you do." His eyes narrowed. "Your father caught Old Sam breaking into the glass case holding the icon. Am I right? Of course I am. And Old Sam panicked and knocked him down getting away. And then you, in a hurry to take over your father's business like you're always in a hurry to take over everything, you seized the opportunity and went in and shoved that big heavy desk over on your father." When Erland's expression changed Jim said, "Yeah, I've seen the crime scene photos. And I'd bet you waited until he died before you called for help, didn't you, you murderous old fuck?"

The old man stared back at Jim, mouth open but no words coming out. Maybe he heard death knocking at his door, maybe he was just unaccustomed to being interrupted in mid-rant.

"Old Sam wasn't a killer," Jim said softly. "But you are. Aren't you, Erland?"

The withered lips twisted from a triumphant grin into a snarl, but he didn't deny it. Because part of Erland was proud of it, proud of killing and getting away with it for all these years.

Jim stepped back. "You're just a common or garden variety killer, Erland. I've seen dozens like you over the years. You're all the same. You see something you want, you take it. Someone gets in your way, you move them out of it by whatever means necessary. Because no one exists on this earth but you."

Kate looked up at Jim with an expression like she'd

seen god. "Once a cop," she said. She turned back to Erland. "I'd like to believe hell exists, Erland, so I could be confident that's where you're headed. I don't, so that's out." She smiled again, and this time the old man shrank into his pillow. "But I'll take you being gone from my plane of existence. Any day now, isn't that right? What a shame."

He spat at her. Literally, a gob of phlegm landing on his blanket too near her hand. She didn't jerk away, just kept looking at him with that expression of amused contempt. "Why didn't you just kill me?" he said, panting. "Why don't you now?"

"Because I'm better than you are, Erland." Her smile was crooked and self-mocking. "Haven't you heard? I'm a fucking hero."

"I'm not a hero," Jim said with a smile that could have been called friendly if it had contained less teeth. "Old Sam was a friend of mine. He died after hunting a moose and cooking it up at a big party that lasted all of one beautiful day on the river he called home, surrounded by family and friends who loved him, all of whom knew better than to believe any of the crap you're trying to peddle here." Jim shook his head. "I'm no hero, Erland, but I'm not killing you, either, because I'd rather your death be long and painful." He looked at Jane. "Surrounded by people you have to pay to endure your company."

This time Kate did leave, Jim hard on her heels.

Kate's phone rang as they were about to climb into the Cessna. It was Brillo. "Hey. That body you found. It's not that McDonald guy."

"I know. You should have his body somewhere in the morgue by now."

"Oh. Him. Yeah, he's on his way. Well. The body you found, we finally got the dental records from that missing orienteer and it's not him, either."

"Okay. Now that we know all the people it isn't, do we know who it is?"

"It's not even a man."

"It's a woman?"

"Yeah. We did a DNA. Given the size of the fragments and the wear and tear on 'em it was our last option. It was a woman. We think maybe somewhere in her forties but it's pretty inconclusive, and I promise you, no one here is going to okay any further expenses on identifying them. Especially since no one seems to be looking for whoever it was."

Kate paused with one foot on the strut. "Can you tell how long they've been out there?"

"You asked me that before." Brillo sighed. "Between five and ten years. No more or less than that. I don't think. Any ideas?"

Kate let her mind sift through Park rats past and present. "Maybe," she said slowly. "Maybe I do."

"Well, good, 'cause I'm out."

Sixteen

THANKSGIVING
the Park, Squaw Candy Creek

BOBBY HAD STARTED A NEW SHOW CALLED "Bullet Points" that began with what sounded like a real-time, you-are-there recording of the shootout at the OK Corral, only with semi-automatics, and featuring as on-air guests those Park rats willing to say out loud what everyone else was thinking. As befitted the "You're all entitled to my opinion" ethic of Bush Alaska, many of them were. "Either the American experiment works or it doesn't," Ruthe Baumann said on Park Air that afternoon. "We've had bad presidents before and the nation has survived them."

"Two of the worst in our own lifetime," Bobby said.

"And I would point out that no law says the American empire lasts forever. Maybe our two hundred years are up, and maybe that might not be such a bad thing. Maybe it's time for us to set the bar about as low as it can go so the rest of the world stops looking to us for every single blessed thing, and for us to stop believing we can do every single blessed thing else."

Bobby, whose legs had been sacrificed in Vietnam on the altar of American exceptionalism, nodded. "Stop us thinking our shit don't stink the way everyone else's shit does."

Ruthe nodded back. "And then maybe the rest of the world can start taking care of its own damn self instead of running to us for all the answers and all the troops and all the money, and maybe we can finally start spending some of it on ourselves. What I hate…"

"What? What do you hate, Ruthe? Tell me. I wanna hate it, too."

She laughed, a rich, mellow sound. "What I hate is that the Boomers have built nothing. We have built nothing. Where's our Panama Canal? Where's our Golden Gate Bridge? Where's our interstate highway system? Instead of building something that might last beyond our lifetime, we've wasted all our treasure and too much of our blood in one war after another, none of which have accomplished anything of benefit for the nation." She shrugged. "Any nation that doesn't first ask the question 'What's in it for us?' is doomed to decline."

"You're not an altruist, then?"

"Sure, I am. I just want to know what's in it for me."

Bobby's laugh rattled the rafters.

Ruthe chuckled. "But before your phone lines melt down—"

Bobby grinned back. "Park Air doesn't have phone lines, Ruthe."

She winked. "One of the many reasons it's my favorite pirate radio station, Bobby."

"Explain to me again how it is you're still single, Ruthe."

"I'm standing right here, Bobby," Dinah said from the kitchen.

"Harvey Meganack's on his way over here right now with a Molotov cocktail, isn't he?" Kate said in Jim's ear.

He choked over his beer but he couldn't deny it.

Thanksgiving dinner was a lavish affair, fourteen Park rats crowded around a table loaded with every good thing to eat. There was Auntie Vi's lumpia, Ruthe's fried salmon bellies, Auntie Joy's fry bread, Auntie Balasha's lowbush cranberry sauce, Bobby's smashed potatoes (which Kate suspected contained more butter and cream than they did potato), Kate's sourdough rolls, Dinah's turkey and stuffing and Anne Flanagan's to-die-for deep-dish pumpkin pie.

"Please don't make us sit here and drool while everyone says what they're thankful for," Johnny said. "Please, Dinah?"

She laughed and gave in.

Jim's phone rang as they were all slowly succumbing to tryptophan inertia. "Jesus, John, it's a holiday."

"You hear Nick Luther's leaving the troopers to join APD?"

"No, I hadn't. Not surprising, though. His service area

tripled over the past year and you gave him a twelve-year-old to help out."

"Which is why we need all the experienced officers we can get. When are you going to knock off this little hissy fit of yours and come back to work?"

"I don't think that's happening, John."

"Well what the fuck are you going to do instead?"

"I don't know. I might go for an A&P. I think this state needs more and better airplane mechanics than it does cops."

"You'd be wrong about that."

"Me being wrong about something would not be a new thing. And who knows. I might just build hours in my new airplane. There's a lot of Alaska I haven't seen."

Barton snorted. "Yeah, well, have fun on your vacation, and let me know when you get bored."

Jim looked at Kate across the room, her face alive with laughter as she advised Katya in a Monopoly game with Johnny, Vanessa and Anne Flanagan's daughters Lauren and Caitlin. "Yeah, you'll be my first call, John."

Right after that Kurt called with the news that Erland Bannister had died in the hospital early that morning.

"Early Christmas present for you," Bobby said to Kate.

"Bobby," Anne Flanagan said.

"What?"

"At least that's over," Jim said later to Kate.

"No," she said. "No, it isn't."

"Why do you say that? Do you know something? Did Erland leave money in his will for a hit on you, or what?"

She shook her head. "I don't know. But Erland wasn't the type to go gentle into that good night."

"Not the room to find any sympathy for Erland Bannister," Jim said later to Anne.

"You don't believe in redemption, then? In the existence of a forgiving God?"

"I've never felt that spark of faith, Anne. Even if I had, it would be for the sole purpose of believing that the judges would take one look at that guy and pull the lever on the trap door." He grinned at her expression "Sorry. Not exactly what a priest wants to hear, I know."

"I don't care what you believe in, Jim, so long as you believe in something."

His eyes wandered involuntarily across the room to where Kate, Katya, the three aunties, Johnny, Val and Dinah were playing a fiercely fought game of snerts on the cleared dining room table. "I believe in Kate Shugak."

"That's a lot of weight to load up on one person."

"Who better?"

"You could try believing in yourself."

But that got way too close to a self-examination he wasn't yet prepared to undertake.

"Yeah," he said later to Bobby, "the McDonalds were buried together in Anchorage last Thursday."

"They ever decide who shot him?"

"DiFronzo says killing Fergus was all Spilotro's doing, none of his. Spilotro says DiFronzo killed him before Spilotro could stop him. DiFronzo says Spilotro was driving when they hit Sylvia. Spilotro says DiFronzo was driving but that it was an accident. And they both fingered Accardo for Campbell."

"He under arrest?"

"There's no evidence, and they weren't even in Anchorage at the time, so…" Jim smiled. "Special Agent Mason is so pleased that Ace and Deuce are going to be locked up somewhere that he didn't, ah, even resent it was Alaska instead of Illinois."

"What were they doing holed up at the Kanuyaq Mine, anyway?"

"They say they needed a place to work Martin over so he'd sign over his shares."

"I still can't believe he didn't. I never would have picked Martin Shugak to have much physical courage, and Matt Grosdidier says they waled on him pretty good."

"So," Ruthe said to Kate, "is Martin going to be rich now?"

"Depends on if Erland's heir decides to develop the Kanuyaq Mine."

"Who is his heir?"

"Well, his daughter's dead, his nephew's in jail, and his wife ran off with her plastic surgeon. His sister by default, maybe? I don't know. We'll have to wait and see."

"And how are you, Kate? You sure got dumped into the deep end before you even got home."

Ruthe's eyes were wise and kind and she'd been in the Park long before Kate came home that winter with her throat cut and her voice gone, when Billy Mike had asked Kate to find the bootlegger and stop him. She had. "I'm really, really glad that Martin being missing wasn't about Ken Halvorsen."

Ruthe nodded slowly. "Yeah. I can see that." She pulled Kate into a hug, warm and maternal. "It's good to have you home, Kate."

"Any news on that guy in Potlatch?" Bobby said.

"He's gone, at least for now. Billy Mike Jr. was down that way and he stopped in. The fire was out, no food on the shelves except for some canned beans. The bedding was bagged. Gone for the winter, I guess."

Kate, overhearing, had a sudden inspiration and called Kurt. "No, not today, there's no hurry. Next Monday when you're back in the office is fine."

"What?'

She hung up and turned to look up at Jim. "Nothing important." She smiled and leaned against him. "Ready for home?"

He kissed her. "Always ready."

And Bobby, shamelessly eavesdropping, marveled, first that Chopper Jim Chopin, erstwhile Father of the Park and the biggest rounder Alaska had seen since Mike Healy scattered offspring from Unalaska to Utqiaġvik, could so easily refer to Kate's house as home, and second that Kate Shugak, that most tightly wired of tightly wired individuals, could be so comfortable with a public display of affection.

Although there was that one time she had climbed Jim

like a tree at the Roadhouse. So maybe not so wondrous a sight after all.

He looked across the room to where Katya was reading *The Paperbag Princess* to Lauren and Caitlin and felt his heart turn over.

Or maybe everyone was just growing the fuck up.

Seventeen

H E WOKE UP ALONE. PULLING ON JEANS and a sweatshirt, he followed the smell of coffee downstairs. There was no sound from behind the door with the sign "Orc Free Zone!" on it. The sign dated from Johnny's *Lord of the Rings* period and remained because Kate thought it was funny. Johnny and Van had stopped to visit Annie Mike on their way back from Bobby and Dinah's and returned home late. Annie was Van's adopted mother, and for all Jim knew—and he'd been a teenage boy with a hollow leg in his time, so he was pretty sure he did know—they'd scored a second Thanksgiving dinner at her house.

The sky was gray for a change, a high overcast with an ominous look to the southern horizon, and the clock read the crack of noon. He poured coffee into an insulated mug, slipped into his parka and boots, and went looking for

Kate. He found her sitting on the glacial erratic that had come to rest at the edge of the cliff that formed one side of Zoya Creek. Its top was worn smooth by two generations of Shugak backsides. He parked the Chopin backside next to the extant Shugak one and they sat drinking coffee together in silence.

The Park was so still this noonday that they could hear the sound of moose stripping bark from an alder, a whuff of displaced air from a golden eagle flying low overhead, the rattle of a porcupine's quills as she licked at a salty rock on the near side of the creek.

It was amazing, what the Park could tell you about itself, if you only stopped long enough to listen. "I forgot to mention."

"What?"

"The doc told me to tell you that you can't get hit on the head anymore."

She laughed a little. "I'll try to avoid it."

"Seriously, Kate. He said you could wind up like Muhammad Ali, with what they call pugilistic Parkinson's. Only with no big-ass gold belt to show off."

"Okay. I'll make sure it doesn't happen ever, ever again."

He knew she was lying, and he knew she knew that he knew.

She stirred. "I have to make a trip up to Keith and Oscar's. No hurry. Next week sometime."

"Okay. Why?"

"I need a DNA swab from Keith."

He looked down at her. "Why?"

"Because he's the last living Gette in the Park."

He frowned, and then his face cleared. "You think it's Lotte."

Seven years before in Niniltna, longtime Park rat Lotte Gette had killed her sister and run from the consequences, straight up into the mountains, never to be seen out of them again. "My first thought was that it was the missing orienteer. Then I thought it was Fergus McDonald. Then I was afraid it was Jennifer or Ryan." Jim was one of two Park rats besides herself who knew that the two were still alive. "But Brillo said the bones had been out there at least five years. Now he says the bones are from the body of a woman."

Jim thought back. "Is Lotte the only woman who has gone missing around these parts in recent history?"

"So far as I know, yes." She was silent for a moment. "When I chased Lotte up into the mountains and lost her, I thought she might have made it down the other side. I kind of hoped she was living off the grid somewhere in the YT." She sighed. "But now I think maybe she didn't make it."

His arm tightened around her shoulders. "We can fly into Niniltna, borrow an ATV, drive up to Keith's."

"Okay." She tipped her head back, smiling. "Kurt texted me a photo this morning. Take a look." She got out her phone.

He frowned and held it at arm's length. "Who—"

"It's Barney Aronson."

It took him a moment. "The missing orienteer?"

"Yes."

"Well, guess what." He handed the phone back. "It's also the guy we found living in Scott Ukatish's cabin in Potlatch."

"Yeah, I thought maybe."

"Why?"

"Gavin Mortimer is married to Barney Aronson's widow."

His eyes closed and his head fell back. "Ah. Okay. Insurance fraud."

"I don't think so, Jim. All three of them would have to be in it. I think maybe he just ran away. Brendan said he and his wife didn't get along. And he's already been declared dead and his insurance has already paid off and she and Gavin are already married."

"Then why is Gavin so anxious for the body to be Aronson's?"

"Maybe he just wants to make sure he isn't a bigamist."

"Maybe."

"Besides. You heard Bobby. Aronson's in the wind."

"He's been hanging around the Park for four years. We could probably find him."

"If we wanted to."

"Yeah. If we wanted to." He found he didn't much. Yes indeed, it was positively liberating not to be wearing the uniform anymore. He saw Kate looking at him. "What?"

"When did you quit? Right after?"

"No. Not long after, but not right after. It really wasn't

a knee-jerk reaction to you getting shot. Or," he said when she raised an eyebrow, "okay, not only."

"What happened?"

He sighed. She'd hear about it sooner or later. "It wasn't any big deal, nothing I hadn't run into a hundred, hell, a thousand times before on the job. The first week of August I caught two of the Yovino boys breaking into the Grosdidiers' clinic. Looking for drugs, although of course they denied it."

"John and Paul?"

He shook his head. "George and Ringo, the twins. They tried to run and it pissed me off, so when I caught 'em, I handcuffed them to the passenger-side rear-view mirror and took them right through town and up to the post at a trot."

"Jim. I'm shocked." And she tried very hard to look like it.

"No, you're not, but I was. That was when—well, that was when I knew it was time to pull the plug. I'd just had it. It was the tipping point. And, come on, Kate, it's a crap job. People lie to you all day every day. They throw up down the front of your uniform and in the backs of your vehicles, always fun when you're in the air. They lie. They—case in point—run and you have to chase them. They lie. And then there's the state, which won't fund enough troopers to do the job in the Bush, so even if you're in the air every other day you can still be three weeks late to a crime scene. And, oh yeah, they lie." He glanced at her. "And on occasion they shoot at you. And, not forgetting, they lie to you. It's just…tiring."

She looked at him for a long moment. "Okay."

"Okay?"

"Really." She kissed him, taking her time about it, before pulling back to look up at him. "Okay."

They sat in silence, drinking their coffee. It was warming up, from the single digits into the twenties. It was still cold but it wasn't biting down to the bone the way it had been.

"Jim." She turned to look up into his face.

"What?"

"I held Jack while he was dying."

He went very still.

"We had time to say goodbye, to say—other things." She shook her head and met his eyes squarely. "I told him I loved him. I'd never said it before." She paused. "He laughed." Her voice almost broke on the word. Almost, but not quite. "And then he said, 'Jesus, now I know I'm dying.' And then he did."

Jim remembered the big, burly, almost ugly man, whose laugh was deeper and richer than James Earl Jones'. One of the last times he'd seen Jack Morgan had been at Bobby and Dinah's wedding, which only marginally preceded the birth of their daughter, Katya. When it was all over Jack had tossed Kate over his shoulder and disappeared into the woods with her and no one had seen them again until well after sunrise. Jim like to have expired of jealousy right there on the spot.

"The thing is," Kate said. "Everyone I've ever loved leaves

me. Stephan. Zoya. Emaa. Abel. Jack. Old Sam. It makes me feel a little…"

"Paranoid?"

Her smile trembled. "Apprehensive."

He put a hand on her neck and pulled her into a long, luxurious kiss that explored her lips, traced her jawline, her cheekbones, her eyebrows and returned again to her mouth. He pulled back to look at her, and was delighted to see that her skin was delicately flushed and her eyes dark with desire. "You don't have to tell me anything. I'm not going anywhere." He kissed her again, once, firmly, and then nipped her lower lip for emphasis. "Anywhere, Shugak. You're like air or water to me."

Her eyes went wide. "And then," he said, "there is your generally nasty attitude, your total lack of sympathy for anyone not up to the job, your complete absence of sentimentality. Also, just FYI, you're the best lay I ever had."

What was even more shocking than his words was the tone of his voice, calm, matter-of-fact, no emotion, no drama. Just the facts, ma'am. Once a cop, she thought. She had to clear her throat twice before she could get the words out. "Good to know. It's a skill set I'm proud of."

"I know you still love Jack, I know that, but I'll take whatever you have to give as long as I can get it, and everything that comes with that, too. You feel the need to hurl yourselves at goons with guns? Right there with you, babe. You have to sequester yourself alone up in the mountains for months at a time? I can deal. Just—" He stopped, thought about it, and started again. "Just once in a while drop by the homestead. I'll be here."

"I kind of guessed that when I saw the airstrip. And the hangar."

"I'll be here," he said again, this time with more force. He wasn't going to let her laugh away what amounted to a declaration, the only one he'd ever made in his life. He leaned forward to kiss her again and then something caught his attention. He nudged her and jerked his chin at the opposite side of the creek.

Shadows glided from beneath the trees. Four of them went to the edge and drank while a fifth kept watch. The watcher was largest of all of them, with a thick pelt so gray the light turned it to liquid silver. Ears were up and alert and the full brush of a tail curled tightly over her behind. She moved easily, lean muscle rippling, paws stepping lightly and gracefully over the frozen ground without making a sound and leaving only the merest trace behind.

The first four stepped back from the creek and vanished again beneath the trees. The watcher took their place at the creek, lapping up water from a lead in the ice. Thirst quenched, she didn't leave but paused to look up, straight at them. It was obvious that she had always known they were there. For all her lean form she projected a massive presence, aggressive with good health, assured in stance, yellow eyes sharp with awareness and intelligence. In a fight you would want her on your side.

And two weeks ago, they had.

Jim let out a shaky sigh. "Did you know?"

From the corner of his eye he saw Kate smile, and had his answer.

"I hoped. I tracked her with the four-wheeler when I got home, as far as I could before I lost the trail. But by then I knew where she was going. I think it's the same pack that comes through the canyon now and then. She knows them. They know her." A fleeting smile. "The big male I'm pretty sure knows her in the biblical sense. I think he was the father of that litter she popped out seven years ago." She was silent for a moment. "They never came down into the hot springs while I was there, not once. But I could hear them howling, almost every night. I could hear her. I thought, maybe, she was letting me know." She leaned her head against his arm. "Like I told you. Nothing to forgive."

They looked at each other, the couple on the rock on one side, the great gray half-wolf, half-husky hybrid on the other. "I couldn't believe it when I saw her at the mine, when she attacked Spilotro. Why didn't you tell me?"

"Better to show you, I thought. Not sure you would have believed, otherwise."

He thought about the blood seeping inexorably into the gray pelt that was the last time he'd seen Mutt before he left the clearing, driving like a madman to get Kate to the docs in Ahtna. He'd been so certain Mutt was dead. Or maybe in his rush to save Kate's life he had just decided she was so he wouldn't feel guilty about leaving her there.

Another thought evolved out of the first. "Kate, did you deliberately put us in harm's way to force Mutt's hand? Is that why we rushed those guys, not knowing if they were armed?"

"No. Of course not."

He wasn't sure he believed her. "Will she stay?"

Kate shrugged. "Up to her." Beneath her deliberately casual tone Jim heard the catch in her voice. "Staying with me has gotten her shot twice. Maybe she'd rather take her chances with assholes in airplanes."

The gray overcast was eclipsed by thick, low-lying clouds coming at them hard out of the Mother of Storms. In the distance, a bird sang, a pure, poignant three-note descant that lingered on the still winter air. A shiver raced up Jim's spine. "Doesn't that bird know it's supposed to have flown south for the winter?"

He listened but the song didn't come again. "I guess some of them are overwintering nowadays. Climate change, maybe." When he looked back across the creek Mutt had disappeared. Something cold kissed his cheek. He looked up. "Hey. What do you know. It's snowing. Finally."

She pulled her glove and held her hand out and watched as several flakes disappeared in her palm. "So it is."

"Maybe we'll get snowed in." He pulled her into his lap, folding her legs around his waist. "Whatever shall we do to pass the time?"

She pulled back and smiled at him, flushed and desirable

and everything he wanted in this world. "But there are children in the house."

He slid to his feet and whispered in her ear. Her legs tightened around his waist and she laughed low in her throat.

Kissing her and walking at the same time proved problematic but not impossible. His foot was feeling for the bottom step of the deck stairs when he felt a strong, sharp tug on the hem of his pants. Caught off balance his legs went right out from under him. By a gymnastic contortion worthy of Simone Biles he managed to land on his ass and not on Kate and to catch her at the same time.

"What the hell—"

They both looked up to see Mutt standing over them, yellow eyes narrowed and sharp teeth bared in the biggest of all lupine laughs. She barked once, a joyous bark, and romped a couple of yards away. She stopped to look at them over her shoulder, tail wagging hard enough to power an electric generator. She barked once more and took off into the gathering snow.

They leaped to their feet and gave chase.

Acknowledgments

My heartfelt thanks go first to Der Plotmeister. Every author of crime fiction needs a friend with a seriously twisted mind.

Thanks to Kevin Gottlieb for the last-minute catch on the E.L.T. Every author of Alaskan crime fiction needs a pilot in her life.

Thanks to Barbara Peters who ferreted out all the "Then a miracle occurs" moments.

Thanks to Rob Rosenwald for buying that gargantuan flatscreen television which now hangs on the wall of Bernie's Roadhouse, keeping the old farts entertained.

No matter how narrow or peculiar or last minute my search parameters, researcher Michael Cattogio always comes up with something I can use, and then, on those very rare occasions when he panics and thinks he might have sent me the wrong information, he knows people I can fact-check him on. This time that would be Dave Reineke. Thank you both, gentlemen.

And, finally, in what previous life did I do something so good that I was rewarded with Nic Cheetham as my publisher in this one? Thanks, Nic, for being so determined to make me an offer I couldn't refuse, and for a working relationship whose hallmarks are humor, sanity and a truly extraordinary willingness to accommodate so many of my suggestions. No author ever had a better auditor, or a more amusing email correspondent.

DANA
STABENOW
A COLD DAY
FOR
MURDER

DANA
STABENOW
A FATAL
THAW

DANA
STABENOW
DEAD IN
THE WATER

DANA
STABENOW
A COLD
BLOODED
BUSINESS

DANA
STABENOW
PLAY WITH
FIRE

DANA
STABENOW
BLOOD
WILL TELL

DANA
STABENOW
BREAKUP

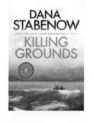
DANA
STABENOW
KILLING
GROUNDS

DANA
STABENOW
HUNTER'S
MOON

DANA
STABENOW
MIDNIGHT
COME
AGAIN

DANA
STABENOW
THE
SINGING OF
THE DEAD

DANA
STABENOW
A FINE
AND BITTER
SNOW

DANA
STABENOW
A GRAVE
DENIED

DANA
STABENOW
A TAINT
IN THE
BLOOD

DANA
STABENOW
A DEEPER
SLEEP

DANA
STABENOW
WHISPER
TO THE
BLOOD

DANA
STABENOW
A NIGHT
TOO DARK

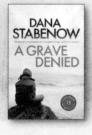
DANA
STABENOW
THOUGH
NOT DEAD

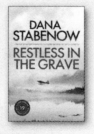
DANA
STABENOW
RESTLESS IN
THE GRAVE

DANA
STABENOW
BAD BLOOD